PORTIA BENCH

a novel by

Robert Boyd

PROMONTORY
PRESS

Portia Bench
Copyright ©2016 by Robert Boyd

All rights reserved. No part of this book may be used or reproduced in any matter without prior written permission.

Promontory Press
www.promontorypress.com

ISBN: 978-1-987857-33-7

Typeset by Edge of Water Designs, edgeofwater.com
Cover design by One Owl Creative

Printed in Canada
987654321

Dedicated to the men who paid the ultimate price in maintaining the Kettle Valley Railway Coquihalla Subdivision from 1916 to 1959.

May their memory never be in vain.

PART 1

1

APRIL 1984

Four men, all members of the same survey crew, were dead. Their own survey equipment had been used as the murder weapons. The surveying transit, mounted on a sharp-legged tripod, had pierced the body of one of the crewmembers and impaled him into a tree. The plumb bob, resembling a yo-yo but with a sharp point on one end, used to measure accuracy, had pierced another crewmember's skull. Pieces of lath, sticks of hemlock wood one foot in length and half an inch in width, used as survey markers, had pierced the head, neck, and chest of the other crewmembers.

"Who made the call?" Constable Friesen of the Hope RCMP asked the two men standing on the scene.

"I did." One of the men stepped forward.

"What is your name, sir, and what is your connection?"

"My name is Clint Matheson. I am the District Engineer for the Lower Mainland Highways Division. I am in charge of this highway project. These men were working under my direction."

"Did you see anything?"

"No, they were already dead when we arrived here. We came up because the crew didn't call in once all day, and they were overdue to return to the office."

"How well do you know these men?"

"Lance Demitrios, the Crew Chief, has worked for me for fifteen years. He was one of my top surveyors. Dan Gibbons, my rod-and-chain man, has worked for me for eight years; Cory Gabriel, my other rod-and-chain man, has worked for me for three years. The survey marker, Tyler Fitzgerald, that young man only started working for me last fall." Clint's face was white as a ghost and he had a blank expression as he said this. His voice was barely audible, and he was fumbling to find the right words.

"My name is Don Lassiter. I am the Project Manager. I am this crew's immediate supervisor." The other man spoke.

Eventually, more police arrived on the scene along with two ambulances. Constable Friesen told Clint and Don that they would have to come over to the police station and answer some questions.

"Don, I'll drive you back to the office and you can take the rest of the day off. I can help the police with their questions by myself," Clint said.

At the Hope RCMP detachment, Clint was led into an interrogation room. Staff Sergeant Dickerson entered the room and sat across the table from him.

"We need to talk. We need some answers," said Sergeant Dickerson.

Clint was still visibly upset.

"Take your time, Mr. Matheson. The best place to start is the beginning."

2

ONE YEAR EARLIER: APRIL 1983

Three years and three months after the announcement that Expo 86 would be taking place in Vancouver, the Provincial Highways Ministry finally received approval to build new highway projects. Over the previous three years, British Columbia's economy was mired in deep recession, so infrastructure projects of any kind were put on hold. On April 20th, the Provincial Government, under the direction of Premier Mike Davenport, was re-elected with a majority, and the Expo 86 highway project was granted approval.

Under the direction of Provincial Highways Minister Bill Plotnikoff and his Deputy Minister, Stan Fisher, the purpose of this highway project was to provide a direct link between Vancouver and BC's Interior, and then eventually link to Eastern Canada.

Clint Matheson, the District Engineer for the Lower Mainland Highways District, agreed to take on this project. In the years that the highway project was on hold, Clint determined that instead of making improvements to the two existing highways to the Interior, a new highway would be built altogether. Otherwise, the expected significant volume of traffic from other parts of Canada during Expo 86 would be too much of a burden on the existing highways.

After careful analysis, Clint determined that the most logical route would be through the Coquihalla River Valley, running in a northern-easterly direction from Hope and along the Coldwater River Valley up to Merritt. Until now, his rationale was based solely on observations made from studying topographical maps and aerial photographs. Now that the project had been approved, and before making his chosen route official, he wanted to take reconnaissance trips along the roads that travelled up both river valleys with the Hope and Merritt Survey Crew Chiefs.

The following day, Clint held a meeting with his three Project Managers: Don Lassiter, Hugh Gormley, and Ed Hildebrandt; his top Crew Chief, Lance Demitrios; and his Office Manager, Ted Harvey. He outlined what was going to happen over the next three years and told them to be prepared to put in a lot of extra hours. He then called Henry Finnegan, the Crew Chief of the Hope survey crew. Henry had been appointed Crew Chief at Hope only ten months ago, and Clint had yet to meet him. When he phoned the office, a man answered the other end.

"I would like to leave a message for Henry Finnegan," said Clint.

"That'll be unnecessary, because you're talking to him."

Clint noticed that he had a distinct Newfoundland twang in his voice, and then wondered why he was in the office at 2:00 p.m. and not out in the field. "We haven't met before. I'm Clint Matheson, the District Engineer for the Lower Mainland Highways District."

"Oh, right. Pleased to hear from you. How are you doing?"

"I'm doing just fine, thanks. The reason I am calling is to let you know that I will be coming up to Hope next Monday, and on Tuesday you and I will be going on a reconnaissance trip. Are you familiar with the road that goes up the Coquihalla River Valley?"

"I've heard of it but never travelled on it before. I heard it's on private property," Henry replied.

"Well, private or not, we'll be taking a trip on it. Does your truck have four-wheel drive?"

"Yes, it does."

"Good. According to the description of the road on the map, four-wheel drive will likely be necessary. Now, I have one more concern. Why are you in the office at this time, and what are your rod-and-chain men working on right now?"

"I'm plotting the elevation shots that Greg and Rudy took yesterday for the new approaches to the American Creek Bridge. You know, the sections that were washed out when we had that heavy downpour last month."

"I thought that project was finished by now," said Clint.

"As it turns out, the ground didn't settle properly, so they had to add extra gravel. I'm working on the western approach today, and Greg and Rudy are taking elevation shots of the eastern approach right now. I'll be plotting their new calculations tomorrow."

"I see. Well, I'll see you next Monday afternoon. Be ready to head out first thing Tuesday morning."

***

The minute Henry hung up the phone, he wiped his forehead. "Holy shit, that was close. You know who that was? That was Clint Matheson, the District Engineer. You know, the *big* boss."

Greg and Rudy, sitting with Henry in the office, seemed rather unconcerned about his reaction. After all, they had never met Clint.

"Okay, Greg, it's your turn to deal. Rudy, I'll raise you ten. Remember, deuces are still wild."

3
MAY 1983

The following Monday, Clint left his office at noon and arrived in Hope at 3:00 p.m. He planned on spending at least three days in Hope, so he obtained a room at the Starlight Motel. From there, he made his way over to the Department of Highways office.

"So, we finally meet. You must be Henry Finnegan," said Clint.

"That's right," replied Henry. "But don't let the name fool you. I'm not really Irish; I was adopted, you see. I'm German and Polish by birth."

"I never really gave the matter any thought," said Clint.

Henry was not how Clint had pictured him. He was a lot shorter than Clint, quite portly, and had very long hair tied back in a ponytail.

"Where's Linda?" Clint asked, referring to the receptionist.

"She only works here part time now, a result of budget cuts. Actually, you were the one who requested a reduction in her hours," said Henry.

"Oh, that's right. I forgot about that. I am going to reverse that decision, effective tomorrow. She will go back to working here full time. Her services will be greatly needed."

It was time to get down to business. After Clint inspected the truck, he went to take an inventory of the survey equipment. It was all stored in a small room at the back corner of the office. While Clint wrote his list, he heard Henry's rod-and-chain men, Greg and Rudy, come into the office. Clint looked at his watch; it wasn't even 4:00 p.m. yet. *What the hell are they doing back here already?*

When Greg and Rudy entered the office, they were hooting and hollering at the top of their lungs, and sounding as though they were just returning from a wild party.

"Hey, Henry, guess what? You know that waitress chick Lola, the one with the huge tits at Spuzzum? Rudy got her phone number, man!" Greg yelled out.

"Henry, my good man, it's only a matter of time before I'll be getting inside her pants," Rudy boasted.

Clint decided to make his presence known. "So, you guys must be Greg and Rudy."

Rudy gave Clint a dirty look and said in a smug tone, "And who the fuck are you?"

Clint was aghast, but before he could say anything, he heard the sound of the toilet flushing, followed by the bathroom door being opened frantically. Henry came running out of the bathroom, quickly doing up his belt. Clint caught sight of him making a slashing motion across his throat while pointing at Clint.

"Oh, that's right, we haven't met yet. I'm Clint Matheson, your District Engineer." Clint noticed the abrupt changes in expressions on Greg and Rudy's faces. "Now that I have all of you here, we'll have a meeting. I know that it has been quite slow for a long period of time, but that is all about to change. Over the next three years, we are all going to be busier than hell. We have to build a new highway, and it must be completed in time for Expo 86 to begin three years from now. Be prepared to put in a lot of overtime. Henry, you and

I will be exploring the potential route tomorrow. Be ready to leave at eight o'clock tomorrow morning. Make sure the truck has a full tank of gas, and the oil and coolant levels are topped up. Greg and Rudy, I hope you both have enough work to keep busy tomorrow. So, I'll be seeing you all bright and early tomorrow morning."

The following morning, Clint was in the office promptly at 8:00 a.m. In preparation for their excursion, he brought his camera, binoculars, notebook, and topographical map. Since he would be taking notes along the way, he told Henry to drive.

Heading eastward from Hope, they turned left when they reached Othello Road at a T intersection. They had barely travelled a quarter-mile farther when they came upon a gate across the road. Beside the gate was a large sign that read, "*Private road—no trespassing. Property of Pacific Coast Gas Trunk Lines. Access beyond this point is strictly prohibited. Expressed written permission is required before access is granted. All enquiries can be directed to: Corporate Headquarters, Pacific Coast Gas Trunk Lines, Suite 1205, 666 Burrard Street, Vancouver, BC, V6B 2A4, telephone: 644-1219. Simon Dale, President.*" Beside that sign was another sign, "*Danger—active logging in progress. Lindeman Logging, Inc.*"

Clint shook his head when he read each sign. "Dale, you lousy son of a bitch," he said angrily.

"I take it you know him," said Henry.

"Know him? I know him all too well," replied Clint. "I've had many run-ins with him over the years. It seems that every time a highway is built over one of his pipelines, he has an absolute shit fit. He always likes confrontation; he never wants to negotiate peacefully."

"But, don't you think we should go back and phone their head office and ask for permission?" asked Henry.

"Are you kidding? If he knew it was me, he wouldn't let us through in a million years. The truth is, the pipeline company owns the pipeline right-of-way, but they don't own the bloody road. I say, fuck him. If there's a problem, I'll deal with him. Besides, what he doesn't know won't hurt him."

"But there's a gate across the road."

"There's no lock on it. Just pull the pin out and put it back in when you close it."

The road beyond the gate was well-maintained gravel. It was wide and completely flat. Clint found it odd that a road used only for pipeline maintenance and logging trucks was in such great shape. Four miles past the gate, they came upon a cluster of four identical sheds on the right side of the road. They were all painted in Tuscan red, and one building had a faded sign that read "Lear". They looked like structures typically found alongside a railroad.

The road eventually narrowed and became very bumpy, which made it difficult for Clint to take notes. When the road crossed a narrow bridge across a creek, Clint requested they stop. He took out his topographical map and checked their position. He was aiming his binoculars westward up the valley of Ladner Creek when he noticed a large steel structure in the distance, resembling a railway bridge. Then it occurred to him. He looked back on his map and saw that all along the valley there was a line that looked like a trail of crosses. The map's legend of symbols stated that meant it was an abandoned railroad. He passed the binoculars to Henry.

"Take a look at that bridge, it's absolutely huge," said Clint.

"Wow, that really is something," Henry replied in awe.

As they headed eastward, the road rapidly gained altitude. The first part of the ascent was through dense forest, and then the road became notched into the side of the mountain, high above the valley floor. Clint could not figure out why they would build the road here when there appeared to be lots of room on the other side of the Coquihalla River.

When the road finally levelled off, Clint told Henry to stop the truck. They were at a perfect vantage point with a panoramic view of the valley and the surrounding mountains, and Clint wanted to take notes. The road was narrow so Henry had no choice but to park the truck right in the middle of the road.

"Uh, Mr. Matheson, need I remind you that this is an active logging road?"

Clint pointed out that he could see the road ahead for about half a mile. Past where they were parked, the road descended, turned to the left, and crossed the Coquihalla River on a Bailey bridge before disappearing into the trees.

"Henry, keep your eyes fixed on that last visible part of the road. If you see any oncoming vehicles, just holler."

Henry would have to be completely dependent on sight, as hearing any oncoming vehicles would be completely out of the question since he had to keep the motor running. The muffler was in desperate need of replacement.

When Clint made his observations, one of the first things he noticed was the long, flat expanse of land on the other side of the valley. It was about a hundred feet above the Coquihalla River, and stretched for at least four miles. *This is perfect. It's more than wide enough to accommodate a four-lane highway, and no blasting will be required. This is my lucky day.* He made a cross-reference on his topographical map. According to the map, this section was referred to as "Portia Bench" and, sure enough, it was exactly four miles in length. *Why were the pipeline and this maintenance road built on this side of the Coquihalla River instead of along Portia Bench?* This side was much more precipitous, and thus more susceptible to slides. *This works out better in my case, anyway. I'll have less wrangling over interference with the pipeline right-of-way over there.*

Clint found it perplexing that all of the forest on Portia Bench was old growth. Being from Vancouver Island, and having many relatives in the logging industry, Clint could tell the difference between old growth and second growth a mile away. There were very tall trees, and many of the Douglas fir trees looked to be nearly 300 years old.

Why has that land never been logged? Ever since he entered the Coquihalla River Valley, he noticed many sections of forest on the surrounding mountainsides had been logged, and on a large number of them, the terrain was quite precipitous. Meanwhile, the terrain on Portia Bench was flat, so from a logger's perspective, it should be a piece of cake.

As Clint continued his observations, he kept his binoculars fixated on the continuous horizontal scar halfway up the mountainside. He was fascinated by what a remarkable feat of engineering it must have taken to build a railroad through this region. He figured that if the railroad passed through Hope Pass, it was understandable why it was built halfway up the mountainside instead of on Portia Bench. With the difference in elevation and the fact that Hope Pass was only fifteen miles away, the gradient was too steep for a railroad.

Clint saw that Henry was relieved once he got back to the truck and began putting everything back in.

"Can we get going now?"

"Just a minute, I have to take one humdinger of a piss." Clint hurried toward the side of the road.

Almost immediately after Clint unzipped his fly and began to pee, a fully loaded logging truck came into view, crossing the bridge in the distance and heading directly toward them.

"Oh shit, Mr. Matheson!" yelled Henry.

Clint frantically tried to finish, but instead he had to end it prematurely. He too hastily tried to put it back in his pants and zip his fly back up. "Ow."

Henry threw the truck into reverse and took off, going as fast as he could go. He stuck his head out the window as much as possible to try to see the road better.

"Look for the turnout that was a little ways back. When you

see it, give me the signal for exactly when I should turn," Henry instructed Clint. There was no room for error. If they went off the road and got stuck, they would collide with the logging truck.

When they reached the turnout, Clint gave Henry the signal, but before he started turning, the logging truck came into view as it came over a rise. It was going at a fair rate of speed as it barrelled right toward them. The logging truck driver looked totally stunned to see another vehicle on the road. He applied his brakes, but he wouldn't be able to stop in time. He let out a continuous blast on the air-horn. Henry gave the truck a mighty turn and hit the gas pedal. The truck was completely in the turnout when the logging truck whizzed by, missing the front of the truck by mere inches. The truck came to an abrupt stop when the back end hit a tree. Afterward, Clint and Henry looked at each other in complete bewilderment.

After he caught his breath, Clint said, "Man, that was close."

"If I'm going to be driving you anywhere in the future, remind me to put a porta potty on the back of the truck," said Henry.

Once they crossed the Coquihalla River on the Bailey bridge, Clint asked Henry to pull over. "Why don't we take a coffee break now?"

Henry nodded in agreement. For him, this also meant a smoke break.

Clint made his way down to the riverbank to wash his hands.

"Mr. Matheson, you should be careful. The river level is higher than normal due to spring runoff," Henry warned.

Nevertheless, Clint bent over to wash his hands and, sure enough, he lost his footing and fell head over heels into the river. Fortunately, it was in a shallow area, so the current didn't carry him away. Even so, the water was freezing. Henry ran over to give Clint a hand, restraining himself from laughing.

Clint made a pot of coffee in the office before they left, and filled his thermos. That helped warm him up. It was sunny outside, so that helped dry his clothes somewhat. It never occurred to him to bring a change of clothes along—he never counted on anything like this happening. In a further effort to keep warm, Clint kept moving around as he drank his coffee, observing the surrounding terrain but he began to feel uneasy. He felt like there was some kind of presence around him. He started to look around suspiciously, as though something or someone was watching him. He then heard what sounded like repetitive drum beats. At first, he thought it was just his head pounding since his adrenaline rush from falling into the river. But, the drumming persisted and was soon followed by a Native chant. Clint couldn't figure out where it was coming from.

"Do you hear anything unusual?" asked Clint.

"No, all I hear is the river," replied Henry.

"I must be hearing things. I keep hearing this Indian-style drumming and those chants they make when they dance. There are no Indian Reserves indicated on my map anywhere around here. Am I going insane or something?"

Clint decided at that point that the coffee break was over. This place was starting to give him the creeps.

"Come on, let's get going. We have a lot of ground to cover," said Clint.

"I'll be right with you. I just want to refill my thermos. This could be my last chance to get some pure mountain spring water." As Henry bent over to fill his thermos with water from the river, he looked into the water and noticed a Native mask, which appeared to be staring straight at him. He screamed out, "Aaaaah! Jesus H. Christ!"

Clint jumped out of the truck and ran toward him, saying, "Henry, what's wrong?"

Henry was white as a sheet. For a moment he was completely hysterical, but eventually managed to blurt out, "Th—the river."

Clint looked down into the river, but didn't notice anything unusual. "Henry, what the hell are you talking about? I don't see a damn thing!"

"There was a ceremonial First Nations mask under the water. It had a real wide-eyed expression, almost like the picture of Charles Manson on the cover of *Life* magazine," Henry told Clint once he managed to regain his composure.

"It was probably just your imagination."

"Oh, I'm the one who's imagining things, eh? What about you?" Henry shot back.

In the ensuing panic, Henry flung his thermos high into the air, and when it landed, it shattered into a million pieces.

Beyond the bridge, the road became very steep. Clint recommended to Henry that he put the truck into four-wheel drive. The road made its way up the side of the mountain on a series of switchbacks. Once they passed the second switchback, there was another road that branched off to the left. This was the road that travelled up the Boston Bar Creek Valley.

"If time permits we'll be going up that road later today," Clint mentioned to Henry.

After they passed the fourth switchback, Clint looked over to the left, and saw what appeared to be a man peering over some bushes.

"Holy shit, look over there!" Clint pointed to the man.

Henry didn't take his eyes off the narrow road nor did he stop since they were on such a steep hill. "Well, sir, what did you see this time? I'll take your word for it."

"A man walked out from behind the bushes. He was dressed in grey-and-white-striped overalls and a matching cap. He was dressed just like the guy who operates the miniature railroad in Stanley Park."

"What?"

Then it dawned on Clint. The guy was dressed like a railroad engineer. *What's he doing here now? That railroad looks like it has been abandoned for some time now.*

After a couple more switchbacks, the road levelled off. A mile farther, they came upon more buildings, none of which appeared to be occupied. Most of them were painted in the same shade of red as the cluster of buildings down the road. On the left side of the road, there was a lone building. It had two stories and was built against the side of the mountain. It was clad in red insul-brick siding, a type of asphalt siding designed to make buildings appear to be made of brick. There was a sign across the side with the word "Iago".

"Iago—that was the name of the Lieutenant in the play *Othello*. Man, he was one bad dude."

"What the hell are you talking about?" asked Henry.

"*Othello* was a play written by William Shakespeare. You know, I've been noticing a trend here. Ever since we've been on this road, everything we've passed has a name associated with Shakespeare's plays. This road we're on is called Othello Road. That first set of buildings we passed was called Lear, as in *King Lear*. Then, there was that sign that pointed to a place called Jessica, and that flat expanse of land is called Portia Bench. Jessica and Portia were both characters in *The Merchant of Venice*. Now, we come to Iago, farther up the canyon is a Romeo Creek, and past Coquihalla Lake there's a place called Juliet."

Henry continued to give Clint a blank stare. "I'm afraid you've lost me. I have no idea what you are talking about."

"I take it that you never read Shakespeare in school," said Clint.

"I only went to high school up to tenth grade. I just had to upgrade my math in order to get into that surveyor's course. In the time I was in school, I don't remember ever learning any Shakespeare," replied Henry.

4

The road eventually wound its way steeply down the mountain to the Coquihalla River where it crossed on a narrow bridge. Beyond there was a series of wooden railroad trestles far up the mountainside. Six miles north of the bridge, Clint and Henry noticed one trestle in particular that really stood out. In the centre was a lattice truss span supported by wooden towers that were at least a hundred feet high, perfectly framing a waterfall.

Clint told Henry to pull over. He got out of the truck and made observations, concluding that the canyon was far too narrow and the mountainsides were too precipitous to support a four-lane highway. He got out his camera, took a series of pictures of the trestle, and then suggested that they stop for lunch.

Just after he got back into the truck, Clint happened to glance over to his right. There, standing in a small clearing, was a young lady with long curly blonde hair, wearing a long white dress.

"What the hell is she doing out here?" asked Clint.

"What are you talking about?" asked Henry.

"I just saw a woman."

Henry slammed on the brakes. "Where?"

"Back there. She had curly blonde hair and was wearing a white dress. She looked quite young."

Henry threw the truck into reverse and took off back up the road. "Gee, I wonder if she wants a ride back into Hope."

Clint indicated when they reached the spot where he saw the woman, and Henry stopped the truck. They both took a look around, but saw no sign of her. Clint rolled down the window and called out, "Hello—ma'am? Are you out there? Miss—can you hear me?"

As was the case with Clint's previous sighting, Henry pointed out that it might have been just his imagination.

"Henry, I know what I saw. She was here, okay? She probably didn't know who we are, so she likely ran off into the woods. Anyway, just forget it. We have to get a move on."

Henry, always one to get in the last word, said, "Well, if you see her again, give her my phone number, will you?"

When the road began its rapid descent into the Coquihalla River valley, Henry flew around the first switchback on two wheels, which proved to be a big mistake. There, right in the middle of the road, was the man that Clint had seen earlier—the man wearing overalls and engineer cap. He appeared to have his arms outstretched above his head as if he was motioning them to stop. This time, Clint and Henry both saw him. They yelled "oh shit" in unison and Henry quickly swerved to the right. The truck went off the road and down the embankment, coming to rest on a sand berm. The rear wheels were dangling in the air, and the rear axle was imbedded in the sand. The front wheels were on solid ground, but with no traction from the rear wheels, they weren't able to go anywhere.

Henry angrily got out of the truck, repeatedly saying, "I'll kill him!" He didn't realize that he was right over the embankment, so when he stepped out of the truck, he tumbled straight down the embankment and landed at the bottom. He scrambled up the other side, and when he reached the road, he yelled out, "Hey, you! Get over here, you lousy son of a bitch! C'mon, quit hiding. Come here and fight like a man, you bloody bastard. Where are you?"

Clint cautiously exited the truck and inspected the damage. Luckily, nothing was broken on the rear axle, but the driveshaft might have sustained some damage.

"Henry, what did I tell you about taking it easy down the grade? All you had to do was keep it in first gear and pump the brakes periodically. You could have lost complete control and we could've both been killed."

"Well, pardon me, sir, but I wasn't planning for some asshole standing in the middle of the road out here. Look, I can call Greg and Rudy on the CB radio and get them over here to help pull the truck out."

"But they'd need a truck with a winch to do that."

"Well, I happen to know a man named Brian who works at the Shell station. They have a towing service and he drives the tow-truck. I know that his truck has a winch. I had to get a tow from him right after I moved here. Then, three days later, I saw him pull a car out of the ditch just south of Yale, right where we were surveying. It turns out that he's a fellow Maritimer, so we became instant friends. I know what channel he's on. I hope he is within range." Henry made the call, but initially did not make contact with Brian. "Quidi Vidi calling Boggy Creek, over. Quidi Vidi calling Boggy Creek, over." It took four tries before a barely audible voice came over the radio.

"Henry?"

"Brian, is that you?"

"Yes, it's me. Jeez boy, I can barely hear you. I'm just passing Hope Slide right now. I got a car that blew its radiator in Allison Pass, and I'm just bringing it into the shop. What can I do for you?"

"We kind of went off the road and got stuck. We're going to require the services of the winch on your truck."

"Whereabouts are you? You sound kind of far away."

"We're about fifteen miles up the Coquihalla road. Way up in the boonies over here."

"Don't you know that's a private road? What are you doing way up there?"

"I'm up here in the company truck with the boss. I'm talking the *big* boss from Vancouver. The big kahuna, the big enchilada, the …"

"Henry, just get to the point," Clint interrupted.

"You know how to get here, do you? You go straight down Kawkawa Lake Road, and when you reach Othello Road, turn left. A mile down, you'll come to a gate. Don't worry, it's not locked. From there, just keep going. You can't miss us," said Henry.

"Before I make the commitment to come up there, how will you be paying me?" asked Brian.

"I'll cover it. I have all the major credit cards," said Clint.

Brian didn't give a definite time for when he would arrive, but he said that he would try to get there within the hour.

Clint handed Henry a shovel and took another one for himself. "Okay, while we're waiting, we need to dig out as much dirt from under the driveshaft as possible. I just hope the damn thing isn't bent. I have a good mind to take some of the towing charge off of your paycheque."

They shovelled each side of the truck, intending to remove an equal amount of dirt from each side so the truck didn't tip over. Clint could tell that Henry hadn't done much physical work lately. It wasn't long before he began gasping for breath, so he eventually had to tell him to take a rest. Clint then began hearing the sound of First Nations drums again, soon followed by chants. Clint tried his best to ignore the sounds, but it wasn't easy. Once Henry caught his breath and resumed shovelling, the sounds became louder.

"Man, I'm sure not used to this much hard work. My head is pounding," said Henry.

"What did you say?"

"I said my head is just pounding, boom, boom, boom—like a non-stop disco song."

"You hear it too? It's not your imagination. It's the sound of that Native drumming. Do you hear the chants as well?" asked Clint.

"Yeah, I do, where the hell is it coming from?"

"I have no idea."

Just then, the image of the First Nations ceremonial mask that Henry had seen earlier flew by. This time, both Clint and Henry saw it.

"There it is—that's the mask I saw! Do you believe me now?"

"Yeah, I saw it. Whatever's going on, I don't like it. That friend of yours had better get here soon."

Brian eventually showed up over an hour after Henry made the initial call. When he saw where the truck was situated, he shook his head in amazement. "Holy shit, how the hell did this happen?"

Once Brian hooked up the winch cable to the truck's front bumper, he pulled the lever to start the winch. Slowly, the truck started to move off the sand berm and down the embankment. When it finally made it onto the roadway, everyone breathed a sigh of relief.

"Oh, thank you, thank you so much," Clint said.

"Hey, it was no problem. But, if you don't mind me asking, why are you guys out here in the first place?" Brian asked.

"We're planning to build a new highway through this area, and I wanted to see where exactly it'll be situated."

"Really? Just so you will know, I've heard talk from the locals that this area's haunted," Brian said, as Henry and Clint looked at each other. "Well, gentlemen, it's been a pleasure doing business with you, but I must get back to work. Henry, give me a call some time. We can go for a beer after work. See you guys later."

Clint glanced at his watch. It was now too late to make the trip up the Boston Bar Creek road, so they would have to wait until the next day to make the trip up there.

"Well, sir, are you sure you still want to build a highway through the haunted forest?"

5

That evening, Clint felt like he needed a drink or two. He decided to reacquaint himself with one of his all-time favourite watering holes, the Hope Hotel, which was within walking distance of his motel. When Clint entered the bar, he immediately spotted some road construction crew workers who had worked for him previously, and they greeted him. Over the course of the evening, they reminisced about past road projects they worked together on, and Clint talked about the forthcoming project.

Clint tried to stay focused on the conversation, but he couldn't help notice the attractive young lady standing by the pool table across the room. She had long, flowing jet-black hair and smouldering brown eyes. She was wearing a tan leather dress with fringes and a necklace with what looked like a First Nations design. She was repeatedly looking over toward Clint, making eye contact with him. Clint waved at her. All he kept thinking was, *Man, she's pretty.*

After three rounds, Clint told the men he had to be in the office early the next morning, so he didn't want to stay out too late. He made a mental note to return to the bar following Friday evening.

The following morning, Clint kept his face buried in his notes again even after they turned onto Boston Bar Creek Road. It wasn't until they came to two massive wooden towers on either side of the road that he looked up. Each tower had trestlework on one side, but the centre span was missing.

"Look at this—it must have been the railway bridge over Boston Bar Creek. Those towers must be at least a hundred feet high," said Clint.

The Boston Bar Creek Valley was somewhat wider than the Coquihalla River Valley, and the mountain slopes on either side were not nearly as precipitous. There was adequate room for a four-lane highway, but there was a great deal of elevation gain. In the upper part of the valley, the gap narrowed, but it was still workable. Some blasting would be required. Once the road levelled off, it carried on for two more miles until it came to a dead end at the edge of a huge gulch. Clint and Henry could see a corner of Coquihalla Lake in the distance, so they knew they had reached the summit. That sealed Clint's decision—this would be the route for the new highway.

"Gee, that's a mighty big gulch. How are we going to cross it?" asked Henry.

"It'll have to be a bridge," Clint replied. "It will be far too much work to make it a fill. That seems funny—this will be by far the longest bridge on the highway, and it won't be over any water."

After a coffee break, Clint and Henry headed back to Hope. Clint couldn't wait to tell Bill Plotnikoff and Premier Davenport about his observations. He was getting nervous about his presentation in Victoria the following week.

After Clint and Henry returned to the Hope office, Clint made a phone call to Anders Johanssen, the District Engineer for the Kamloops-Thompson region, at his office in Kamloops. He wanted to arrange a meeting at the Merritt office within the next couple days. Clint then called Matt Yablonski, the Crew Chief for the Merritt survey crew. He wanted to arrange for them to take a reconnaissance trip up the Coldwater River Valley as far as Hope Pass.

As Clint prepared to leave the office, Henry said, "So, you're heading back to Vancouver today?"

"No, I'm heading up to Merritt tomorrow morning. I'm going to meet with the District Engineer from Kamloops, and the Crew Chief and I are going to take a trip up the Coldwater River valley. Is that okay with you?"

"Sure, but how do you plan on getting up there?"

"I'm going to drive. How else would I get there?"

"I mean, what road are you going to take?"

"The Fraser Canyon, of course. What difference does it make?"

"The Hope-Princeton is very scenic this time of year."

"That's a much longer route, and I don't really have the time. Besides, I'd like to see how they're coming along with the replacement approaches for the American Creek Bridge. I'd like to find out what's taking so long."

Henry started walking in circles. It looked like he was deep in thought.

"Henry, what's your problem? Is there something you're not telling me?"

Henry just kept stammering.

Clint finally got fed up. "Out with it."

Henry eventually managed to squeak out, "The project is finished."

"Okay, then what the hell are Greg and Rudy working on now?" Clint asked angrily.

"Well, I kind of have them on standby."

"What the hell does that mean?"

"I—I just wanted them to patrol the highway and see that everything is in place. You know, I wanted to have them see that all the survey markers are where they're supposed to be, and stuff like that."

"You're still not making any sense. So, basically, Greg and Rudy are spending all day either driving around or sitting in a restaurant, or god-knows-what. Is that it?"

"That's about the extent of it," Henry said, but Clint was about ready to explode. "Sir, I was just worried that if I told Hugh we didn't have any assignments we might get laid off. I mean, I don't care so much if I get laid off—I'm single and I got no kids. But, Greg has a family to support and Rudy has to pay child support. Look, you can fire me, but please don't fire Greg and Rudy. I'll take full responsibility."

"Henry, nobody's going to get fired," assured Clint. "But, in your case, don't push your luck. Where are Greg and Rudy right now?"

"Well, it's two-thirty. They're probably either at the Tunnels Café, the Charles Hotel in Boston Bar, or the Kanaka Bar Restaurant."

"Call them on the CB radio and tell them to get their asses back here *now*," ordered Clint.

It took four tries before Rudy finally answered the CB radio, and when he answered, he was barely audible.

"Rudy, what is your position?" asked Henry.

"We're just the other side of the Ainslie Creek Bridge."

"What are you doing there?"

"We are taking some elevation shots."

"What are you doing that for? I never asked you to do that."

"We were just checking to see if any of the roadway was undermined when we had that heavy rainstorm last month."

"Rudy, don't go bullshittin' me. I know what you're up to. I need you and Greg to come back to the office right away."

When Greg and Rudy returned to the office, Clint gave them assignments for the rest of the week. Clint then handed Henry a stack of field notes to be entered into the computer.

"Greg, Rudy, meet me at the Highways Department maintenance yard at eight o'clock tomorrow morning. I have an assignment for you," Clint said.

The following morning, Clint arrived at the maintenance yard at 7:45 a.m.

"Ah, Greg, Rudy, how nice to see you. As you know, camping season is about to begin. All the provincial campgrounds are set to open on Victoria Day weekend, which is coming up quick. Of course, the perennial favourite part of any camping trip is the campfire, and in order to have a campfire, firewood is needed. That's where you guys come in."

Clint handed Greg and Rudy an axe each. Then he pointed to a massive pile of cut-up logs beside one of the maintenance sheds. Clint could tell by the look on their faces that they were in complete disbelief.

"Now, I want each log section split into at least four pieces and stacked neatly over there," said Clint, pointing to an empty space beside another building.

"Mr. Matheson, sir, I'm awfully sorry about what I said the other day. I take it all back," said Rudy.

"Oh, I wasn't even thinking about it," replied Clint. "You guys have had it pretty easy for the past while. But now, your ride on the gravy train is officially over. I just thought I would give the both of you a taste of what hard work is really like."

"Mr. Matheson, how long are we going to have to do this?" asked Greg.

"Until I say so. For the rest of the week at least. But don't worry, I don't expect all of it to be chopped. This is an entire summer's worth. Just do as much as you can. See you guys later."

As Clint left, he could tell from the look on the faces of Greg and Rudy that they would rather do something else with their axes.

Clint arrived in Merritt that afternoon, and after checking into a motel, he headed over to the Department of Highways office. He was greeted by Matt Yablonski, the Crew Chief. There was a phone message from Anders Johanssen, stating that he would be coming up the following afternoon from Kamloops.

The next morning, Matt drove and Clint took notes. After they turned off of Highway 5 onto the Coldwater Valley Road, Clint began surveying the mountainsides on either side of the valley. Eighteen miles south of Merritt, a road branched off to the right. There was a sign at the intersection for Coquihalla Lake with an arrow. The road ahead carried on to the village of Brookmere. They turned onto the road to the right, and it immediately climbed up the hillside. The road eventually entered a valley that was wide and flat—lots of room for a four-lane highway. Fifteen miles later, they reached Coquihalla Lake. From there, they turned right onto a seldom-used logging road and continued until the road ended. They then walked a short distance to the edge of the same gulch that Clint encountered the other day, observing the very spot he stood across the gulch.

"Well, Matt, I believe I have the route for this new highway determined. Let's head back and we'll discuss it with Anders this afternoon."

When Clint met with Anders Johanssen, he outlined his proposal for the route of the new highway, using a topographical map as a reference. He could tell that Anders liked the idea of building the highway on the eastern hillside away from the populated areas.

"Clint, I can take responsibility for the section between Coquihalla Lake and Merritt if you like," Anders offered.

"That would be great, but it is not one hundred percent definite yet. I'll have to receive approval from the Premier and the Highways Minister when I make my presentation in Victoria next week."

6

After the meeting, Clint returned to his home in Vancouver. When he passed through Hope, he stopped in at the local museum and enquired about the railway line that used to run through the Coquihalla Valley.

"If you want any information on the Kootenay Central Railway, you'll have to travel to Penticton and visit their museum. It has an entire exhibit dedicated to the Kootenay Central Railway. The only KCR items we have at this museum are some artifacts from the Hope station and the old mile-board from Lear Station," the man at the desk informed Clint.

With this in mind the following morning, Clint obtained the phone number for the Penticton Museum through long-distance information. When he phoned the museum, the lady at the other end informed him about the KCR exhibit.

"Yes, we do have an extensive database of written articles and photographs of the history of the KCR. I'm Barbara Middleton, the Director. I'm always at the museum on Saturdays, but the rest of my schedule isn't quite concrete. If you can, definitely come down on a

Saturday and I'll help you find what you're interested in."

"Splendid, I'll be there one week from today," said Clint.

When Clint arrived at his office the following Monday morning, his secretary, Sandra, gave him a list of phone messages from the previous week.

"Simon Dale, the President of Pacific Coast Gas Trunk Lines, has been phoning repeatedly since last Wednesday, and he needs to talk to you immediately."

"Oh God, what the hell does that asshole want? This better be important."

Clint went into his office and closed the door behind him. He took a deep breath and made a vow that he would keep his composure.

"Simon, how are you doing? It's Clint Matheson. I've heard you've been trying to reach me for the past few days. What's on your mind?"

"Matheson, I want to launch a formal complaint against two of your highway workers. They were seen driving on my road without my permission, and they nearly collided with one of Lindeman Logging's trucks. The driver nearly had a bloody heart attack."

"How did you know that it was one of my vehicles?"

"Your two-tone colour combination was a dead giveaway. I demand that you fire those two workers immediately."

"Gee, Dale, that's going to be very hard to do."

"Oh, why's that?"

"How am I going to fire myself?"

"What the hell are you talking about?"

"You see, Dale, that was me. I was in the passenger seat. The Crew Chief from the Hope crew was driving because I told him to."

"What the hell were you doing up there in the first place?"

"Look, that is none of your goddamn business, okay?"

"Well, we'll see what my lawyer has to say about that. I can have you charged with trespassing. Maybe then you will realize that it is my goddamn business."

"Dale, just because you own the pipeline right-of-way it does not automatically mean you own the road. If you must know why we were on the road, we are planning to build a highway through the region, and I wanted to determine the exact route. I've made observations on my topographical map, and the proposed route will be nowhere near your pipeline. There will be no disruption of any kind, so you have nothing to worry about."

"A highway? Over my dead body."

Before Clint had a chance to say anything else, Simon hung up. He went back out to the lobby and told Sandra, "If Simon Dale ever phones again, don't even answer the phone." While Clint was at Sandra's desk, he couldn't help but notice the plastic figurine that was on her desk. It was of a man dressed the same way as the man Clint and Henry saw above the fourth switchback. "What is that?"

"It's Tommy the Train Engineer," replied Sandra. "You know, the cartoon character. I got that for my little grandson, since he's a big fan of the show. He'll be turning four soon, and I'm just keeping it here until then."

Clint continued to stare at the object in complete bewilderment while flashbacks of that moment flooded back to him.

"Tell me something. Do railroad engineers still dress like that? I mean, they wore that outfit when I was little, but do they wear that outfit nowadays?" asked Clint.

"I don't know, I've never noticed whenever I see a train go by. It's possible, but I doubt it," replied Sandra.

"My case in point. Why don't the creators of this so-called cartoon character get in tune with the times. If you ask me, that's stereotyping."

Sandra seemed quite puzzled by Clint's sudden change in demeanour. "Sir, are you feeling okay?"

"Oh yes, I'm feeling just ducky," Clint shot back.

The following day, Clint travelled to Victoria and made his presentation to Premier Davenport, Bill Plotnikoff, and his deputy, Stan Fisher. He outlined the route that the highway would take, including the new sections to be built west of Hope, the three major bridges, and the snow-shed needed. All of them approved the proposal, but they were wary of the estimated cost.

7

The following weekend, Clint travelled to Penticton. On Saturday morning, he visited the museum. At the front desk, he asked to speak to Barbara Middleton. A few minutes later, she emerged from the back.

"You requested to see me?"

"Yes, my name is Clint Matheson. I spoke to you on the phone last week. I was the one who's interested in learning about the history of the rail line that used to run through the Coquihalla Valley."

"Oh, yes, the Kootenay Central. Come with me, and I'll show you our exhibit on the railway. I'll tell you this much. The section through the Coquihalla was the most problematic on the entire rail line, so it's no wonder that it was the first part to be abandoned."

"Why is that?"

"You'll see."

The room containing the KCR exhibit was filled with such artifacts as lanterns, handcars, signals, mile-boards from many stations, engineer and conductor uniforms, time-tables, and numerous photographs. Barbara directed Clint to one wall, where there was a brief written essay giving an overview of the history of the KCR

"Feel free to take your time, read it over, and tour the exhibit. If you have any questions, I'll be by the front desk."

According to the essay, the Kootenay Central Railway once ran between Nelson and Hope, and was constructed between 1897 and 1916. The purpose for its construction was to provide an all-Canadian rail link from the Kootenays to the West Coast, and tap into the vast mineral wealth of the Kootenay Region. It played a vital role in the development of the Southern Interior of British Columbia. Clint noted that the Chief Engineer of the KCR during the construction phase was a big fan of Shakespeare, so much so that he named all but one of the stations on the Coquihalla Subdivision after Shakespearean characters.

The essay mentioned that during its years of operation, the Coquihalla Subdivision was constantly plagued by heavy snowfalls, rockslides, and washouts. Except during WWII, the line was always closed during the winter months, and all rail traffic was diverted to the line that ran between Spence's Bridge and Merritt. The Coquihalla line was the last section to be completed, and the first section to be abandoned, which happened in 1961. It was active for only forty-five years.

I wonder if building a highway through that region is a good idea after all, Clint wondered for a moment. He shook his head. *With heavy snow removal equipment now available, the outcome will be a lot better this time around.*

Half an hour later, Barbara re-entered the exhibit room.

"So, what do you think?"

"Most impressive. That must have been quite the railroad. I can just imagine all the stories from people who worked on the line during the years it was operating."

Clint spent the next two hours admiring the many photographs as well as all of the memorabilia. He had to remind himself that the museum closes early on Saturdays.

"Well, I better be getting off. Thank you very much for all of your assistance. I've gained a lot more information as to what the railroad meant to this region. It seems so sad that it all had to come to an end," Clint said as he returned to the foyer and made a generous cash donation.

"It was my pleasure. I hope you will make a return visit here sometime in the future," said Barbara.

"I most definitely will."

Over the next three weeks, Clint had many closed-door meetings with Don Lassiter, Hugh Gormley, and Ed Hildebrandt, along with Lance Demitrios and the other Crew Chiefs, to determine how the work would be divided. Of all his Project Managers, Don Lassiter had the most expertise. But, as for Don himself, Clint couldn't stand him.

After one of the Project Management meetings, Clint asked Don to stay behind so they could have a one-on-one discussion.

"Don, I want to make this perfectly clear. You are not to make any decisions without my approval, all monthly progress and budget reports are to be handed in on time, you must attend all Project Manager meetings with no tardiness, and, most importantly, you must treat all surveyors working under you with respect. If there are any complaints against you, or if any of the rules are not met, that's it. Your bum-buddies in the union will not be able to help you this time. This is your last chance. You *will* accept that *I'm* in charge, and I will not tolerate any shit from you whatsoever. Do you understand?"

Despite Don nodding in agreement, Clint still anticipated trouble.

8

JUNE 1983

Clint's next order of business was to arrange the logging of all the forested areas on the proposed highway right-of-way. Originally, Clint had planned to choose which outfit would log the areas through a bidding process, but since Lindeman Logging already had the contract to log in the Coquihalla Valley, Clint decided to stick with them.

Clint then travelled to Hope to meet with Herb Victor, the Superintendent of Lindeman Logging. The evening he travelled up there, instead of having dinner at one of the diners along Highway 3, he decided to head downtown. There was one particular restaurant that caught his attention—the Kootenay Central Restaurant.

Inside, the walls were adorned with old photographs of the KCR, as well as a huge mural of the old Hope station. There was even a large picture of the big trestle with the waterfall in the background—taken in the same spot where Clint took his picture.

Right after Clint received his order and began eating, a middle-aged First Nations man approached him.

"You're Clint Matheson, is that correct?"

"Yes, that's right," replied Clint.

"I thought so. I remember seeing you on the CBC News. Mind if I join you?"

Clint was surprised that he was so recognizable from the brief news coverage after his meeting with Premier Davenport. "Sure, why not."

The man sat down across from Clint and ordered a coffee.

"What can I do for you?" asked Clint.

"My name is Edwin Baptiste. I am the Chief of the Hope Indian Band. I understand that you are planning to build a highway through the Coquihalla River valley."

"Yes, that is correct."

"When I read the article in the *Hope Standard*, I noticed that in the area between Ladner Creek and Boston Bar Creek, you plan on building the highway on the lower bench."

"Yes, we are. Is there a problem with that?"

"Indeed, there is a very serious problem. I ask you to reconsider that routing."

"What's the problem? Oh, wait a minute—let me guess. There's an ancient burial ground there. Listen, Chief, I hate to burst your bubble, but I have heard this story far too many times over my career. It seems that every time we plan a new highway, the local Indians start screaming bloody murder that we're building it over an old village site or over an old burial ground. So, unless you have documented proof that there was a burial ground there, you, my friend, are out of luck."

"Are you finished?" replied Edwin. "No, that's not what it's about. It's something completely different."

"Well then, just what the hell is this all about?"

"It's a long story."

"Out with it, then. I have all evening."

"I have a better idea. Why don't you come over to my house tomorrow evening? I'll explain in detail. I will even serve dinner." Edwin gave Clint directions to his house on the Reserve.

"That sounds okay. I shall take you up on your offer."

"You will still be in town tomorrow evening, won't you?"

"Of course. As a matter of fact, I have a meeting with the Superintendent of Lindeman logging tomorrow."

"Oh, that'll be Herb."

"You know him?"

"I've known him all his life. He's one of our people. We go fishing together quite often."

Oh boy, that meeting tomorrow may not go as well as I hope.

The following morning, Clint met with Herb at the Hope office. At first, Herb seemed very interested in taking on the job, but when Clint pointed to the area around Portia Bench and told him that would be where the largest portion of trees would have to be cut, Herb abruptly changed his tune. His enthusiasm immediately changed to concern, and he almost appeared to be frozen in fear. After a few minutes of total silence, he finally said, "No, we won't do it."

"What do you mean, you won't do it?" asked Clint.

"I—I said we are not interested. We'll only do the first part, but we're not touching the trees on the bench."

"It doesn't work that way. It's either all or nothing."

"If that's the case, then we don't want the job at all. Forget about it."

"What the hell is your problem with logging there? We are willing to offer your company a generous amount."

"We don't want your *goddamn money*. We will never do anything that will anger Siaman."

"Who the hell is Siaman?"

"Look, I have to go. The deal is off."

"Don't ever come back," Clint said as Herb left. "Man, now I'm back to square one. I've got to get to the bottom of all this starting tonight."

"Oh, what's happening tonight?" asked the receptionist, Linda.

"Big Chief Baptiste wants me to come over to his place for dinner. It appears he wants to discuss the area in question."

Clint arrived at Edwin's house a little before 6:00 p.m. Edwin led him directly to the dining room, and just as he sat at the table, a familiar face entered the room. It was the pretty young lady who Clint had seen at the bar.

"Clint, I'd like you to meet my daughter, Cindy,"

Clint, still looking very surprised, started to say, "Pleased to meet you. But I think we already ..."

Edwin shifted awkwardly before he went into the kitchen.

"You saw me at the Hope Hotel recently," interrupted Cindy. "I thought you were going to come over and talk to me, the way you were eyeing me all evening. What's the matter? Are you too shy? Or were you too busy with your friends?"

"It turned out that I ran into some guys who worked for me years ago, and I haven't seen them in a long time. But I'll also admit that yes, I'm sometimes shy. I wasn't trying to be stuck up or anything."

Their conversation was interrupted by Edwin announcing that dinner was ready. Cindy then called out, "Alex, dinner's ready! Let's go!"

Clint thought to himself, *Alex? Who's Alex?*

Just then, a little girl came running down the stairs and into the dining room. She couldn't have been more than three years old.

"This is my daughter, Alexandra," said Cindy.

At that point, Clint assumed she was married. He wondered where Alex's father was, but he didn't want to ask questions.

As they sat down to dinner, Clint couldn't help but notice the First

Nations mask hanging on the wall. It looked identical to the mask that he and Henry saw that time they were stuck at Portia Bench.

"So, tell me about that mask," said Clint.

"It was a ceremonial mask that was used by my tribe for many generations," replied Edwin. "It was used specifically for funerals."

This sent a shiver down Clint's spine.

"I had a meeting with Herb earlier today. The minute I showed Herb on the map the area to be logged on Portia Bench, he had an absolute fit. He completely freaked out and said that he didn't want the job."

"That goes to show you that our people respect the spirit of Siaman. If we do anything to anger his spirit, bad things will happen."

"Tell me about this Siaman, please, Chief."

"It looks like Herb gave you a head start, but you didn't hear the whole story. To get a full understanding, it's best to know who Siaman was, and what he meant to our people," said Edwin. "Many years ago, the Hope Nation was ruled over by the Grand Chief named Siaman. He was known as an excellent hunter and fisherman. He ruled the tribe with great authority; many elders claim that even to this day, he was the greatest Chief our nation ever had. He had a son, who was named Siaman Jr. He was very proud of his son, and always wanted the best of everything for him. He was grooming him to eventually take over as Chief, and his dream was that his son would be an even greater Chief than he was. He believed that his son would one day lead the Salish people to victory in their many battles with the Haida Nation.

"When Siaman Jr became a man, his father made arrangements with the Chief of the Nicola Nation to provide him with a bride. In exchange for twelve bear pelts, the Chief arranged for him his niece, Nooaitch. She was considered the tribe's princess, although there was never any ceremony to crown her. The arrangement was that Nooaitch would travel from the Nicola Village, near the present town of Merritt, toward the Hope Village, and Siaman Jr would travel from Hope toward Nicola. They would rendezvous somewhere in between, and then they would travel back to Hope together. They would travel on the trade route between our nations, which ran through the Coquihalla River valley. We didn't have horses, so all travel was done on foot.

"The night of Siaman Jr's first day of travel, the earth shook very violently. He was awakened from his sleep by the earth shaking and the trees swaying. He barely escaped a tree falling right where he had slept. But he was more concerned about his bride-to-be, who was camping farther up the canyon. Unbeknownst to Siaman, Nooaitch had set out two days earlier, so she was only four miles from where he camped that night. He waited until daybreak to set out to find his bride-to-be, but even with daylight, he had difficulty making his way along the trail, as there were many fallen trees and boulders, along with crevasses that were newly formed. The landscape had changed completely. It had taken him nearly a day to cover four miles, and at that time, he came across the remains of a makeshift camp. Although several boulders had come down from the mountainside, he could distinguish the remains of a lean-to, and he also came across the ashes of a campfire, which were still warm. He then found a poke made from moose hide, and inside he found some trinkets with distinct markings. He could tell immediately that they were the markings of the Nicola Tribe. He knew that he had found the last camp of Nooaitch, and she had met an untimely end at the hands of the mountain.

"After making this unpleasant discovery, Siaman was absolutely devastated. He made his way back to his village, climbing over fallen trees and boulders. When he finally reached the village, he found it in ruins. Many people from the village had perished, including Siaman's parents. A massive cedar tree had crushed their hut. This became too much for Siaman to bear. But he was more devastated for the loss of his bride-to-be than his parents. He decided at that point that his life was over. He made a vow that he would put a curse on the spot where Nooaitch breathed her last breath. A few of the survivors of the tremor remember seeing Siaman standing on a bluff right over the Fraser River, just north of where the Highway One Bridge is now. They remember him yelling out, '*Nih shuquim quahayskahstan sha-tla `tkw*,' which means, 'Whoever treads upon my beloved's final resting place will perish.' Ever since then, the spirit of Siaman has been guarding Nooaitch's final resting place. To this day, nobody has tried to disturb it, and it is greatly feared that anyone who does will face dire consequences."

Clint took a moment to digest all this information, and then a thought came into his head. "You know something, this story sounds very familiar. It sounds exactly like the story of Slumach and his lost gold mine. You may remember that just before he was hanged, he put a curse on the site of his mine, and anyone who came across it would die. Gee, what a coincidence. It just so happened that he was a Salish Indian, too. So, what is it with you people? Do you have nothing better to do with your time than to put curses on places with sentimental value?"

"No, it's a completely different story," replied Edwin. "Even so, the case of Slumach shows you what can happen when spirits' warnings are not heeded. Look what happened—every person who tried to find Slumach's mine died a mysterious death. Do you want a similar fate to happen to your workers if you build that highway?"

"Well, let's get one thing straight. It's not a case of *if* the highway will be built—it's *when*. As for this Siaman dude, it's just Native folklore. It's only a legend; there's no documented proof. Just for the record, when did this incident happen?"

"The best estimate was that it was around three hundred years ago," replied Edwin.

"If that's the case, how would anyone be sure that this incident happened on Portia Bench? Was the exact location ever determined?"

"As the story goes, when Siaman returned to the village, he told one of the survivors that he found the remains of Nooaitch's camp on a flat expanse of land now called Ladner Creek. That survivor was one of my ancestors, and the story has been passed down from one generation to the next."

Clint admitted to himself that he found the whole story quite fascinating, but he still had no intention of backing down.

"Isn't it possible to build the highway on the opposite side of the Coquihalla River?" Edwin refused to give in.

"Look, this whole incident happened three hundred years ago. If this Siaman character is still guarding his lover's burial place, it's time to let it go. The fact is you can't stop progress. At the rate this region is growing, a highway has to be built through the area sooner or later. If there really is this ghost up there, he'll just have to get used to it; it's a fact of life. However, what we could do is erect some kind of memorial to him—maybe a monument or something."

"Well, I guess there's not a lot I can do. Your highway has been approved, and that area is not on any Indian land."

"Look, Chief, I'm not trying to be an asshole. What it boils down to is the demand for a new highway, and it has to go somewhere. The Coquihalla River valley is the most ideal route."

"I'm still not convinced this highway is a good idea."

"Another point I want to make is that the reserve and the entire Hope area has a very high unemployment rate right now. This project will create many jobs in the short term, and will result in many economic benefits in the long term. The new highway will also give a boost to the tourism industry, ease congestion on the existing highways, and provide easier access to the Lower Mainland from other parts of Canada. It'll be a win-win situation for everybody."

When it was 9:00 p.m. Cindy said that she had to get back home, which was half a block up the road. It was way past Alexandra's bedtime.

"I have a very busy day tomorrow. I work as an Administrative Assistant at the local Band office. It isn't easy working full time and being a single parent," said Cindy.

"I sort of know how that is," said Clint. "I'm a single parent, too. But my kids live with their mother, and they're now teenagers."

"Your kids are teenagers? You must have been married awfully young," said Cindy, looking surprised.

"Well, I am forty-four."

"Wow, you sure don't look it."

"Why, thank you. I always try my best to stay in shape. By the way, can I walk you home?"

"Sure, why not," Cindy said as she put on her jacket. She gave her father a hug.

"Chief, thank you for having me over for dinner. You've given me some things to think about before we get started," Clint said, extending his hand.

Edwin shook Clint's hand and nodded, concern still written across his face. "Good night, Clint."

Clint and Cindy stepped outside with Alexandra. "Don't mind my father. He's so set in our old ways. To be honest, I've heard that story a million times. A lot of our people swear by it, but I think it's a load of bullshit."

"I'm not the least bit worried. My only concern is getting the highway completed in time for Expo." When they reached Cindy's house, Clint said, "Look, I want to make it up to you for snubbing you that night. Would you like to go to dinner tomorrow night?"

"That sounds like a nice idea, but why so soon?" Cindy said, playful.

"I have to go back to Vancouver the next day. I'll be back, of course. I'm just not sure when. I would like to see you one more time while I am still here. So, what do you say?"

"I would be most delighted."

"How would you like to go to that Bavarian restaurant downtown?"

"That sounds good to me."

"Good, it's a date then. Can I pick you up at seven o'clock?"

"Actually, why don't we meet at the restaurant? I'm not sure if my father would like the idea of his daughter dating the man who wants to destroy a sacred Indian site. I'll get my sister to look after Alex. So, I shall see you there."

9

Clint arrived at the restaurant precisely at 7:00 p.m. that evening, but Cindy was nowhere to be seen. After a few minutes, he began to wonder if she had stood him up to get back at him. Finally, she arrived at 7:10 p.m.

"I'm sorry I am late. My sister didn't get to my place until seven o'clock; she couldn't get away from work on time," said Cindy.

"Don't you worry about it," Clint told her just as the hostess saw them to their table. "Have you ever tried Schnitzel before?"

"No, I haven't."

"You should give it a try—you don't know what you're missing." Clint smiled.

Over the course of the evening, Clint wanted to ask Cindy what happened with her and her husband, but he knew that it was none of his business. But somehow, it seemed as though she could read his mind.

"I suppose you're wondering what happened between me and my old man," said Cindy.

"Actually, I wasn't really giving it any thought."

"Oh, I bet you were. I could tell by the look in your eye. If you must know, a year and a half ago, he ran off with some white woman, and I haven't seen him since. The last I heard was that he was somewhere in the Queen Charlotte Islands."

"Oh, I see. Well, in my case, I put in way too many hours at work and spent too much time on the road. She didn't understand that it was all part of the job. I guess I'm a bit of a workaholic."

"You're sure a far cry from my ex. I don't think he even knew what work was."

The waitress brought a bottle of wine and poured them each a glass. Clint then raised his glass and said, "Enough of our past failures. Here's to the future."

Clint then noticed that hanging on the wall was a picture of the large trestle with the waterfall in the background, identical to the picture hanging on the wall in the Kootenay Central Restaurant. He pointed out the picture to Cindy.

"It's really weird. Before I began surveying for the new highway, I didn't even know that the Kootenay Central Railway existed."

"You've got to be kidding," replied Cindy. "I rode that train for the first time when I was four years old. My family and I were going to a potlatch on the Wild Horse Reserve near Cranbrook. From what little I can remember, the train ran way up on the side of the mountain. It was really scary. After the line was abandoned, my siblings and I used to ride our bikes up the Coquihalla road all the time. We didn't give a shit if it was a private road. My brothers used to ride right up to where the road goes under the big railway bridge. You want to hear something funny? One time, my brother said he saw a tiger run across the road, and another time, my older brother said he saw an elephant by the side of the road. Weird, eh?"

"Yeah, that does sound pretty weird. The only places you can see tigers and elephants here is at the circus and the zoo."

They had both lost track of time until Cindy realized that her sister had to be up early in the morning, so she had to get back home and relieve her of her babysitting duties.

"When will you be returning to Hope?" Cindy asked as they left the restaurant.

"As soon as I can, but it will be at least three weeks from now."

"Well, you know where to find me."

10
JULY 1983

Mitchell Logging, based in Mission, won the bid for logging the Coquihalla Valley once Herb had refused Lindeman Logging to take on the highway project. Clint was astonished by Mitchell Logging's low bid. He wondered how they would be able to pay their workers, but figured that they must be pretty desperate. He phoned the company headquarters and delivered the good news to the President, Buzz Mitchell.

"Congratulations, Mr. Mitchell, you are the successful bidder. I would like to meet with you in the Hope office next Monday morning. I'll outline the specific areas that you will log. I want you to set up a camp in the Coquihalla River Valley—it would be better if your workers live on the site rather than drive back and forth each day since most of your workers live in Mission."

"Do you have any spare ATCO trailers?" asked Buzz.

"Excuse me, but isn't it your responsibility to provide portable buildings? We only use ATCO trailers when we're working in very remote areas, and they're only for Highways workers. Don't you have any of your own?"

"We own six ATCO trailers, but they are all tied up right now."

"They can be rented."

"Isn't that expensive?"

"Look, this project will only take about a month. They can be rented short term."

"Okay, I'll look into it. But, in the meantime, I have some portable tent-like structures, and my guys can bunk in those."

"Whatever. Just be at the Hope office first thing next Monday. We'll discuss it then."

After he hung up the phone, Clint shook his head. *Maybe choosing Mitchell wasn't such a good idea after all ... but if they can get the job done, they'll keep my expenses down.*

The following Monday morning, Buzz arrived at the Hope office bright and early. He looked well past retirement age. He was accompanied by a very scruffy looking man with numerous tattoos.

"This is my son, Buzz Jr, the foreman of the logging crew," Buzz introduced the man.

Clint gave a detailed analysis of the areas that will be logged, using his topographical map as a reference. "It would be in your best interest if you were to set up two camps due to the sheer size of the operation. The best site for camp one is three miles north of Lear Station, and the best site for camp two is on the clearing right after the Bailey bridge over the Coquihalla River just before the road begins its ascent up the mountain."

Henry, who was standing behind Clint, spoke up. "Say, isn't that the spot where you and I ..."

"Henry, why are you still here?" Clint interrupted him. "It's eight-thirty, and you have a lot of work to do. Greg, Rudy, and that new guy of yours are just sitting around, doing nothing. Now, get going." Clint then turned back to Buzz Sr and Buzz Jr. "Okay, gentlemen, how soon can you start?"

"We will set up the camps and move the men and equipment in tomorrow, and the logging will commence on Wednesday. You know, it's so great to have my son back working for me after being away for seven years. It's hard to find decent help. I had to basically run the company all by myself," said Buzz Sr.

"Well, that's great to hear. So, what were you doing in that time—travelling?" asked Clint.

"I was in jail," replied Buzz Jr.

"Oh, I see. If you don't mind me asking, what were you in for?"

"Manslaughter."

"Are you serious?" asked Clint, astonished.

"Do I look like I'm joking?" Buzz Jr said aggressively, and turned to leave. Clint guessed he wasn't.

Right after Buzz and Buzz Jr left, Clint summoned Don into his office.

"Don, I want you to keep a close eye on this outfit. I want a daily report on their progress, and if you run into any problems with them, I need to know immediately."

"Why would there be any problems with them?" asked Don.

"For one thing, the owner of the company sounds like he's starting to go senile. Secondly, his son is apparently a convicted killer, and he's the foreman. Need I say more?"

Don nodded in agreement and left the office. Clint sat down at his desk.

Another of Clint's main priorities was to get in touch with Cindy. The last time he had spoken to her was two weeks ago over the phone while he was still in Vancouver. Since she gave him only her home phone number, he had to look up the phone number for the Band office in the telephone directory.

"Cindy! Guess who's back in town?"

"Well, hello there, stranger. I was beginning to wonder if you were ever coming back."

"Are you kidding? I jump at every available opportunity to come to this great community, especially if there is an opportunity to see you. So, I was wondering, would you like to go to lunch?"

"That sounds great, but today is out of the question. I'm in meetings all day today with representatives from the Department of Indian Affairs, and tomorrow I am meeting with officials with the Department of Fisheries and Oceans."

"Hey, what is this? Work, work, work—is that all you think about?" Clint teased.

"You should talk! By the way, I'm free on Wednesday. Is that okay?"

"Sure, that'll be just fine. Let's meet at the Kootenay Central Restaurant at noon."

"I'll see you there."

The following day, the crews from Mitchell Logging set up their respective camps with temporary tent structures. Buzz Jr supervised the camp near Portia Bench. Later that evening, the crew at the Portia Bench camp made a huge bonfire. They were going to have a wiener roast before turning in. At first, everything was going fine. But then, the wind began to pick up. A storm seemed to be coming in, but there was not a cloud to be seen. The wind did not let up; it intensified. Trees began to sway violently, and the crew had an impossible time keeping the fire going.

With every passing moment, the wind grew stronger and stronger. One by one, the portable tent buildings blew over. Wind speeds soon reached hurricane force, and each man was flung against a tree or the ground. One company truck blew up onto its side while the other flipped onto its roof. For nearly a half an hour, the wind blew relentlessly. Then, for no reason, it suddenly stopped. Everything from the camp was strewn all over the place. Most of the men's belongings and sleeping bags were blown way back into the bush.

Tonight, they would have to sleep on the ground.

The men tried to sleep that night, but it was a difficult task. Buzz Jr decided to stay awake and keep a vigil over the camp, looking out for wild animals and anything out of the ordinary. One of the men offered to relieve him after a couple hours. The sound of First Nations drumming and chants was unmistakable, but the men couldn't determine where the sounds were coming from. None of the men got very much sleep.

***

At 7:00 a.m. the following morning, Don arrived at the camp near Lear. The crew was already at work, so everything looked in order. He assumed everything would be the same at the Portia Bench camp, so when he passed by the site of the camp, he never even looked over; he kept on going.

***

When Clint arrived at the Hope office at 8:00 a.m. he had the feeling he needed to head up to the Portia Bench area. He couldn't explain why—it was his intuition talking.

When Clint arrived at the Portia Bench camp, he couldn't believe his eyes. Each man was lying in a fetal position, and most of them were still asleep. Buzz Jr was sitting in a crouched position with his eyes wide open, acting like he was in a catatonic state. The camp looked like a disaster area. Debris was strewn about everywhere, all of the tents had blown over, and both vehicles were overturned. Clint was absolutely furious.

"Buzz, what the fuck happened here?" yelled Clint.

Buzz Jr gave no response. He continued to give a blank stare, as though his mind was on another planet. Clint shook him vigorously and slapped him twice across the face.

"Tell me what happened *now*."

"What are you talking about?" asked Buzz Jr in a puzzled tone.

Clint was completely aghast. He pointed all around the site of the camp and said, "The camp is a fucking disaster! Everything is all over the goddamn place, and the trucks—why the fuck are they on their roofs?"

"Didn't you feel the windstorm last night?" asked Buzz Jr, still in a state of disbelief.

"What windstorm?"

"There was a major windstorm last night—it was like a bloody hurricane! I'd never seen anything like it."

"We never got no windstorm last night. I don't remember any wind, period."

"How do you think our trucks ended up on their roofs? They couldn't have flipped over on their own—"

"I don't give a shit how any of this happened. Now, clean this place up. Everybody, get up and get to fucking work. I am going to check in this afternoon, and I want to see results."

Back in Hope, Clint met with Cindy for lunch at the Kootenay Central Restaurant as planned. After catching up on the past couple weeks, Cindy told Clint that she had tomorrow afternoon off.

"I was wondering if you might be able to arrange to have tomorrow afternoon off as well?" Cindy asked.

"Of course, I can take time off whenever I want. I am the boss after all."

"That's good," she said. "Why don't we plan something?"

"Sure, why don't we go for a drive up the Fraser Canyon? I can show you some of my earliest achievements with the Highways Department. I can pick you up some time after one o'clock," Clint suggested.

When Clint returned to the logging camp near Portia Bench later that afternoon, nothing had changed. Not one tree had been cut down, and all the loggers were repairing their chainsaws.

"Alright Buzz, start explaining," said Clint.

"I don't understand it … the minute any of us start cutting into a tree, the chain breaks. These were supposed to be brand-new chains."

"That doesn't surprise me. These chainsaws have got to be older than me." Clint pointed to a chainsaw that wasn't being used and said, "What's the matter with that one?"

"I tried and tried and tried to start it, but it just wouldn't start," said Buzz Jr.

Clint picked up the chainsaw, primed the pump, and gave the cord a mighty pull. It started right away. "Would you look at that? There's nothing wrong with it."

"I don't understand it—it wouldn't start for me, I swear."

One of the members of the logging crew, who had the name "Trevor" written across his hard hat, approached Clint.

"Mr. Matheson, last night there was some First Nations guy banging on his drum and chanting all night, but we never saw him."

"Trevor, is it? That was just your imagination, son."

"You know what I saw over there this morning?" Trevor pointed east and said, "An elephant."

Clint had to restrain himself from bursting out laughing. "Oh, really? An elephant? What colour was he? Was he striped? Checked? Polka dotted?"

"Why, you smart-assed son-of-a-bitch," Trevor retorted as his face grew red.

"What did you call me?" Clint could tell from the look on Trevor's face that he wanted to take a swing at him. "I wouldn't do that if I were you," he warned.

"Trevor, it was probably just a bear. You didn't sleep much last night, so you might have been blurry eyed," said Buzz Jr, stepping in between them.

Clint, still very annoyed, pointed to one of the overturned trucks and said "Why are these trucks still overturned? You guys are all big, tough lumberjacks. You should be able to turn them upright without any difficulty. Everybody, over here *now*."

Clint motioned for all of the men to come over to the truck on its roof. He showed each man where to grab onto, and told them to give a mighty push on the count of three. Sure enough, the truck went up on its side. He gave the command again to push on the count of three, and when they did, the truck landed upright.

"There, that wasn't so hard, was it?" Clint looked down on the ground and noticed that a hash pipe had fallen out of the window of the truck when it was up-righted. He picked it up and said, "Well, what do we have here? This is probably why you guys were seeing things. Who here is doing drugs?"

"We all do a few hoots now and then," said Buzz Jr.

"Alright, I've had enough. You guys are absolutely pathetic. Buzz, I am reporting this to your old man. I better start seeing some results, or else."

After Clint left, he couldn't help but tie in what Trevor said to what Cindy had said about her brother seeing an elephant in the area when they were kids. *There can't really be an elephant up here, can there? How could it even get here?*

11

The following morning, Clint requested Don come into his office.

"Don, I want you to stay with the logging crew working at Portia Bench. Watch their every move, and stay in constant contact with Buzz Jr."

"I don't know about you, but I find that guy a real asshole."

"Well, if there is anybody who is an expert on assholes, it's you."

"That guy constantly berates his workers and treats them like absolute garbage. He's always on their case. He acts like he enjoys being a prick."

Clint found this strange coming from Don.

"Oh, yes, you are really Mr. Congeniality. You treat your workers with the utmost fairness and respect. Personally, I think the two of you were meant for each other."

"Look, I didn't choose that outfit—you did. Why should I be their babysitter? I'd rather supervise the survey crews," said Don.

"Okay, I'll make it easier on you. You only need to check on them periodically and report back to me their progress at the end of the day."

After lunch, Clint drove up to the Administration Office for the Hope Indian Band. Cindy was finishing some documents as Clint arrived.

"Ready to take the afternoon off?" asked Clint.

"Yes, just give me a minute here," replied Cindy.

Just then, Edwin emerged from his office. "Clint, what a surprise. What brings you here?" asked Edwin.

"He's taking me out, Dad," said Cindy.

"I see … well, what are you two planning to do?"

"I'm taking her for a ride up the Fraser Canyon, Chief," said Clint.

Edwin continued to look concerned.

"It's okay, Dad. I'll be back in time to pick up Alex from Joanne's place. I'll see you at six," said Cindy, reassuringly. She gave her dad a kiss. "I'm ready, Clint,; let's go."

Clint drove up the Fraser Canyon Highway up to a rest area one mile north of the Alexandra Bridge. From there, they walked down a section of the old highway to the old Alexandra Bridge, replaced by the current bridge in 1962.

Afterward, they agreed to stop in at the Spuzzum Café. Once inside, Clint noticed the one waitress that was on duty. She was a tall, attractive blonde, and her nametag read "Lola". He figured she must be the girl that Rudy liked. Clint muttered to himself, "Man, Greg was right—she does have huge tits."

"What did you say?" asked Cindy.

"Oh, nothing."

"Hi, Cindy, how are you doing?" asked Lola.

"Just fine, how about yourself?" asked Cindy.

"You two know each other?"

"Of course; we went to school together, although I was a grade ahead," said Cindy.

"Oh, by the way, Rudy sends his regards," Clint said as Lola brought their order.

"You know him?"

"Yes, he works for me. I'm his boss. Actually, I'm his boss's boss."

"If you see that son of a bitch, ask him why he hasn't called me in ages."

"I'm afraid that might be my fault. With this new highway project, I've got him working many long hours. But, as far as I know, he still has weekends off. I'll be sure to tell him that you'd like to hear from him."

When they returned to Hope, Cindy asked Clint if he was free on Saturday.

"For you, I most definitely am."

"Super! I want to show you a little-known piece of local history just east of town."

"I'd be delighted."

Don came into the office shortly after 5:00 p.m.

"Don, how are things going with the logging crews? Especially that crew working on Portia Bench."

"Same shit, different day. None of their chainsaws were working again, and that Buzz Jr guy was just yelling and screaming at them. He eventually got fed up and made them use axes. Since then, they managed to cut down four trees."

"Four trees? Wow, in two days, they actually cut down four whole trees … Only ten thousand trees to go. The problem is we're building this highway for Expo 1986, not Expo 2006. This is the last straw."

Clint called Buzz Sr at the company's head office in Mission.

"Buzz, you'd better come up to Hope and meet me in the office first thing tomorrow morning," Clint said, unable to hide the anger in his voice.

"What seems to be the problem?"

"Well, it's very basic. Your logging crew is not getting the job done."

"Please, Mr. Matheson, sir, don't give up on them just yet. Let's try and work things out."

"Okay, meet me here at the office tomorrow morning like I said, and you had better have a game plan worked out. Be forewarned—my patience is wearing thin," said Clint.

When Buzz Sr arrived at the office the next day, he tried to go straight into damage control mode, but Clint didn't give him the chance.

"The performance of the crew working on Portia Bench is the absolute shits. That was quite the poor excuse where your workers claimed their camp was destroyed by a windstorm, and their chainsaws supposedly were sabotaged by tree-huggers. They were just severely outdated. Your workers are also doing drugs; some to the point where it was making them hallucinate."

"Okay, here's what I plan to do. I'll place all of my men on Portia Bench and completely focus on that section. I have a friend in Maple Ridge who owns an equipment rental company. He has a bunch of chainsaws that I can rent, and they are all brand-new. I also have a helicopter available to haul the logs out, bring them to where the other camp is, and then they can be loaded onto a truck there. What do you think?" said Buzz Sr.

"You guys have a helicopter?"

"Yeah, it's a Sikorsky model. Bought it at a military surplus auction at Fort Lewis, Washington, ten years ago. It was used in the Vietnam war."

"So, in other words, it's out-dated, just like every other piece of equipment you own."

"Oh no, it runs like a dream. It will definitely get the job done. Look, give my guys until next Tuesday. If you don't see any improvement by then, you can do whatever you want."

"Alright, but that is my ultimatum."

At the end of the day on Friday, Clint decided to forget about the logging company for now and just enjoy the weekend. After receiving Cindy's invitation, he decided to stay in Hope all weekend. He was especially curious about this piece of local history she wanted to show him.

When Clint returned to his room at the Starlight Motel, he phoned Cindy.

"So, what time will be convenient for me to pick you up?"

"No, no, I'll pick you up this time. I'll come by around one-thirty in the afternoon," Cindy said.

"I'm at the Starlight Motel, room fourteen."

When Cindy picked up Clint the next day, she drove down a very familiar road—right where the new highway would be constructed.

"Hey, I'm familiar with this area, or so I thought. I didn't know there was a part of the local history around here. What is it?" asked Clint.

"You'll see." When they reached the T intersection at the junction with Othello Road, Cindy hung a right. "You probably always turn left here. Have you ever thought about turning right for a change? I didn't think so," she said.

They soon passed a cluster of buildings painted in that familiar shade of Tuscan red. One of the buildings had the word "Othello" written across the front.

"These were the buildings from the Othello station on the Kootenay Central Railway. Someone purchased the old section house and converted it into a private residence."

The road continued for another hundred yards until they came to a huge log blocking the road. There was a small turnout on the left side of the road, which was where Cindy parked the car.

"A group from my Band placed this log to block the road from vehicular traffic beyond this point."

Clint asked, "How come?"

"You'll see," replied Cindy.

The road was built upon a large fill, and there were discarded railroad ties all down the embankment. The road continued along the bank of the Coquihalla River until it came to a tunnel. The tunnel portal was lined with decaying wooden beams.

"Wait a minute—I remember reading about this place. When I was at the museum, I read a written history of the Kootenay Central Railway, and it mentioned a canyon four miles east of Hope where the Chief Engineer designed a series of tunnels and bridges that went straight through the canyon instead of bypassing it," said Clint.

"Correct," replied Cindy. "These are called the Quintette Tunnels."

The tunnel was curved at one end, so when they were in the middle, it was pitch black. Right after they exited the tunnel, they came to a second much shorter one. Just past the second tunnel, they came to a missing bridge over the Coquihalla River. Across the river were third and fourth tunnels. On both sides of the river were sheer cliffs over a hundred feet high. Cindy pointed to the tunnel across the river.

"You see over there on the right—there's an opening. That made it appear as though there were five tunnels. That's why they're called the Quintette Tunnels, but in reality, there are only four. My friends and I used to come here all the time when we were kids. The KCR took out this bridge right after the railway was abandoned, and the bridge at the other end is damaged, so we were never able to explore the tunnel across the river."

Clint was awestruck by the breathtaking scenery. "Man, if this was made into a walking trail, can you imagine the tourist dollars it would generate?"

"Is that all you think about—money?"

"No, I think about you, too."

"You know something, if there were tourists here, we wouldn't be alone," said Cindy.

"That's a very good point. But, despite this magnificent scenery, I would much rather gaze into your smouldering dark eyes, anyway."

"Oh, I bet you say that to all the girls."

"On the contrary; you're the first."

"You know what I've noticed most about you, Clint? You're shy, admit it. Since I've known you, you've never tried to kiss me …" Cindy threw her arms around him, gave him a kiss, and said, "You're free now. Let your inhibitions run wild."

They kissed again, only this time, it was long and passionate. They were oblivious to everything around them except for the sound of the rushing water of the Coquihalla River.

Clint and Cindy eventually made their way back to her car.

"Why don't you join me at the motel later for dinner?" Clint invited.

"That sounds great, but I do have to pick Alex up from Joanne by nine tonight."

It was 6:00 p.m. that evening when Clint answered Cindy's knock on his motel room door.

"Top of the evening to you. I want to inform you that dinner will be courtesy Chan's Kitchen. The cookware that comes with this room is about as old as the motel itself, so if I was to make anything, it would be limited to Lipton Cup-A-Soup and toast."

"Chinese food will be just fine with me," said Cindy.

"I don't know why I bothered getting a room with a kitchenette; I only use it for breakfast anyway. The dining room at my house is bigger than these rooms combined. You'll definitely have to come up to Vancouver some time and see my place."

"That sounds like a good idea, since you've told me so much about it."

After dinner, they both flopped down on the sofa, and Clint

tried to see what was on television. They started to watch an old movie, but they soon became more focused on each other than the movie and completely lost track of time.

"Holy shit, Joanne is going to wonder what happened to me," Cindy quickly put on her shoes and grabbed her purse. "When can I see you next?"

"I hate to tell you this, but I have my kids next weekend. Maybe we can get together during the week. I'll give you a call." Clint gave her a quick kiss good night before she hurried off.

12
AUGUST 1983

On Monday, the morning air was punctuated by the sound of a helicopter flying overhead. The helicopter was big and bulky, still had its United States Air Force colours, and was piloted by none other than Buzz Jr himself. Buzz Jr landed the helicopter at a clearing formed from the twenty trees felled on Friday before the chainsaws malfunctioned again. Two choker men applied chokes to two logs each, as the helicopter would take four logs at a time to the loading area. When the chokes for the logs were all on tight, one of the choker men gave the signal to Buzz Jr.

At first, the take-off went smoothly, but right after the last log was off the ground, the helicopter's engine began to sputter, and Buzz Jr was unable to gain any more altitude. It then began to rock violently, smoke started to pour out of the engine, and then it started to spin around like a top. Buzz Jr frantically tried to regain control, but to no avail. The two choker men on the ground looked up in horror, and signalled Buzz Jr to jump. Buzz Jr screamed for help, but his screams were drowned out by the noise of the sputtering engine.

When Buzz Jr realized that there was nothing he could do with the controls to make the helicopter go up or down, he decided to jump. By then, smoke was filling the cockpit. He climbed onto the railing and jumped clear. He landed in some bushes, but he still landed quite hard. Buzz Jr screamed in agony while the choker men carried him clear from where the helicopter would crash. Just then, there was a massive explosion, and the helicopter erupted into a huge fireball. A few seconds later, the helicopter crashed into the ground in a flaming heap.

"Call an ambulance! He's hurt real bad," one of the choker men screamed.

***

Up in the Boston Bar Creek Canyon, Don heard what he thought was an explosion, but it sounded like it was far away. At first, he didn't think anything of it, but then he decided to check on the logging crew.

When Don arrived at the logging camp, he could see smoke rising from up the hill. He saw a group of the loggers carrying a man down the hill. He got out of his truck and went up to the loggers.

"What the hell happened here?" he asked.

"Little Buzz jumped out of the helicopter just before it blew up. He broke both legs when he landed, and his pelvis is probably broken, too. We have to get him to the hospital," said Trevor.

"The helicopter blew up?" repeated Don, astonished. He then ran up the hill toward the clearing. He saw the smouldering remains of the helicopter and noticed that no further trees had been cut down. He climbed back down the hill, went to his truck, and called Clint on the CB radio.

"Yes, Don, what can I do for you?"

"Clint, I need you to come up to the logging camp on the bench."

"What for? I'm very busy."

"I'd rather you see it for yourself."

"What's the problem?"

"It's the helicopter—it blew up."

"What do you mean it blew up?" Don could hear Clint's anger over the radio.

"I thought I heard an explosion so I came over to investigate. When I got here, all I saw was a flaming heap of metal. Can you please come up here—*now*?"

***

"I don't have time for this shit." Clint slammed down the receiver. After taking a deep breath, he changed his mind and decided to investigate.

When Clint arrived at the Portia Bench camp, he climbed up the hill in the direction of the smoke. When he reached the clearing and saw the pile of charred metal that was once the helicopter, and also took notice of the lack of progress with clearing any further trees since Friday, he was absolutely furious. He returned to the Hope office and phoned Buzz Sr.

"Buzz, I've had it. Your logging crew is fired. Get all your men and equipment out of my area *immediately*," Clint growled, not even giving Buzz a chance to defend himself.

It took over a day for Clint to cool off. It was Wednesday morning before he regained his composure enough to contact his second choice of a logging company. Clint called Leonard Exelsior, the General Manager of Livingston & Daniels Timber, and arranged to meet with him the following afternoon.

"I will admit that I fell victim to the old adage ... I got what I paid for. I wish I chose to work with your company in the first place, Leonard. If you are still interested in the job, it's yours."

"Yes, I am very much still interested. I can have one crew available to start next week, and once the section has been completely logged, I can put my remaining crews, who are currently occupied with other projects, onto the project in the Coquihalla Valley."

"That'll work well. By the way, how new is your equipment—mainly your chainsaws?"

"All of my loggers use Husqvarna models that are less than one year old."

"Super, I'll see you next week."

The following Monday morning, Leonard stopped in at the Hope office before his logging crew set up camp in the Coquihalla Valley. Clint showed him on the topographical map where to set up the camp and the area that will need to be logged.

"I have two ATCO trailers available, and they will be delivered to the campsite today. The crew will start first thing tomorrow morning," said Leonard.

"If there is anything you need, the office can be reached on the CB radio on channel seventeen, and if you run into any problems whatsoever, contact me immediately."

The next day, Clint headed up to the logging campsite after lunch. When he arrived at the site, he noticed the two ATCO trailers, and everything else seemed to be in order. What was the most appealing was the sound of chainsaws running. This was music to his ears. He got out of his truck, put on his hard hat, and walked up the hill toward the clearing. He saw that a huge section had already been logged.

Clint met up with David, the logging crew foreman.

"You guys are doing great work so far. Keep it up," Clint complimented him. "Did you experience any weather problems last night by any chance?"

David gave him a puzzled look. "No, why do you ask?"

"This valley has been noted for sudden wind gusts. It's a weather phenomenon that nobody has been able to explain."

"Nope, we didn't have any wind last night. It was calm as could be."

"Okay, just thought I'd ask. There's one more thing—I have a zero tolerance policy to drug use on any project that I'm running."

"That's okay; none of us do drugs anyway."

"Good. I'll check back in a day or two."

Later that afternoon, Clint received a welcome phone call from Cindy.

"Hi, Clint. How was your weekend?" He could sense her smile over the phone.

"Well, when you're trying to entertain two precocious teenagers, you definitely have your hands full. Even so, I still miss them; I wish I could see them more often."

"Yeah, it makes me glad that I have custody of Alex."

"Would you like to go to lunch tomorrow?"

"Sure, that sounds like a good idea."

"Let's make it the same place—the Kootenay Central. I'll meet you there at noon."

While he was at the restaurant with Cindy, Clint couldn't help but bring up the subject of Siaman. "If there really is the ghost of that Siaman character up there, is he selective in the people he spooks? I don't get it … The first logging crew had nothing but trouble. I have no idea if it had anything to do with the ghost or it was just the fact that they were a bunch of incompetent idiots. With the crew up there now, everything is going smoothly. Does this Siaman dude judge people on their attitudes or something? The foreman on the first crew was an absolute prick, but the foreman of the crew there now seems like a nice guy. So, if anyone is going to work up there who's an asshole, will Siaman scare him, but if he's nice, he won't? What am I dealing with here, the ghost of Miss Manners?"

"Are you finished? Wow, Dad was right—you can be a smart ass sometimes. Look, I don't know any more about the legend of Siaman than you do. Even though I've heard the story a million times, and it has been passed down from one generation to another, it's exactly what it is—a legend. I've learned that the story has become distorted over the last six or seven generations. If you want my honest opinion, I believe in Santa Claus more than I believe in Siaman. At least he gave me a bike and a Barbie doll."

The crew from Livingston & Daniels completed all of the logging on Portia Bench by early November, just in time for the first snowfall. Surveying on the bench would not commence until the following spring. Clint only kept Henry's and Lance's crews operating throughout the winter, surveying the realignment of Highway 1 west of Hope.

13

MARCH 1984

Spring had arrived in the Coquihalla River valley. The thick blanket of snow that had covered the valley for the past three months was now melted. For Clint, that meant one thing only—surveying could now resume in the region. The only two sections where preliminary surveys still needed to be performed were the section between Deneau Creek and Ladner Creek, and Portia Bench.

The task of surveying Portia Bench would fall on the shoulders of Lance's crew. Before winter set in, Lance's crew were working all along the summit area. They surveyed the greatest distance of any of the crews with pinpoint accuracy.

Clint gave Don specific instructions for the direction in which the survey would be conducted. Lance would man the transit, while Dan and Cory would take turns being the head and rear chainmen. Tyler would bring up the rear, pounding marker stakes into the ground from indentations from the marker pole.

Now that surveying had resumed, Clint could stay in Hope again.

All throughout the winter, he worked out of his Vancouver office. As a result, he had not spent much time with Cindy over the past three months. He had not able to come up to Hope every weekend and, whenever he did, it was just for the day, not leaving much time for him and Cindy. She only travelled to Vancouver once, and that was just for the day. They only had time to meet for lunch. Most of their communication in that time frame was by phone. Now that Clint was back in Hope, he was anxious to make up for lost time.

His first priority was to call Cindy.

"Hello there, my dear, guess who's back in town?"

"Clint, what a surprise! I was beginning to think you'd forgotten about me."

"Me—forget about you? That's absolutely absurd. I would never forget about you." Clint couldn't help but smile at the sound of Cindy's voice. "I'm now back in Hope, and I'm here to stay. So, I was wondering, would you be free to join me for dinner tonight?"

"Of course, I would be delighted. What's on the menu?"

"How does fish and chips sound?"

Over dinner, Clint and Cindy talked about their children. "So, my friend Donna, who has a daughter the same age as Alex, is taking her daughter and Alex to a camp at Alert Bay for a week and they left this morning. Today is the first day of Spring Break. They're going to learn tribal dances at the camp. When they return, she can show what dances they learned."

"That sounds interesting; maybe she can do a rain dance. Believe me, we sure can use it."

"We can have a big ceremony, and she can perform a rain dance."

"That is, however, weather permitting."

"You know something, that joke is getting pretty old." Cindy had a mischievous grin on her face. "You know what? I feel like going for a night on the town."

"What a great idea." Clint smiled. "But we're quite limited in the choice of night spots since this is such a small town. Where do you suggest?"

"How about the Silver Chalice? They have live entertainment this weekend."

Being a Friday night, the Silver Chalice was packed. They walked into the pub and right away Clint saw Henry with his friend Brian, from the Shell station, playing a game of pool. No sooner had Clint and Cindy found a table and sat down to order their drinks when Henry approached them.

"Hi, Mr. Matheson! How's it going? I'll have those field notes on your desk Monday morning. The going has been pretty good; the ground is nice and level, so it's been a piece of cake. I think I'm going to need my transit adjusted—one of the mechanisms is coming loose. Anyway, we'll talk about it on Monday. I can see that the two of you would like to be alone, so I won't be a bother. Seeing you later."

Once Henry had wandered off, Clint turned to Cindy. "That was Henry, the Crew Chief for the Hope crew. Do you think it'd be alright if I set him up with your sister?"

"I don't think Joanne would appreciate that."

"Oh, come on; Henry's a really nice guy. Don't judge him by his appearance; he's a good worker and quite the colourful character. You never know, he and Joanne might hit it off."

"I don't know. I think Joanne would prefer to meet a man on her own. Besides, between her work schedule and her kids, she doesn't have much time for dating."

"Oh well, it was just a suggestion."

Just then, some guy slammed an empty beer bottle down on the table. When Clint looked up, he realized that it was Trevor, one of Buzz Jr's loggers.

"Well, look who we have here. I got fired, and it's all your fault, you fucking asshole," said Trevor.

"Wait a minute, why is it my fault? What happened to you had nothing to do with me. That was strictly between you and Buzz."

"You embarrassed me, you bastard, remember? I tell you, I did see an elephant, but you thought I was full of shit. You made me look like I was some fucking lunatic."

"Okay, I believe you. But you are still responsible for your own actions. Now, get lost."

Instead of leaving, Trevor got right in Clint's face. "I'm going to make you pay, motherfucker. I'm going to bash your fucking brains in," he slurred.

"Clint, just ignore him," said Cindy.

"Shut up, bitch. When I'm finished kicking the shit out of you, I'm going to rape your fucking squaw girlfriend."

"That does it." Clint raised his fists as he stood up.

"Yeah, that's it. Come on, old man! Are you sure you don't need your walker?"

Clint delivered a series of rapid-fire jabs left and right, nailing Trevor square in the jaw, nose, and forehead. Within seconds, Trevor was a bloody mess. Clint didn't let up—he continued to nail Trevor with vicious upper cuts. Trevor didn't put up any offense whatsoever, allowing Clint to knock him out cold with a hard roundhouse right hook.

Henry watched the entire event, went up to Clint afterward, and said loudly, "Wowee, Mr. Matheson, you really gave him the ol' one-two. Hey everybody, let's hear it for my boss!"

The crowd erupted in applause. Clint felt totally embarrassed. As far as he was concerned, he was just defending himself. It wasn't anything he wanted to boast about.

In all the commotion, a man came out from the back room and approached Clint. "What's going on here?" the man asked.

"Who are you?" asked Clint.

"I'm Ian and I own this place. Now, can someone please explain to me what the hell happened here?"

"Ian, this asshole here started threatening him for no reason, and he was just defending himself. I swear, that guy instigated the whole thing. I'll vouch for Clint any day," said Henry. Trevor was still on the ground.

"Yes, Ian, that guy started the whole thing. I would have done the exact same thing myself," Brian chimed in.

"Get this piece of shit out of my bar," said Ian to his kitchen staff. "Well, as a token of my appreciation, I'd like to buy you and your lady friend your next round."

"Clint, don't you think we should leave?" asked Cindy.

"Of course not, the evening is just starting," replied Clint.

They stayed at the pub until closing time.

As they were getting ready to leave, Clint asked Cindy, "Would you like to go over to your place, since you have the place to yourself for a week?"

"Actually, I'd rather go to your place since my dad and the neighbors are so nosy. They all seem to know my every move; it's like I have no privacy at all. That's the trouble with living in a tight-knit community. So, what do you say, can I come over for a nightcap?"

"Sure, no problem. But as far as a nightcap is concerned, all I have is beer."

"Sounds good to me."

"Even though I've been away from this motel for a few months, I admit it'll be nice to be back in my own bed for a couple nights next week." Clint commented once they were back at the motel. "The furniture in this place should have been replaced years ago." He flopped down on the couch and a spring stuck out as if on cue.

"It does have that nostalgic look, though, doesn't it? By the way, I had a great time tonight. I learned that you're a boxer as well as a highway engineer. You are a jack-of-all-trades," said Cindy.

"I never looked at it that way. I guess I …"

Cindy never gave Clint a chance to finish his sentence. She took his hands and got him to stand up, threw her arms around him, and kissed him passionately. She led him toward the bedroom and flung herself down onto the bed, taking Clint with her. She undid the buttons on Clint's shirt and helped him remove it, did the same with his belt and the button on his pants, and allowed him to lower the straps on her dress and unzip it on the back. They continued in a passionate embrace all the while caressing every inch of each other's bodies.

***

On Monday morning, Lance's crew began their task. When the crew from Livingston & Daniels logged the forest on Portia Bench, they had only cut down a swath wide enough for a four-lane highway plus road allowances. On the west side, there was still some forested area before the mountain resumed. Clint viewed this as an advantage, because the trees could act as a buffer in the event of an avalanche.

On the following Thursday morning, as the crew stopped to take a coffee break, Dan happened to glance over into the nearby forest and saw something unusual.

Upon closer inspection, Dan saw that it was a long slab of iron about an inch thick. It was mostly rusted, but parts of it were black, indicating that it had been through a fire. It had a row of bolts down the middle, and all of the edges were jagged. He pointed it out to Lance and, as they inspected the object, they spotted more panels of iron in various sizes, all with jagged edges. They then came across what appeared to be a large wheel. They had no idea what the objects were, but figured that they had to be from a major piece of machinery.

When they took their lunch break, Lance and Dan decided to take another look at the objects. Cory and Tyler tagged along.

"What do you think this is?" asked Dan.

"Looks like it was part of a big engine," replied Lance.

As they hacked their way through the dense forest, they found more iron panels, another large wheel, a huge rod assembly, and a set of steel wheels, like the ones found on a railcar.

"Do you have any idea where these objects came from?" asked Tyler.

"Did you know about the abandoned railway up here?" said Lance.

"No, I didn't."

"Oh, come on, you can't miss it. You can see it from across the river. It's way up on the side of the mountain. I think this is all part of a steam locomotive."

"Wow, do you really think so?"

"I'm pretty sure. I'll call Clint to see if he can come here and take a look at this. Carry on and see if you come across any more parts."

***

Lance hurried back to the truck and called Clint on the CB radio.

"Highways Office, Clint speaking."

"Clint, it's Lance."

"Yes, Lance. How is everything going?"

"Oh, just fine. Listen, my crew and I came across something quite unbelievable in the woods right near the baseline we're running."

"Really, what is it?"

"It looks like the remains of an old steam engine, but it's hard to tell, because it's all in pieces."

"It's very possibly a steam locomotive, given the fact that the KCR line used to run up the mountain behind where you guys are working. I'd really like to take a look at it. I need an excuse to get out of the office anyway; I've been cooped up here all day."

***

When Clint arrived at the jobsite, the crew had uncovered further remains. The area was now becoming a debris field. They showed Clint what they had uncovered so far.

"Yes, these parts were definitely once a steam locomotive," Clint confirmed.

Clint wanted to take a further look into the woods to see if they could find any more remains. He eventually came across what used to be the cab. The faint outline of the words *Kootenay Central Railway* could still be discerned. Right nearby was the tender, which landed upside-down with its wheels in the air. Chunks of coal were scattered everywhere. Beyond that, he found remains of the railcars; most of them were smashed beyond recognition. The wheel assemblies were the only parts that remained intact.

"How could this have happened?" asked Lance.

"The locomotive most likely derailed and the entire train careened down the mountain," Clint speculated. "When it landed, the boiler must have ruptured, causing a massive explosion. That would explain why the locomotive is in many different pieces and all of the edges are jagged. This had to have happened at least fifty years ago, judging by the amount of rust on each fragment and the advanced stage of overgrowth."

On Clint's return to Hope, he stopped at the same spot where he had made his observations of the valley with Henry. He observed where the abandoned railway grade was on the mountainside across the valley, and estimated the distance between there and the bench. He figured that the train would have fallen at least three hundred feet.

Why has the wreckage remained there all these years?

14

The following week, Clint received a call over the CB radio from Lance on Wednesday morning.

"Clint, Dan has just made another discovery."

"What is it?" asked Clint.

"You have got to see it for yourself," said Lance.

Clint wasted no time heading up to the jobsite. He was anxious to find out what Dan had discovered now. When he arrived on Portia Bench, the men were on their coffee break.

"Man, you sure came up here fast," said Lance.

"Yes, well, I am a fan of early railroading."

"Let me show you what I found this morning." Dan directed them toward the spot where he made his discovery, and when Clint saw what he had found, he couldn't believe his eyes. It was another steam locomotive.

Despite the fact that it would have fallen three hundred feet down the mountain, it looked rather intact. There was severe front-end damage and the cab was crushed, indicating that the front end likely struck a tree and that it had rolled several times during the descent. Somehow it had managed to land upright.

"So, what do you think?" asked Lance.

"This is definitely another steam engine, but judging by the distance between this one and the other locomotive, it would have to be from a different accident entirely. I plan to do some research this weekend at the Penticton museum. Hopefully I can determine the whole story behind both train accidents."

"Good idea. I'd like to know myself what exactly happened and when," said Lance. They started to head back to where the crew left off. "By the way, does the local Native Band ever hold ceremonies up in this area?"

"Why do you ask that?" Clint asked, concerned.

"Lately I've been hearing someone doing a Native drum chant but it sounds like only one person."

Clint pretended to not know anything about it. "I'm not sure. I'll have to look into it."

"Thanks, Clint. I'd appreciate it. You know, Tyler claimed to see a tiger the other day. He seemed really sure of what he saw, and he swears he doesn't do drugs. I tried to reassure him that it was probably a cougar, since there can't be any tigers in these parts."

"I'll drop by again next Monday and I'll let you know what I find out at the museum," Clint told Lance before he made his way back to Hope. As Clint started to head toward his truck, he happened to glance over to a large white boulder at the edge of the forest. There, on the face of the boulder, was the image of the Native mask that he and Henry had seen before. He stared at it nervously as he slowly walked away, and his immediate thought was concern for the surveyors. *Will the spirit of Siaman strike again?*

That evening, Cindy invited Clint over to her place for dinner. Unbeknownst to Clint, Edwin joined them.

"Hey, Cindy, how would you like to accompany me on a trip to Penticton this weekend?

Cindy showed little interest. "What do you want to go to Penticton for?"

"I want to do some research on the Kootenay Central Railway and get in some spring skiing at Apex Mountain resort."

"So, you're going to Penticton, eh?" Edwin chimed in. "When you're there, do me a favour. Go see the Chief of the Penticton Indian Band, and tell him he owes me money."

"Oh, really? What for?"

"That's none of your damn business. Just tell him he owes me money. If he denies it, tell him that I say he's a cheap asshole."

"Okay, I will try to remember."

When Clint arrived at the Penticton Museum on Saturday morning, Barbara was there as usual.

"Clint, I wasn't expecting to see you back here so soon."

"I was so impressed with your KCR exhibit, I couldn't wait to come back and see it again … but really, I'm here because I'm looking for some information about a train accident that happened on the Coquihalla line many years ago."

"Oh yes, that would be the wreck of Engine 3401, which happened on September 5, 1926," Barbara responded without missing a beat. "It was the result of loss of brake power, which caused it to run away down the steep grade of the Coquihalla line. It finally jumped the tracks a mile west of Portia and plunged down the mountain. That wreck is famous in that it will always rank as the worst wreck in KCR history. What makes it even more legendary is that the total death toll will never be known. The only confirmed deaths were those of four crewmembers, but there were many transients riding on top of the boxcars."

"Wow, it's amazing that you know all of this from your research. Why were there transients on the boxcars? What were they doing?"

"It was on Labour Day weekend, so there were a lot of kids who travelled to the Okanagan for fruit-picking jobs and were returning to the coast to go back to college. It was at the end of peach and apricot season, and it would be a few weeks before the apples were ready for picking. There's a transcript on file of an article from the *Penticton Herald* written one week after the accident. It was the lead story of that particular issue, and it was the testimony of the only survivor of the accident. He gives an eyewitness account of the events leading up to the tragedy. I'm amazed that anyone could have possibly survived the accident—it would have to have been a true miracle. I would have liked to have met the lone survivor but I've never had the chance." She invited Clint to continue looking at the exhibits while she retrieved the lone survivor's transcript. "Take your time and look it over."

Clint started reading. "It was a beautiful late summer morning when engineer Tom Kramer, brakeman Oly Sigurdsson, and I left the station at Brookmere. The train was twenty-four cars long. Of those twenty-four cars, eighteen of them were loaded with lead and zinc bars from the Trail smelter. A helper locomotive attached to the caboose would assist with the upgrade haul to Coquihalla Station and then provide extra braking power on the long descent into Hope. The helper locomotive was manned by engineer Clive 'Smoky' Gibson and fireman Andy Simms. Ray Parker and rear brakeman Bob Hennessey would ride in the caboose. We were required to stop at Coquihalla and pick up twelve hopper cars loaded with coal from the Coalmont mine, which were parked on the siding.

"When the coal cars were coupled to the train and all of the necessary switching was complete, the brakemen flipped on the retainers on each car, which is a requirement when travelling down a heavy grade. After that, the brakes were tested. Everything seemed to be in working order. Ray then gave the signal, and Tom eased up on the throttle. Oly threw open the switch, allowing the train back onto the main track. When the tender of the helper engine passed the switch, Oly closed it and ran back to the head engine.

"Normally, westbound trains stop at Iago Station to cool their brakes, since that is the halfway point between Coquihalla and Hope. This time, however, we would make our first stop at Romeo in order to allow eastbound Extra 2475 to pass.

"From Coquihalla to Romeo, everything went smoothly as the train slowly made its way down the steep 2.2-percent grade. I kept a watch over the air pressure gauge, making sure it didn't go below the minimum thirty PSI. At Romeo, we pulled into the siding and waited for the eastbound train to pass. It was just enough time to cool the brakes. Tom made another stop at Jessica to cool off the brakes again. He phoned ahead to the Section Master at Jessica to get the go-ahead to pull into the siding when we arrived there. We could have continued right through to Hope, but he said he didn't want to risk burning the brake shoes on the railcars.

"About five minutes after we left Romeo, the train started to accelerate beyond our control, but Tom didn't panic; he merely activated the brake lever. But when he moved the lever, nothing happened. He tried to let out some air, but there was only a brief hissing sound, followed by silence.

"I looked at the air pressure gauge, and I yelled out, 'Where's your air?'

"Tom yelled back, 'Oh my god, I've given it all it has.'

"Tom blew the whistle cord, giving the signal to every crewmember to man the hand brakes. Oly grabbed a club and climbed over the tender, and once he was on top of the boxcars, he furiously turned the handbrakes. Ray and Bob left the caboose immediately when they heard Tom's whistle. Tom ordered me to save myself and jump, but I ignored the order. Instead, I grabbed a club, climbed up to the top of the boxcars, and gave Oly a hand setting the handbrakes. At this point, every second was crucial. If enough of the handbrakes could be set before the train's speed became excessive, the train could be brought under control. But the steep grade would not let them have that option. As fast as each crewmember turned the handbrakes, the more the train accelerated. Obeying the law of gravity, the train ran faster and faster as it tore through the blackened tunnels and over the high trestles.

"Seeing that the situation was now hopeless, the two men in the helper locomotive knew that the only way they could save themselves would be to unhook their engine from the train. Andy Simms, the young twenty-three-year-old fireman, decided that he would do it. Venturing from the cab, he bravely walked down the narrow catwalk alongside the wildly swaying locomotive. With the wind blowing furiously and the train rocking violently, he reached down and pulled the coupler lever. Immediately, the locomotive was freed from the caboose. Smoky was then able to bring his locomotive under control. A half a mile later, he was able to bring the locomotive to a complete stop. But as for the train he was helping, there was nothing he could do. Andy stood on the pilot and watched helplessly as the runaway train rounded a curve ahead, with every crewmember except Tom on top of the railcars manning the handbrakes.

"When the runaway train passed Iago, there was no one there to notice. That was because Mel Scarpino, the Section Foreman, was out on his morning patrol. He was down the line at Portia, where he took the handcar off of the track and went inside the phone shack to make a pot of coffee on the portable stove. Just as he stepped out onto the shack's porch to enjoy the Sunday morning sunshine with his coffee and a cigarette, there was a loud roar coming from up the canyon, growing louder and louder. Soon, it sounded like continuous thunder. Then the runaway train rounded a curve to the east of the Portia siding, with flames pouring out from the brake shoes. Three coal cars and the caboose broke off the end of the train and smashed into the mountainside. Mel had said he was completely horrified when he saw the train disappear from sight almost as quickly as it appeared. Less than thirty seconds later, there was the sound of a tremendous explosion, followed by the sound of multiple railcars crashing, which echoed throughout the canyon. Less than a minute later, there was complete silence.

"Mel immediately phoned the dispatcher, and then he ran down the tracks at a full clip. Just to the west of the passing track, there were three more coal cars smashed against the mountainside. About a half a mile past there, on a sharp curve, were two dislocated rails. Mel looked down the mountain at that point and saw the shattered remains of a locomotive and twenty-five railcars in a flaming heap. They all fell three hundred feet and landed on the bench above the Coquihalla River. The locomotive had exploded into a thousand pieces, and the hot ashes from the locomotive firebox had scattered over the wreckage, setting it on fire. Fed by the six remaining cars of coal, the fire soon reduced most of the railcars to blobs of molten lead. The fire momentarily set the surrounding trees on fire, but due to the recent heavy rains, it did not spread. If the weather had been its usual hot and dry, the whole forest on the bench area would have been ablaze.

"As for myself, the last thing I remember was that while I was turning the handbrakes on top of one of the boxcars, we rounded a sharp curve and I was flung from the train. I hit some tree branches and then fell onto some bushes. Even though the bushes broke my fall, I still landed pretty hard. At that point, I momentarily blacked out. I don't remember hearing any of the crash. As it turned out, the curve where I was thrown from the train was the last curve before the fatal curve. I was semi-conscious when Mel found me and asked me if I was all right. I remembered Mel from our many stops at Iago before. When he saw that I was alive, he said that he would run back to the phone shack and notify Hope to send a special train up here to get me to the hospital."

Clint noted that that was the end of the survivor's transcript part of the article and kept on reading. "In the end, Tom Kramer, Oly Sigurdsson, Ray Parker, and Bob Hennessey were killed. Even though the dozen or so young men riding on top of the boxcars were all killed, there is no official record of any of them being among the casualties. The official death toll remains at four. It is estimated that the train was travelling over one hundred miles per hour when it broke free from the track. It flew off the edge with such force that it became airborne and remained that way all throughout its descent to the bench. As a result, it was decided that none of the wreckage was worth salvaging. After the Canadian Transportation Commission held an inquest, it was determined that the overall weight of the train's cargo exceeded what was acceptable on a 2.2-percent grade. Eighteen boxcars loaded with lead and zinc bars were pushing the weight limit already, but the addition of twelve cars of coal made the end result inevitable."

Clint then read a short snippet from a later and much shorter related article. "KCR crash survivor Conner Linden sustained a separated shoulder and a broken ankle, as well as some cuts and bruises. He spent a week in the hospital and was back on the job two months later. He has remained as an employee of the KCR until the mid-1950s when he retired. Young Andy Simms, the hero of the helper engine, received an award for bravery from the Kootenay Central Railway. His act of heroism was recognized by railroaders from all over Canada. Shortly afterward, he was promoted to Engineer."

It all makes sense now why the train ran away like it did, Clint thought. He flipped the page to see photographs belonging to the newspaper article clippings. The picture showed the crashed locomotive as well as a picture of Andy Simms. *That young guy Andy sure had a lot of guts.*

The second picture showed Tom Kramer and Oly Sigurdsson standing side-by-side in the Penticton rail yard, taken two weeks before the accident. When Clint saw the picture, his jaw dropped.

Tom, the one standing on the left, looked identical to the man standing on the road the day Clint and Henry made their first trip up the Coquihalla River valley. In the photo, Tom was wearing the customary Engineer's outfit in the picture, just like when Clint saw him. For a few moments, he stared at the picture, completely stunned.

Clint couldn't shake the feeling that he had actually seen a ghost. There was no other explanation. *Maybe the locals in Hope are right after all ... the Coquihalla Valley is haunted.*

15
APRIL 1984

Upon Clint's return to work on Monday, he met with the men from Lance's crew when he headed up to the job sites. He told them all about what he learned from his most recent visit to the museum. From there, he headed up the Boston Bar Creek Valley to check on the survey crews working up in that area. On the way back to Hope, he took a side-trip up the Pipeline road as far as the site of Iago Station. He parked his truck and decided to take a look around to see what was left of the old station site. In addition to the section house, there were a number of abandoned buildings in the immediate area, including the bunkhouse and the tool shed. A couple of them looked like they were still in good condition. The water tank foundation was clearly discernible. There was still water flowing out of the intake pipe.

Clint decided to walk up to the site of the switch at the west end of Iago siding. After going a hundred yards, standing there in the middle of the road was the same woman with the long curly blonde hair wearing the long white dress that he saw when he travelled with

Henry through the area almost a year ago. The dress she wore looked quite formal yet old fashioned. She did not say anything—she just stood there with a blank expression.

"Oh, hello there, you startled me. I wasn't expecting to see anybody up here. What brings you here? Where did you come from?" asked Clint.

There was still no response from her. She continued to stand there staring at him, expressionless. Her hair was blowing in the breeze, which was strange, since there was no wind. Clint continued to try establishing some form of communication with her.

"Ma'am, what is your name? What are you doing up here? Are you lost? I'm not trying to be a pest; I'm just trying to be of some help," he said, as friendly as possible.

Just then, the woman went into convulsions. She reached out to Clint with her right arm, and blood began to pour out from her mouth.

Clint was horrified. "What the hell—ma'am, are you all right? What's the matter? You need to go to the hospital! Let me take you."

As blood continued to pour from her mouth and onto her dress, she pointed to the treetops behind Clint, as if she wanted to warn him about something, or someone, approaching from behind. Clint immediately looked behind him, sensing some kind of danger, but he didn't see anything out of the ordinary.

"I don't see anything ..." When he turned around, the woman was gone. She couldn't have run into the woods that fast without him noticing. It was like she had completely vanished.

"Ma'am, you don't have to run away—I'm here to help," yelled Clint. He looked down at the ground and noticed that there were no traces of blood anywhere. There were no footprints nor was a single sound made when the woman ran away. *That couldn't have been real, could it?*

16

By mid-April, the weather warmed up. In fact, it was absolutely spring-like. After encountering bad weather over the past couple weeks, Lance and his crew were behind schedule. Now they could make up for lost time.

They were now on the third kilometre. They started out with the centre line for the westbound lane and worked their way outward. On the second day of surveying kilometre three, they took their morning coffee break at their usual time of 10:00 a.m. They found shelter from the sun under the trees at the edge of the clear-cut. Cory immediately noticed a large number of boulders in between the trees. They were covered in a substantial amount of moss, indicating that they had been there quite a long time.

"Holy shit, look at the size of these boulders," said Cory.

"They must have rolled down from way up the mountain," said Dan.

"Can you imagine if one of those fell on top of you? You'd be history," said Tyler.

Dan began moving one of the small boulders.

"What are you doing?" asked Lance.

"This boulder looks like it's made of slate. It can be cut into lengths and be used as ornamental garden rock. I'd like it in my backyard garden. I'm going to get my brother to come up here in his truck with me next weekend to take some of these boulders home."

As Dan and Cory continued to move the smaller boulders and examine them closely, Lance began hearing a drumming sound. He looked around, trying to see where the drumming was coming from, but saw nothing.

"Hey, guys, do you hear anything unusual?" Lance asked.

"Yeah, I hear a pounding sound, like a Native drum or something," said Tyler.

"I hear it too," said Cory. "Where's it coming from?"

"I don't know," said Lance.

The drumming sound became louder and the wind began to pick up. When Cory turned around, he noticed that the surveyor's transit, which was thirty feet from where they were standing, had levitated and was hovering in mid-air four feet above the ground.

"Look at the transit!" Cory shrieked, horrified.

The transit turned until it was horizontal, still in mid-air, its legs pointing at Dan. Dan, standing in front of a large tree, appeared totally awestruck by what he was seeing. Then, without warning, the transit shot forward like a rocket, heading right toward Dan. He didn't have time to react. The three legs of the transit impaled him through his chest and stomach, exiting through his back and into the trunk of the tree, where they lodged deep inside the trunk.

"Dan!" Lance cried out as he and the others ran toward him.

Dan's body convulsed for a few seconds as blood poured from his mouth. Soon, his eyes rolled into the back of his head, and his head slumped forward.

In their horror, the others were momentarily oblivious to what else was happening. The plumb bob had levitated up from Cory's tool belt, which was placed next to where the transit was. When

Tyler turned around and saw it suspended in mid-air, it had pivoted into a horizontal position.

"Holy shit," yelled Tyler.

The plumb bob shot forward like a missile, heading right toward Lance. It nailed him right between the eyes.

"Run for your life," Cory yelled out to Tyler.

But Cory and Tyler never had a chance to run away. The many pieces of lath levitated up from the bag that Tyler had carried on his shoulder. Even though they were only a half-inch thick and one-and-a-half inches wide, the slabs of hemlock had a sharpened point at one end. One by one, the slabs levitated into mid-air, turned horizontally, and projected with rocket propulsion toward Cory and Tyler. Because of the warm weather, they had removed their jackets, and since they were on a break, they had removed their hard-hats. Therefore, they were no match for the slabs of lath hurtling toward them with such force as being shot out of a cannon.

The first slab nailed Cory in the lower back. Despite the excruciating pain, he tried to keep on running. The next two slabs nailed him between the shoulder blades and his right shoulder, respectively. After a couple of them missed him, one more slab hit him in the neck. It entered in the back, grazing his spinal cord. It went right through and out the front, ripping out Cory's oesophagus in the process. At that point, he collapsed face first into the dirt. As for Tyler, he took a total of six slabs in the back before one nailed him in the back of his head, piercing his skull and lodging itself deep in his brain. He, too, collapsed face first.

***

Back at the Hope office, Clint and Don were going over the elevation shot calculations the survey crews had made. They were engrossed in their work to the point where they were oblivious to the fact that Lance hadn't called in over the CB radio to give a progress report as he usually did every day at 12:15 p.m. like clockwork. It was 3:00 p.m. when Clint realized Lance hadn't called.

"Lance hasn't called in yet," Clint voiced his concern to Don.

"He's probably extra busy. After all, he still has five kilometres left to survey and doesn't have much time," said Don.

"They still have to stop for lunch. This isn't like him."

"Let's give him one more hour, and if he hasn't called by then, we'll call him." An hour later, there was still no word from Lance. Clint called Lance on the CB radio.

"Hope base to Lance Demitrios, over."

Clint repeated the request at least six times. Each subsequent time he called, his voice became more frantic.

On his final call, he yelled out, "Lance, are you there? Answer the radio. Please call the Hope base *immediately*, over."

"Clint, you're being paranoid. Lance and the boys are working over a kilometre from where they park their truck. They probably decided to pack all of their gear and stay right where they're working. It makes more sense to do that than walk all the way back to the truck at lunchtime," said Don.

Clint could sense that something was wrong. "Well, you may be right, but I'm still heading up there to make sure. Are you coming with me or not? Let's get going."

Right after they crossed the narrow bridge over Ladner Creek, they turned left onto a rough road that eventually turned into a crudely built access road, winding steeply up to Portia Bench. Clint and Don saw the crew's truck parked at the end of the road. They got out of their truck and looked around, but saw no signs of the crew. They followed the survey markers until they ended, and still saw no signs of life. Clint and Don both repeatedly called out Lance's name but got no response.

When Clint looked toward the woods, he saw what looked to be a man leaning against a tree with his head slumped forward. He also noticed the transit in a very unusual position. He motioned to Don, "Over there," and they ran toward the tree. When they got up close, they saw just the upper portion of the transit. The transit legs were imbedded deep inside the tree, and had pierced right through the man's chest and stomach. Clint lifted the man's head and saw that it was Dan. His body was cold, and there was blood everywhere.

Don looked behind him and said, "Look, over there."

There was Lance, lying on his back, and the pointed end of the plumb bob was imbedded deep inside his forehead. His eyes were still open, and it looked like he still had an expression of shock on his face. Nearby to Lance, they came upon the bodies of Cory and Tyler. They were both lying face down, and both of them had at least six slabs of lath imbedded in their backs. Clint noticed the gaping hole in the back of Cory's neck. When he lifted Cory's head, he noticed that a large portion of the front of his neck was missing. It appeared that when the lath pierced his neck, it hit his jugular vein; there was a considerable amount of semi-dried blood on the ground. When he examined Tyler, he noticed that the fatal slab nearly went right through his head.

Clint was in a total state of shock. He couldn't begin to comprehend how someone could have killed his top survey crew, especially like this. But then he noticed the pile of boulders in front of him, and saw that on one of the smaller boulders the moss had been removed, and there were recent hammer marks.

"Who the fuck would do this?" said Don, as he surveyed the carnage.

"I don't know. This had to have been the work of more than one person …" replied Clint. He tried his best not to let on that he knew anything else. *Oh my god, this is where Siaman's bride was killed. They disturbed her final resting place. Why didn't I heed the Chief's warning?*

"Let's try to remove the transit from the tree and free Dan's body," Don suggested.

"Don't touch it, there are probably fingerprints all over it. Besides, that would interfere with a police investigation. Leave everything as you see it, and I'm going to radio for help." said Clint.

Clint turned the CB radio to channel nine, the emergency channel. The voice at the other end said, "Emergency services, how may I direct your call?"

Clint was frantic. "Yes, I'm calling from mile fifteen on the Coquihalla road. My survey crew has been attacked. All four men are dead. I need an ambulance and the police."

"Sir, you said that your crew was attacked? Were they attacked by animals?" said the voice at the other end, sounding rather puzzled.

"No, by humans. They were most likely ambushed or something. I am not sure, as I was not here when it happened."

"Sir, the police and an ambulance will be with you as soon as possible."

Oh God, oh God, Chief was right ... Siaman is for real. Now I'm responsible for this. I should never have let them work here. Four men are dead ... and I'm responsible.

17

The meeting with Clint, Constable Friesen, and Staff Sergeant Dickerson lasted well into the early evening.

"Mr. Matheson, I have been with the RCMP for over twenty years. I can tell when people are trying to hide something," said Staff Sergeant Dickerson.

"I'm telling you—neither myself nor Don saw anything out of the ordinary," Clint said with his voice quivering.

"If the crew was in any kind of danger, how come they were not able to contact you? Or anyone else for that matter?" asked Constable Friesen.

"The crew had a CB radio in their truck, but from their position, it would have been at least a five-minute walk to the truck. There have been times where crews have brought along military-issue portable radios, but that's only in very remote areas."

"Didn't the crew have any kind of protection, like a firearm or something?" asked Constable Friesen.

"There's no need to. The only possible danger they would have is with a bear or a cougar. We teach them what to do if they encounter a bear or a cougar. Normally, they're afraid of humans especially if they encounter more than one. In their case, there were four of them."

"Mr. Matheson, would you have any reason to want them dead?" asked Sergeant Dickerson.

"What?" Clint was nearly hysterical. "That's preposterous! I had the utmost respect for them. Lance and I have been good friends for many years ... How could you even ask such a question?"

"You have been evasive and defensive all the while you've been here. I can sense you are not telling us everything," said Sergeant Dickerson.

"How the hell am I supposed to react? I cared about those men—I would never deliberately put them in any situation where their lives could be in danger. I'm just as stymied as you are."

By the end of the meeting no progress was made, but Clint agreed to cooperate and pass any information along if he learned of any new leads.

The bodies of the four men were taken to the coroner's office. As for Clint, he had by far the grimmest task of all. He had to notify the families of the victims. The real hard part was he didn't know what to say, and the nightmare would not end there. He would still have to face the media, and there would also be an extensive police investigation. There were many unanswered questions. The backgrounds of all four men would be extensively analyzed to determine if any of them had any known enemies.

Back at the Hope office, it was an absolute zoo. All of the survey crews had assembled there after hearing of the tragedy. There was a number of police officers present, asking all of the survey workers who were working in the valley if they saw anything suspicious. Several members of the local media were there as well.

"Your attention, please, everyone ... I will be holding a press conference at my office in Vancouver tomorrow afternoon at two o'clock," Clint announced to the Hope office just before he left that day.

The next day, it was a total media circus at the BC Department of Highways office. Clint vowed to do his best to maintain his composure and to answer all questions from the media personnel as concisely as possible. When it came time to go on the air, Clint made the following statement:

"Ladies and gentlemen, it is with deepest regret that I must announce that a tragedy of unspeakable proportions has occurred on the Coquihalla Highway project. Yesterday, at approximately 10:30 a.m., four survey workers, working under my direction, were blatantly and viciously attacked by a group of assailants. They were surveying fifteen miles northeast of Hope in an area known as Portia Bench when they were attacked and killed. The names of the four deceased men are Lance Demitrios, age forty-four; Dan Gibbons, age twenty-nine; Cory Gabriel, age twenty-six; and Tyler Fitzgerald, age nineteen. Their own survey equipment was used as the murder weapons. They were fired from some kind of projectile device. As of now, there are no suspects, and no known motive. The area where they were working is quite remote; there is only one road through the valley, but it goes in two different directions. Therefore, there were two possible escape routes. All surveying in the immediate area will be suspended pending the investigation. This will not cause any disruption in the construction schedule. The construction of the highway should be able to commence on schedule in mid-May."

The Superintendent for the RCMP Lower Mainland Division then said, "The RCMP is working on any possible leads. If anyone listening to this has any information, please contact the RCMP in Hope."

Clint didn't think the press conference went over very well. Nothing was gained, and there was no clearer understanding of what happened. He was also now living with the fact that he was hiding a deep, dark secret—one that nobody would likely believe. For now, all he wanted to do was go home and be alone.

That evening, Clint was sitting alone in his living room when the phone rang. It was Cindy.

"Cindy, what a nice surprise. It's so good to hear from you," he said, despite the fact that he wanted to be alone.

"I heard about what happened, and then I found out that you rushed back to Vancouver the same day. Oh, Clint, I'm so sorry."

"I appreciate that you're thinking about me. Yes, they were good men. I just can't make any sense out of it."

"Are you coming back up to Hope soon?"

"Yes, I'll be up there the day after tomorrow."

"Super, why don't we get together then?"

"Sounds like a good idea. I'll talk to you then."

The following day, Clint received a call at his office. It was the coroner, Dennis.

"Mr. Matheson, I need you to come out to my office as soon as you can."

"What is this about?" asked Clint.

"To be honest, I have never seen anything quite like this in my seventeen years of being a coroner."

"I understand what you must be thinking. They died under such unusual circumstances that I can't even explain myself."

"I was hoping you might be able to shed some light as to what happened. This case completely boggles my mind."

"Well, I'm afraid I won't be much help."

"Regardless of what you know, I still want to meet with you. I want to show some of the observations I've made. Can you come up here today?"

"Today is impossible. I'm tied up in meetings all day. I can head up there tomorrow. Would that work for you?"

"I don't want to wait too much longer; the families are anxious for me to release the bodies so they can make funeral arrangements.

Tomorrow it is."

At the lab, which was attached to his office, Dennis showed Clint some of the discoveries he made when he examined the bodies. The first thing he showed him was what he referred to as "Exhibit A", one of the pieces of lath that was removed from the bodies of Cory and Tyler.

"It was a major chore to remove all of the pieces of lath. It was not a simple case of pulling them out by any means. Every piece had to be painstakingly removed using surgical instruments. Once each slab was removed, I marked on it exactly how far in it penetrated. The slab I'm holding was the one that was lodged in Tyler's head. Look how far in it had penetrated. The pointed end is now barely recognizable." Dennis picked up another slab with his other hand and compared the two. "Here is an unused piece of lath I obtained from the local Department of Highways office. It is indeed sharp, but not sharp enough to make it a lethal weapon."

Then he gave a demonstration. Holding the new lath in his hand, he swung his arm in an upward motion over his head.

"Now, let's say I was going to stab you in the back with this sharpened piece of wood. If I was to use full force," he brought down his arm, "the most damage I could do is a flesh wound. The same holds true if I aimed for the back of your head. No matter how strong anyone is, nobody in the world could exert that much force. Whatever these things were fired from, the amount of force exerted was absolutely unbelievable."

From there, he showed Clint "Exhibit B", the plumb bob.

"In order to penetrate Lance's skull that far, it would have to have been fired from a .308 Remington rifle at close range. However, it would never fit inside the barrel." Dennis shook his head in disbelief. "Now, let's move on to Dan's body. The emergency crews had to cut halfway into the tree trunk and cut out a huge chunk before the transit could be removed. The tree had to be chopped down in the process. The three transit legs each had to be surgically removed, so to make a long story short, there wasn't much left of him to examine. One of the transit legs pierced right through his heart, so his death was instantaneous. He wouldn't have suffered. Now comes the proverbial question. What device could have been big enough and powerful enough to project the transit with that amount of velocity? The transit would have to have been fired from a cannon. The barrel is the only device I could think of that would be big enough to fit the transit, but it would take a substantial amount of gunpowder to make it project with that much force. Herein lies another problem. If that were the case, the blast would make one hell of a racket. Considering how narrow the valley is, a blast of that magnitude could easily be heard ten miles away." Dennis picked up a clipboard with some notes on it. "The report says that the nearest survey crew was working five miles south—half the distance. None of them recall hearing anything that resembled a blast or gunfire."

"There is one more inconsistency to this theory," Clint spoke up. "If a cannon was indeed used, one of that size would weigh nearly a ton. It would take at least four men to lug it to within firing range from the nearest road, and that is over a mile."

"So, you see what I'm getting at here? There are so many inconsistencies. None of this adds up. I'm not able to provide any conclusions, and frankly, I find it very frustrating," said Dennis.

"I see where you're coming from; I'm also at a complete loss myself to provide any explanation as to what happened. I was not there, so I didn't see what went on. If I knew anything, I'd let you know," Clint replied.

Over the next couple of days, a dejected Clint occupied the Hope office. He had a lot of work to catch up on, but his mind just wasn't in it. It was a welcome relief when he received a call from Cindy on

Friday afternoon.

"Hi, Clint, how about we get together after work today?"

"I'd be happy to." Right now, Clint could use anything to cheer himself up.

Even though it was Friday, he didn't feel like going home, at least not until the next day. An hour after he arrived back at the motel, Cindy knocked on the door. She was carrying a picnic basket and a bottle of wine. For a moment, he just stood in the doorway, not saying a word.

"Can I come in?" Cindy finally asked.

"Yes."

"I thought I would come by and cheer you up. I hope that old saying is true—the way to a man's heart is through his stomach."

"What's in the picnic basket? It smells good."

"I made lasagna. But instead of the traditional garlic bread, I brought something close to my heart—bannock. It's my grandmother's recipe."

"What a coincidence—Italian. I was thinking of ordering pizza."

During dinner, Clint felt he had to confess to Cindy that he felt responsible for what happened to his men.

"Cindy, I've been thinking a lot about it and it has been weighing heavily on my conscience. I can't help but think that it was Siaman who killed them. Why did I let them work there?"

Cindy seemed rather startled by his allegation. "Clint, don't be silly. I know my father has a way of making himself sound convincing, but it's all just an act. He's told that story so many times that he has even convinced himself that it is true. Trust me, I've never believed that story for one minute."

"Yeah, but everything that happened is impossible to explain otherwise. There is one other thing I noticed when Don and I found the bodies ... I saw a pile of boulders that was hidden in the trees. They looked like they had been there for quite some time. It looked like one of the boulders was disturbed. That's why I think they may have come across the spot where Siaman's girlfriend was killed. They disturbed it."

"Look, I know this has been hard on you, but don't let what my father said get to you. He believes anything he hears from our elders, and never once thinks about questioning their sources. Besides, rocks fall down from that mountain all the time, so it is unlikely that they stumbled upon the site of her demise. That is, however, if there *is* such a site."

Clint was lost in his own thoughts for the next little while. The two of them each had three more glasses of wine.

"Now, go and stretch out on the bed; you've had a hard day at work," said Cindy.

Clint did as Cindy suggested and she flopped down beside him.

"Do you know what I admire the most about you, Clint? You're a go-getter. You have a real get-the-job-done attitude, and you never let anything stand in your way. I also find you very charming and witty. I can't figure out why your ex-wife would want to leave you. Oh well, her loss is my gain. That's how I see it. You need to relax and get your mind off all that has been happening. I need to make you feel special again."

Cindy began to gingerly undo the button on his pants and unzip the fly. She got up and removed her tan leather dress, revealing that she had nothing on underneath.

"Make love to me, Clint."

He graciously obliged. That definitely took Clint's mind off things if only for a little while.

18

Clint didn't get a chance to leave Hope all weekend. When he returned to work on Monday morning, his mind was still not focused completely on the project. In the afternoon, he had to make a trip to the bank. Since it was only two blocks from the office, he decided to walk there. Just before he entered the bank, he ran into none other than Edwin Baptiste.

"Clint, how are you? I heard about the tragedy."

"Yes, it was a terrible shock. These last few days have been very difficult; they were my number one crew," said Clint.

"I also heard about where it happened. Can't say I didn't warn you."

"What are you talking about?" Clint grew defensive.

"I told you that area is guarded by the spirit of Siaman. Those who disturb it bear his wrath. Now you see that the power from the great beyond is more than anyone can imagine."

"Look, I don't have time for this bullshit, Chief. I have had to try and answer questions for which I have no answers. I don't need you making things worse by bringing that goddamned fairy tale into the picture."

"That's where you're wrong. It is not a fairy tale; the spirit of Siaman is very much real, and must be taken seriously."

"Well, you believe what you want to believe, but all I'm concerned about is catching whoever is responsible."

"Oh, one more thing. You stay the hell away from my daughter," Edwin snarled.

"Your daughter is a grown woman. She can date whoever she wants to, and it just so happens that she wants to date me."

"I know you have been fucking her. I wish her and Claude never split up."

"That guy ran out on her, and with another woman to boot. He also ran out on your granddaughter. And by the way, the sex is completely consensual. Now, if you don't mind, I have business to attend to." Clint abruptly turned his back on Edwin and entered the bank.

Later that afternoon, Clint had a meeting with his Project Managers. Throughout the meeting, Clint was very evasive, and couldn't hide that he was not the least bit interested in what anyone else had to say. Clint was afraid that Ed, Hugh, and Don all noticed that he was not acting like his normal self. "Now, gentlemen, I have an important phone call to make." Clint adjourned the meeting early.

As it turned out, Clint's timing as he called Bill Plotnikoff was perfect; the Legislature had adjourned for the day, and he was back in his office.

"Hello Bill, it's Clint Matheson."

"Clint, what a pleasant surprise. How are you coping?"

"What can I say? I guess I'm coping. Listen, I need to see you."

"Sure, Clint, what's it about?"

"I'd rather talk about it in person. I'll come meet you and Stan in Victoria."

"Okay, how does tomorrow afternoon sound? Around four

o'clock?"

"Yes, that will work out just fine. Let Stan know, because I would like to talk to both of you."

Clint went back home to Vancouver that night, and the following morning, he caught the ferry to Victoria. Bill and Stan didn't arrive at Bill's office until after 4:30 p.m. since the Legislature session ran longer than planned. Clint was already sitting down in Bill's office when the other two joined him.

"Hi, Clint. What was it you wanted to talk about?" asked Bill.

"I think we should cancel the project," Clint said, wasting no time.

Bill and Stan looked momentarily stunned.

After a near minute of silence, Bill finally spoke up. "Did I hear you correctly? Did you just say that you want us to scrap the highway project?"

"Yes, you heard me correctly. I've given it a lot of thought, and I've come to the conclusion that the whole Coquihalla Highway project was one big mistake."

"Clint, have you lost your mind? Do you realize the expenditure we have put into this project already? You can't quit on us now."

"What are we going to do about the highway situation with Expo coming up? How are we going to handle the extra volume of traffic if there's no highway?" asked Stan.

"Personally, I think all of this extra traffic that we have been talking about is being blown out of proportion. Sure, there'll be extra traffic, but not the magnitude we projected. We can make some cosmetic changes to the Fraser Canyon and Hope-Princeton highways, and we'll be just fine," replied Clint.

"Clint, you're not making any sense. Just one year ago, you were in this same office with an enthusiastic attitude toward the new highway. We liked your proposal, and approved it. You were all gung-ho to get this project going. Now, all of a sudden, you want to stop the whole thing? I don't know what the hell has gotten into you," said Bill.

"I want this project stopped out of respect for my crew that got killed. Those men were some of my best workers, and I feel responsible. If it weren't for this stupid project, they'd still be alive."

"Look Clint, what happened to the crew was not your fault, and if it weren't for this project, they would have been out of a job. I realize you're taking it pretty hard, but if the highway project is cancelled now, they would have died in vain. My heart goes out to the families of the victims, but as the saying goes, the show must go on."

Bill and Stan repeatedly pleaded with Clint to change his mind, and in the end, they were somewhat successful.

"Well, maybe you guys are right. I guess I've been rather irrational lately, but you can't exactly blame me. It has all been such a terrible shock," said Clint.

"Clint, in all of the years that I've known you, you've never been a quitter. You've always shown the attitude of getting the job done no matter what it takes. Don't ever become a quitter, especially now. We're counting on you, so please, hang in there," said Bill.

Clint thought long and hard about what Bill said. He began to realize that it was a case of him not being in the right frame of mind lately. It wouldn't be right to give up at this stage. But right now, he had to focus on the upcoming funerals for the four men. Over the next six days, Clint attended each separate funeral. At each funeral, there was not one ounce of resentment toward him by any of the family members. This made him realize that he should once and for all stop blaming himself for the tragedy.

19
MAY 1984

Three days after Lance's funeral, and with the official start of construction of the Coquihalla Highway only weeks away, Clint received a call from Bill.

"Hi, Clint. Could you come and meet me at your Vancouver office? I need to discuss a matter with you in person."

"If it's so important, why can't you come up to Hope? I'm very busy; I can't just take off and come up to Vancouver."

"Clint, it's very urgent. Can you please get up here ASAP?"

"Oh, all right. I will be there in a couple hours." The man did pay Clint's salary, after all.

When Clint arrived at the Highways District office in Vancouver, Bill was waiting in Clint's office. Clint expected to see him, but he did not expect to see Anders Johanssen in his office as well. Clint noticed that Bill had a distinctively sad look on his face. Something wasn't right.

"Clint, I've been thinking this over for the past couple weeks, and I have been discussing the matter with Premier Davenport at great lengths. We have come to an agreement that will be in everyone's best interest. You are no longer in charge of the Coquihalla Highway project."

Clint's heart sank, and he slumped down in his chair. After a moment of silence, he said, "You mean I'm fired?"

"Oh, no, not fired—just reassigned. As you are aware, Myles, the District Engineer for Vancouver Island needs to undergo triple-bypass surgery. So for now, there's nobody running the show on Vancouver Island, and there are a couple of major projects on the go right now—that's where you come in. Meanwhile, Anders will be in charge of the entire Coquihalla Highway project. He has made tremendous progress at his end in Kamloops, and since Phase Two will not be built until 1987, his talents can be used on the southern portion."

For the first few moments, Clint was in total disbelief. Then he realized that he had really stuck his foot in his mouth when he had met with Bill and Stan at the Legislature. At the time he didn't think that he was potentially digging his own grave.

"Bill, I was not in my right frame of mind when we had that meeting—I take back everything I said that day. My number one goal right now is to complete the highway on time and as much on budget as possible."

"Clint, that's not what we're seeing. Your section of the highway project is way behind schedule, and the official start of construction is only two weeks away. You have three miles of roadway that aren't even surveyed yet, for God's sake. This is totally unacceptable. Your Project Managers have been complaining that you have been evasive, and have not been giving them any sense of direction. I'll admit, though, you have shown great leadership in the past, and you were instrumental in getting this project off to a great start. But, we need someone who can see this project through to the end. I am sorry to have to do this, but you have left me no choice. I want you to keep in mind, though, that this is only a temporary arrangement. You can resume the position of District Engineer for the Lower Mainland District after the Coquihalla Highway is completed. But for now, you are needed at the Victoria office right away."

"I hope there'll be no hard feelings. I will do my best to oversee the completion of the project," said Anders.

Clint had no choice but to grudgingly accept his fate. He headed to Victoria to start his new position.

20

Anders got right down to business. From now on, he planned to base his operations out of the Hope office and return to Kamloops on weekends. Anders' first priority was to meet with Don, Hugh, and Ed. He outlined his strategy for the next three months, starting with completing the remaining surveying on Portia Bench. He would go over the field notes to determine where the doomed crew left off, and would assign a crew to complete the surveying over the next couple days. On his first day, he also received a phone call from Clint.

"There's a stack of field notes and calculations for the first three miles west of the summit. I never had a chance to go over them, so can you go through them to see if all of the calculations are correct? Since that section will be part of the early stages of construction, it is a definite priority," said Clint.

"I'll look at them right away," said Anders.

On Anders' second day in charge, he began going over the calculations and survey notes from that section. After going over them for a couple hours, he almost wished he hadn't. Much to his horror, nearly four kilometres were completely out of alignment. Once he realized this, he stormed out of the office.

"Linda, call Don over the CB radio and tell him to get his skinny ass over to the office *right now*."

It took Linda six tries before Don finally answered on the CB radio. "Don, you need to come back to the Hope office right away. Anders wants to see you."

"What is this all about?" asked Don.

"I don't know, but he says it's important," said Linda.

"Linda, I'm very busy. I don't have time to drop everything just so I can listen to his crap. Tell him that I will meet with him when I return this afternoon."

"I'm not sure if you are aware of this, Don, but he's our boss now. I don't want any trouble, so you should do as he says and get back here now. Don't make this any harder than it has to be—just do it."

"Oh, alright. I'll be there in a half hour."

When Don arrived at the office, he was visibly annoyed.

"Okay, what is it the big Swede wants that is so damn important?"

"I don't know. You will have to find out for yourself. But I had better warn you, he is not in a good mood."

"How can you tell?"

"He has been swearing in Swedish all morning."

When Don entered Anders' office, Anders took the detailed map of the section in question, unrolled it, and pointed out the problem.

"Don, there's a problem with the highway layout and your corresponding calculations for the first four kilometres west of the summit."

"Oh, what's wrong?"

"Basically ... everything. First of all, when the highway begins its descent, there's a two-kilometre straight stretch, followed by a curve, then another straight stretch, followed by another curve. These curves are too sharp, considering that the gradient is sixteen percent. It's too easy for vehicles to go out of control, and is especially dangerous for large trucks." Anders pointed out where the roadway corresponded to the mountains and Boston Bar Creek. Using his enlarged contour map as a reference, he drew a line beside the course of Boston Bar Creek. The line followed the natural contours of the canyon and the mountainside from the summit to the site of the proposed snow-shed. "The end result is one continuous curve. There will be far less blasting required, and no need for retaining walls."

"Anders, don't look at me—this was all Clint's idea," Don defended himself.

"Don't give me that bullshit. I don't think you have ever taken responsibility for any of your actions in your entire life. It was your responsibility to design a roadway that best suits this terrain. Now, I want you to start making calculations using the coordinates I showed you. Assign Henry Finnegan's crew to redo the surveying, and get on it right away."

"Yeah, yeah," replied Don in a snarly tone.

"Don't you *yeah yeah* me, you son of a bitch," Anders shot back. "From now on, you have two choices: either respect the fact that *I* am in charge now or look for another bloody job elsewhere."

One week after Anders took over as coordinator, he received a call from Bill, reminding him that the date for the official start of construction was only one week away.

"Is all the surveying proceeding on schedule, Anders?" asked Bill.

"Yes, everything's on schedule," Anders replied with a tone of apprehension. Anders didn't want Bill to know that the surveying was way behind schedule, and this most recent debacle was only compounding matters. He didn't want to cause any alarm that would result in negative publicity.

"Where will be the best place to set off the ceremonial 'first blast'? Premier Davenport will push down on the plunger and set off a large explosion, which will dislodge a mound of rocks, thereby signalling the official start of construction. I want a spot where blasting will be required, but is currently accessible by road. Many dignitaries representing the Provincial Government and Expo 86 will be present, as well as all of the local television stations."

"The best spot would be a half mile east of Falls Creek. There's a small rock outcropping there, and it is right at the end of the Coldwater River Forest Service Road. By the way, how come the Premier is doing the official first blast and not you?"

"For one thing, the Coquihalla Highway is more Davenport's baby than it is mine. Another thing is that my people have a history with explosives, and not for the better. As a result, I have quite the aversion to explosives. After all, my father went to prison for blowing up a BC Hydro transmission tower, so I don't think it would be appropriate."

Bill was the first ever Doukhobor to be elected to the Provincial Legislature. His family belonged to the radical Sons-of-Freedom Doukhobor sect, who opposed Government intervention in their way of life. Throughout the late 1950s and early 1960s, members of the sect waged a war of terror throughout the Kootenay region, committing acts of bombings, arson, and naked protests. Bill's father even served time in Agassiz Mountain Prison for bombing a BC Hydro transmission tower.

On the momentous day of 17 May 1984, Anders was the first person to arrive at the site of the ceremonial first blast. Using a rope, he outlined the spot where the media would be positioned, and marked the spot where the Premier would stand when he set off the charge. When the workers from Britannia Blasting arrived, they immediately went to work setting the charges. One by one, representatives from the media, the Government, and Expo 86 arrived. Finally, Bill and Premier Davenport arrived. At 11:00 a.m. Davenport pushed down on the plunger, setting off a series of charges that went in rapid-fire succession. The sounds of the blasts were deafening. When the dust finally settled, over one hundred tons of rock had been displaced.

"The construction is now officially underway," Davenport announced as the crowd erupted in applause. The ceremony did not go off without incident, though.

After Davenport finished speaking, a reporter for the *Nelson Daily News* yelled out to Bill, "Hey, Plotnikoff! The Premier blows things up as good as your old man!"

Stan had to restrain Bill from taking a swing at the reporter. It seemed like some of the wounds of the Sons-of-Freedom Doukhobors terror campaign of the early 1960s had not yet completely healed.

It took over two months to resurvey the section west of the summit. There were many places where the terrain was precipitous, so it was difficult to properly mount the transit on solid footing. The crews were mostly working high above the creek bed, and one false move could make them fall right down to the creek. Another complication was the fact that the ground was solid granite, so an iron pin had to be pounded into the ground with a sledgehammer before a survey marker could be placed.

As if all of this wasn't enough to stress out the workers, Don added insult to injury by being an absolute slave driver. He was constantly on the workers' cases—almost to the point where they were ready for mutiny at times. Despite all of this, they managed to work it all out in the end. The alignment was perfect.

"Well done, Henry, keep up the good work," said Anders. "I don't want Don to take all the credit."

Now with the section west of the summit done, Anders returned his attention to Portia Bench. But this came with a new dilemma. The elevation shots now had to be done immediately on the newly surveyed section since it would be part of the early stages of construction. Therefore, as much manpower as possible would be needed for that task, but they were already short-staffed. The roadway along Portia

Bench would not be built until spring of next year at the earliest. Even so, he wanted the surveying to be completed, and he wanted it done by an experienced crew. After careful consideration, he decided to pull his top crew from Kamloops. He would place them in charge of the surveying on Portia Bench.

The following Monday morning, Dwight Tannen and his crew reported to the Hope office. Dwight's crew consisted of Farrell Collins, Bud Wilkinson, and Tom Greenbrier. Their duties alternated between head and rear chainman and pounding in the survey stakes. As was customary with all of the survey crews, they took turns with each task every day. Dwight was always the one who manned the transit and took survey notes.

    Anders gave them the rundown on where they would be working and what was expected of them. Using his detailed topographical map, Anders showed them where they would be starting from and the direction they would be heading. "There is still a total of five kilometres that needs to be surveyed. Unlike the previous crew, you will be starting from the eastern end and will work westward. You will work in the same pattern as the previous crew. The surveying will be done one kilometre at a time, starting with the centre line for both the eastbound and westbound lanes, and will then survey the road allowance lines in each direction for both lanes. Once an entire kilometre is completed, you will move on to the next. You'll also need to bring a chainsaw along, because there was an area that Livingston & Daniels neglected to pull out all of the stumps for some reason." He pointed out that particular area on the map.

    "I have experience with operating a chainsaw," Dwight piped up.

    "Excellent. One other item you should be aware of is that the ground is very uneven; there are lots of small hills. This could affect the accuracy somewhat. Now, do any of you have any questions?"

    Farrell asked, "Isn't that the place where those surveyors were killed?"

"Well, it's in the same region, but that happened three miles further west. It was determined that it was an isolated incident; somebody must have had a personal vendetta on one of the men. Even so, I want all of you guys to watch each other's backs. If you see anything suspicious, get out of there and call me on the radio at once. Keep your CB radio on my frequency at all times."

***

It took the crew nearly two weeks to complete their first kilometre. As Anders predicted, the going was fairly rough. Dwight had to constantly use the chainsaw to cut stumps down to ground level, and the uneven ground kept them questioning their accuracy. The next kilometre was not any different. Dwight decided to work on the westbound lane first, as the ground where the eastbound lane would be appeared to be easier. After three days, they had not made much progress. On the fourth day, by 10:00 a.m. Dwight had already cut down three tree stumps, and another one was directly in their path, and was only forty feet away. He decided to take their coffee break at that point.

Dwight was always annoyed whenever Farrell ran deep into the woods to relieve himself.

"There are only men on the crew, and there is nobody else around us for miles. You could get lost, or you could encounter a bear or a cougar," Dwight reminded him before he went off.

But, Farrell never listened, and today was no exception.

"I know the real reason you go back into the bush to pee so often is so you can play with yourself," Dwight resorted to teasing him.

On this particular break, Farrell had a very blank look on his face when he returned. Tom looked over at him, and saw the really glazed look in Farrell's eye. Farrell wandered past the men and down the hill, acting like he was in a daze.

"Alright, everyone. Coffee's over," Dwight informed everyone a few minutes later.

Bud and Tom had rod-and-chain duty that day, and Farrell's job was to print markings on the survey stakes and pound them into the ground. Dwight was anxious to get past the next tree stump before lunch.

"Men, get into your positions," said Dwight. He looked around, but could see no sign of Farrell. "Collins, get your ass over here *now*." After Farrell didn't show up for several more seconds, Dwight decided to start without him, and he fixed his eye in the transit's viewfinder. "Bud, Tom, proceed to the next thirty-metre marker."

Bud was the head chainman, so he took the end of the chain and started forward. When thirty metres of chain were unravelled from the spool, Tom yelled out, "Stop."

With Dwight focused on his survey notes and the rod Bud was carrying, he was completely unaware that Farrell was sneaking up behind him. Contained in the bag of survey stakes that he carried was a hatchet; the flat end used to pound the stakes into the ground. As Farrell snuck up behind Dwight, he took the hatchet out of the bag and, with a mighty swing of his right arm, he struck Dwight in the back of the head. He struck him with such force that the blade of the hatchet pierced his skull and lodged deep within his brain. Dwight didn't have a chance to scream; instead, his eyes rolled back and he fell sideways, landing with a loud thud. He didn't even knock the transit over.

For the moment, Tom and Bud were unaware of what just happened to Dwight. Since Bud didn't hear Dwight yell out "left" or "right", he assumed he was supposed to travel in a straight line. After yelling out the word "mark" and dropping the plumb bob right over the thirty-metre mark, he made an indentation in the ground for Farrell to place the survey stake.

"Farrell, get over here with the stakes," Bud called. "Dwight, we're ready to head over to the next thirty-metre mark."

When Bud got no response, he stood up and looked back. That's when he noticed Dwight lying on the ground with the hatchet protruding from the back of his head.

"Oh my god—Tom, look at Dwight!" yelled Bud, hysterical.

They both ran over to where Dwight was lying face down. When they saw that he had no movement, they knew he was dead. They looked around to see where Farrell was, even called out his name repeatedly, but there was no sign of him.

"Uhh, Bud? The chainsaw is missing." Tom gulped.

Just then, they heard the sound of a chainsaw starting up. Farrell stood up from behind a small hill, revving the chainsaw and swinging it wildly in the air.

"Run for your life!" Bud yelled.

Bud let the much younger Tom run ahead of him, but they still had to run toward the edge of the bench, as Farrell blocked their path in the direction toward the truck. Tom got a good head start, and Bud tried to run as fast as he could. Bud didn't get very far when he tripped on a snag. By the time Farrell caught up to him, Bud had not been able to get up on his feet. Farrell aimed the fast-running saw blades right at Bud's leg. Bud flung his legs in an effort to dodge the saw blades, but to no avail. He got him right above the right knee, opening a huge gash. Bud managed to roll away before the saw could cut deeper, and he screamed in sheer pain. Before Farrell could get in another swing, Bud managed to kick him in the right shin with his left leg. That momentarily threw him off balance, and allowed Bud time to get to his feet. He managed to start running, despite the intense pain and profuse bleeding. With Farrell in hot pursuit, Bud ran toward the truck. He got a hundred yards ahead when he made a terrible mistake. Instead of looking forward and keeping focused on where he was going, he looked back to see where Farrell was. It was then that he tripped on another snag and hit his head on a tree stump. His head hit the stump with such force that he was completely dazed.

When Farrell caught up to him, he took full advantage of the situation. He aimed the end of the chainsaw right at Bud's neck. His neck muscles offered no protection from the fast-moving chainsaw blades, which sliced effortlessly through the soft tissue and tendons. Farrell received a shower of blood as the blades tore through Bud's carotid artery. The spinal cord was no match for the blades, either. In less than five seconds, Bud's head was completely detached from his body.

With both himself and the chainsaw covered in blood, Farrell now set his sights on Tom. By now, Tom had reached the truck, but the keys were with Dwight. Luckily, the driver's side door was unlocked, and the CB radio had its own power source. Tom had never operated the CB radio before, but he watched Dwight operate it many times. He turned the "on" switch and pushed the button on the microphone. He didn't look to see what channel it was on—he just spoke into the microphone.

"Hello, is there anybody there? Mayday, mayday! Can anybody hear me?"

The person closest to a vehicle with a CB radio was Hugh, who was ten miles away, taking elevation shots near the site of Lear Station. He picked up the receiver and said, "Yes, come in."

"I'm with the Highways Department," said Tom.

"I'm with the Highways Department, too. Who are you, where are you, and what is your problem?" asked Hugh.

"My name is Tom Greenbrier. I'm somewhere up the Coquihalla River, but I'm not sure where. It's Collins, my crewmate—he's gone completely berserk. He murdered our Crew Chief and now he's coming after me."

"Listen, I need to know your position. Are you near any milepost marker or some kind of landmark?"

Tom looked back and saw that Farrell was catching up to him, still running with the chainsaw going. But then, the chainsaw unexpectedly gave out. Either it ran out of gas, or the blood on it caused the chain mechanism to seize. Either way, when Farrell realized this, he immediately ditched the chainsaw and began running full-tilt toward the truck and Tom. Seeing him, Tom said into the CB radio, "Please, you have to help me—Collins is gonna kill me!"

At that point, he abandoned the call and began running down the makeshift road at full speed. When he heard the truck starting up, he looked back and saw that Farrell had taken the keys from Dwight. Farrell put the truck into gear and took off toward Tom.

Tom left the road and ran through the open logged portion of Portia Bench that they had surveyed last week, running over snags, mounds, and tree stumps. Farrell did likewise, taking the truck off the road. The four-wheel-drive pickup moved effortlessly over the rough terrain. Tom saw that Farrell was gaining on him, so he ran toward the edge of the bench. When he got within ten feet of the edge, he turned around and saw that Farrell was barely thirty feet away from him.

Tom could plainly see Farrell through the windshield; his eyes appeared illuminated, and he had the most sinister look on his face. At the last second, Tom bolted out of the way and tumbled to the ground. Farrell did not get a chance to turn. The truck went over the edge and down the embankment. It was airborne for a few seconds, and when the nose hit the ground, it flipped over end-to-end six times before coming to rest ten feet before the Coquihalla River. There was a loud explosion, followed by a massive fireball. When Tom witnessed it, he sat down on a tree stump and wept.

***

When Hugh heard the call, he didn't know what to make of it. He couldn't tell if it was somebody playing a prank or if somebody really was in trouble. He could hear the chainsaw running in the background, so it was probably legitimate. The names didn't sound familiar; he was never introduced to the Kamloops crew since they were working under Don. He decided to check with Anders, so he radioed the office.

"Hugh Gormley calling Headquarters, Hugh Gormley calling Headquarters, over."

"Yes, Hugh, this is Anders, over."

"Anders, what did you make of that last transmission? Did you hear it?"

"I didn't hear it very well. I was in the bathroom, and I had the fan on. By the time I came out, the call had stopped. Linda is at a dentist's appointment, so I'm here by myself. What did you hear?"

"Do you know somebody by the name of Tom Greenbrier?"

"Yes, he's one of my men I brought here from Kamloops. They're working up on Portia Bench."

When Hugh learned where they were working, he began to feel very uneasy.

"Is there also someone on that crew named Collins?"

"Yes, Farrell Collins. Why do you ask?"

"Oh my god. Tom said that this Collins guy has gone berserk and was trying to kill him. He said that he has already killed the Crew Chief."

"Hugh, get up there immediately. I'm leaving the office right now, so I should be ten minutes behind you."

***

Anders was in a total state of shock. He couldn't believe his ears. Farrell seemed like the last person on earth who would go insane and kill somebody. He knew something was terribly wrong.

21
AUGUST 1984

Anders could only think that the same people who killed the other crew were now attacking his crew. That's the only way it could make sense. He could not imagine Farrell going on a rampage and killing anyone. He had only known Farrell for a couple years, and in that time, he had never seen him get angry. He was always very easy going and always seemed cheerful, no matter how stressful the job was.

***

As Hugh made his way toward Portia Bench, he didn't quite know what to expect. All he could think of was those four surveyors who were killed in the same area. He wondered if this crew had met a similar fate. As he drove along the section of roadway high above the Coquihalla River overlooking Portia Bench, he could see a fire way down below, almost at the river. Even from a distance, he could tell it was a truck that was on fire. He knew at this point that there was something seriously wrong. Right after he crossed the Coquihalla

River and started up the hill, he saw the man dressed in a train engineer's outfit standing beside the road. Hugh didn't think much of it; he merely waved at the man, but the man didn't wave back. *Who the hell could that be?*

After he passed the second switchback, Hugh saw what appeared to be a young man wandering down the road in the opposite direction. He appeared to be in a daze.

Hugh pulled over. "Is your name Tom?"

The young man just nodded, not saying anything.

"My name is Hugh. You made the call to me. Can you tell me what happened?"

Tom continued to give a blank stare. A few minutes later, Hugh had almost given up trying to get any information from the young man when he managed to squeak out, "I really don't know what happened."

Anders eventually arrived, and when he got out of his truck, he asked, "Tom, what happened?"

Tom was still unresponsive, and evidently in a state of shock.

As a last resort, Anders slapped him across the face.

"Tom! Snap out of it, man—tell me what happened!" yelled Anders.

Tom came to his senses somewhat, and finally said, "Farrell just went crazy for no apparent reason. Here, follow me. You can see for yourselves."

Just then, Don came around the switchback in the distance. When he saw Tom, he stopped his truck and got out.

"Tom, what the hell are you doing here? Get back to work. What do you think you're doing, leaving your crew like that?" Don berated him.

"Back off, Don. We have a serious situation here," said Hugh.

"What are you talking about?" asked Don.

"Don, where the hell have you been all morning? You were

supposed to be checking on Dwight's crew on a regular basis," said Anders.

"Hey, I was working with Henry's crew all morning. I was just coming here now to check on them. I can't be everywhere, you know. Why are you guys here?"

"Tom called us on the radio and said that Farrell snapped and went on some kind of rampage. We came up here to investigate," said Anders.

"He went on a rampage? What did he do?"

"That's what we're trying to find out. Now, quit asking questions and come with us. We need an extra pair of eyes just in case there's something suspicious."

"I saw everything when Farrell drove the truck over the embankment. He didn't get out of the truck, so he was inside when it crashed and exploded. There's no way he could have survived," said Tom.

After they turned off of the main road onto the makeshift road, they soon came across the discarded chainsaw. It was still in the "on" position, but it had long since stalled. It was covered in blood, and there were bits of flesh and bone still stuck to the blades.

"This doesn't look good," said Anders.

They followed the survey stakes until they ended. It was there that they saw the lifeless body of Dwight. He had landed face first into the dirt, the hatchet blade buried deep into his skull.

Anders, who had always regarded Dwight as his number one Crew Chief, cried out, "Oh my god, no—Dwight!"

There was still no sign of Bud. Tom pointed them in the direction in which they ran, and shortly thereafter, they came over a small rise and spotted a body lying on the ground. When they got up close, they realized that it was indeed a body, but no head. They then saw Bud's head two feet away. It had rolled down an incline after it was severed. The four men stood in silence for a few minutes, totally stunned. Tom completely broke down and cried, and Hugh turned around and threw up.

From there, the men headed over to the spot where Farrell drove the truck over the edge. They could see the truck still burning over a hundred feet below them. It was painfully obvious that it was too late for Farrell. They then made their way back to their vehicles.

While they were walking, Hugh asked, "Anders, did you see a man standing beside the road, just past the Bailey bridge, wearing grey-and-white striped overalls with a matching cap?"

"No, I didn't see anybody. That sounds like a train engineer, but there hasn't been a train through here in over twenty years," said Anders.

***

Once they arrived back at their vehicles, Anders immediately radioed for police and ambulance service. Within an hour, the place was surrounded by police and medical service personnel. An RCMP officer wanted to get a statement from Tom, but Anders told him that Tom was still in too much of a state of shock to say anything right now. One of the ambulance drivers offered to take Tom to Fraser Canyon Hospital in Hope, so Tom would be taken there and treated for shock. He would be kept in overnight and released the next day. The bodies of Dwight and Bud would be taken to coroner Dennis's office. As for Farrell, there was nothing left of him for Dennis to examine—they would have to use dental records to positively identify him.

"There isn't much point in you guys sticking around, Mr. Johanssen. This is now a crime scene," Staff Sergeant Dickerson told Anders a little while later.

"I guess you're right. I have to head back to the office, anyway. I'll likely give a statement to the media sometime later today," said Anders.

As Anders drove off, all he could think about was what he would tell the families of his workers who were killed, especially Farrell's wife. This took most of his concentration off of the road. When he rounded the last switchback before the Bailey bridge, the man that Hugh had described was standing right in the middle of the road. Anders slammed on the brakes and let out a yell. He couldn't swerve out of the way in time, and was sure he was going to hit the man. He expected the man to go flying into the windshield, but instead, it appeared as though he went right through the truck. When his truck came to a stop, Anders hurriedly got out and looked around, but saw no sign of him. He looked down at the dirt road, but saw no footprints whatsoever. He was totally bewildered.

Later that day, Anders issued a statement to the media, where he stated as much as he knew about the incident.

The next day, Anders offered to give Tom a ride home to Kamloops. That would also give him the opportunity to meet personally with the families of Dwight, Bud, and Farrell. He wanted to express his deepest sympathy for each man. He also wanted to have a talk with Farrell's wife, so he could possibly shed some light as to what would cause him to snap like that and go on a killing spree.

In Kamloops, Anders met with officials from the RCMP, and stressed to them to not start questioning Tom until he was mentally fit. This was a very traumatic experience for him, so it was in his best interest that he was given some space for now. Anders gave the RCMP his account of what happened from what he had witnessed, so for now, that was all they had to go by.

When Anders met with Farrell's wife, she could not provide any answers. She was just as dumbfounded as everybody else. In all the years that she and Farrell were married, he had never shown any aggression or anger whatsoever toward her, the kids, or anyone in their families. He was always a very happy-go-lucky person, so this came as a total shock.

Anders did not return to Hope until the following Monday. When he checked his phone messages, he heard one from the coroner, Dennis. The message concluded with Dennis stating that it was urgent Anders talk with him. Anders made the return call a priority, but Dennis didn't divulge any details over the phone; he instead told Anders to come to the lab right away.

"You know something, I never imagined that I would be examining the bodies of survey crew workers within three months of each other, who were all working in the same area, and were killed under very mysterious circumstances. Something is very wrong here," said Dennis, once Anders had arrived at the coroner office.

"Yes, I am very aware of that. But I don't have any answers," replied Anders.

"I didn't think you would. It was the same case with your predecessor. Now, let us proceed with Exhibit A, which is Dwight."

Dennis proceeded to pull the cover off the corpse of Dwight. The hatchet had been removed, revealing the deep gash in Dwight's head.

Anders felt like he was going to be sick at the sight of this.

"What's the matter, Anders, are you squeamish? Consider yourself lucky you don't have my job. You need to have a strong stomach to be a coroner. I have to examine dead people all the time, so I'm used to it. Now, I need to show you something."

Anders reluctantly got up close to the body of Dwight, but he had to restrain himself from looking the other way. Using the end of a scalpel as a guide, Dennis outlined the extent of the wound.

"This Farrell guy sure knew what he was doing. His aim was bang on. The hatchet blade pierced Dwight's skull precisely between the hemispheres of his brain. There was virtually no damage to either of the occipital lobes, but the corpus callosum was completely severed. His head was just short of being split into two pieces. Tell me something, was Farrell a very big guy?"

"No, not really. He was somewhere around five feet, nine inches tall. But he was really skinny. I swear he couldn't have been more than one-hundred and thirty pounds soaking wet."

"Did he have big muscles?"

"No, I don't think he ever lifted weights in his life."

"Well, he must have swallowed a bottle of steroids or something, because he somehow became the world's strongest man in one hell of a hurry."

"I don't get it—what are you talking about?"

"Here, Exhibit B—the hatchet. It would be next to impossible to inflict a wound this size with a hatchet. This type of wound would be possible with a standard-size axe, and using a full-throttle swing with both hands. Considering how hard the human skull is, Farrell would have had to take a very hard swing, and even that would barely penetrate beyond the scalp. If he were built like Arnold Schwarzenegger, it would be possible. But if he had skinny arms, he wouldn't even come close. What makes this even more bizarre is the fact that he used only one hand, as there were fingerprints from only one hand found on the handle." Dennis then proceeded to give Anders a demonstration using a block of wood. He took a swing with the hatchet, holding it with just one hand. When it landed, it penetrated the block only a half an inch. He then took another swing, this time using both hands. It penetrated the block further, but not by much. He then produced an axe, took a swing with both hands, and when it hit the block, it split in two. "You see my point?"

"Yes, very much so. I guess you've seen your share of head wounds caused by hatchets."

"On the contrary, this is the first."

From there, they casually walked over to the table containing the body of Bud. Dennis pulled the cover off, revealing that his head was still detached from the rest of his body.

"What can I say? When you get into an argument with a chainsaw, you're going to lose. Chainsaws can cut down huge oak trees; a neck is no match. His family wants an open-casket service, so I have to stitch the head back on. The people at the funeral home will have to be careful dressing him."

Anders had no response as Dennis put the cover back over Bud's body.

"I hope I was able to shed some light on the situation. If you could provide some answers, that would be greatly appreciated."

"I wish I could."

When Anders returned to his office, he received a surprise phone call from Clint.

"Anders, I've been trying to reach you for the past two days. I wanted to see how you're doing."

"My apologies, Clint. It has been so hectic since the recent tragedy."

"I'm very sorry about the loss. If it's any consolation, I went through practically the same thing three months ago, and I've managed to pull myself together."

"It was a complete and total shock … I still can't believe it happened," said Anders.

"Do you have any idea what could have caused this?"

"My best theory is that Farrell must have been hiding a deep, dark secret from everybody, which was that he had anger management issues, and for no apparent reason, he finally snapped."

"The guy who survived—did he mention anything about hearing the sound of drums or seeing a Native ceremonial mask?"

"What are you talking about?"

"Never mind … Did he see anything at all?"

"He's not saying anything right now. He's still pretty traumatized."

"Yes, that's quite understandable."

"They're having one large funeral service for all three of them. Would you like to come to it?"

"Yes, I would. Let me know when and where they're having it."

"Say, Clint, I was wondering, would you like your old job back?"

"Yes, I definitely would. There is not much to do here, and District Engineer Myles is getting anxious to get back to work. He is pretty much completely recovered from his heart surgery, so he has been coming into the office almost every day and getting under my feet. I keep telling him to take it easy, or else he might have another heart attack. Yet, he never listens."

"Well, if you want it, it's yours. I'm finding now that it's too heavy a workload. Coordinating the entire project is too much for one person; it's much better if we work as a team. That way, we can focus on our respective sections."

"You must realize, though, that it's not up to me; it's entirely up to Bill. He has the final say in the matter. Your best bet would be to talk to him personally. I believe he's at the Vancouver office right now, since he has a meeting with my Office Manager, Ted Harvey. Give the office a call and see if he's still there."

"Thanks Clint, I really appreciate your call."

Fortunately for Anders, Clint was right. When he telephoned the Vancouver office, Bill was still there. Sandra directed his call to Ted Harvey's office, where he and Bill were in a meeting. Anders asked Ted if he could speak to Bill.

"Sure, he's right here."

"Anders, it's so nice to hear from you. How is everything going?"

"Well, things are going along alright, considering what just happened."

"Yes, I'm so sorry about your loss. I understand that they were your top survey crew."

"Yes, I did consider them my top crew, which makes it even harder to comprehend. We're all trying to cope as best as we can."

"So, what was it you wanted to speak to me about?"

"I was just wondering, were you planning to come up this way in the next few days?"

"Yes, as a matter of fact, I was planning to come up there and see how the highway project is coming."

"Good. There's something important I want to discuss with you."

"Well, what is it, Anders?"

"I want to have Clint reinstated as Project Coordinator. My workload is too overwhelming; a project of this magnitude is too much for one person to coordinate. I want the arrangement to return to the way it was before, where Clint and I focus on our respective sections.

"I empathize with you, Anders, and I promise to give it serious consideration. It was actually Mike's idea to reassign him in the first place, so I'll have to talk to him. I plan to go to Victoria tomorrow, so I can meet with Clint in the next day or two."

22

Bill arrived at his office at the BC Legislature the following day as planned. One of the first items on his agenda was to meet with Premier Davenport to discuss reinstating Clint. After a little coaxing, Davenport finally gave in and agreed to reinstate him. Bill's next priority was to call Clint at the Highways District Victoria office.

"Hi, Clint, it's Bill. Could you come down to my office and meet with me today?"

"I can be there within an hour."

When Clint arrived at Bill's office, Bill got right to the point. "Clint, Anders talked with me and has made me realize that the highway is too much work for one person. Would you like to be in charge of the Coquihalla Highway project again?"

As expected, Clint accepted. "Of course, I'd be delighted. Well, what are we waiting for? Let's get the job done," said Clint.

"I'm glad to hear that Clint—welcome back. But, just to confirm everything, let's call Anders and make it official."

Bill called Anders at the Hope office, and Clint took part in the conversation on the other extension. "This is excellent news. I look forward to us working together for the rest of the project." Anders concluded the call.

***

Once they were off the phone with Anders and they were alone again, Bill gave Clint a sheepish look. "Uhh, Clint, can I ask you a question?"

"Sure, what is it?"

"Do you believe there's a spirit up there?"

"Up where?" This caught Clint by surprise. Clint was very much aware that admitting anything like that might sound crazy to Bill and could put his job in jeopardy again.

"On the route for the Coquihalla Highway."

"Oh, that spirit. I'll tell you something—the local Natives sure believe it's real. They refer to it as Siaman. Myself, I think it's just a figment of their imagination. Whether it's real or not, I'm not going to let it stand in the way of this project."

"Well, overall, do you believe in ghosts?"

"I've never really given it much thought. It's possible that they're real."

"Well, I believe in ghosts. When I was eighteen and working at the Doukhobor Village Museum in Castlegar, I saw a man who looked exactly like our Spiritual Leader, Peter Verigin, walking down the hallway. It couldn't be him, since he was killed in 1924. It had to be his ghost. I wonder if there are any real-life ghostbusters, like in that movie now playing."

"Yes, I saw the movie myself; I found it rather amusing. But as for a real-life person who removes ghosts, I'm not sure about that. I'll tell you what, that can be a project you and Stan can work on. You guys have easier access to research material."

"I will definitely look into it. By the way, are you going to the funeral for those three men who were killed?"

"Yes, even though I didn't really know them. I think I only met two of them. Even so, I want to pay my respects."

"I wish I could go, but with the Legislature reconvening soon, Mike has scheduled a series of meetings with the Cabinet over the next week, so I'm stuck here. Anyway, say a prayer for me."

The following Saturday, the church was packed for the funeral of the three men. Clint went over to speak with Tom, who was standing nearby.

"Hi, Tom. I wanted to introduce myself—I'm Clint Matheson. I work with Anders and Hugh." They shook hands. "I heard you opened up about the incident to the RCMP the other day. I want to commend you for your efforts, son."

"Mr. Matheson, I still have no idea why Farrell went so crazy all of a sudden."

"Did you see anything out of the ordinary that day—anything unusual?" prodded Clint.

"No, I didn't see anything unusual. Anders told us to watch each other's backs, so I kept a lookout at all times, but I didn't see or hear anything strange."

"Okay, just thought I would ask."

After his conversation with Tom, Clint found Anders.

"Anders, I just wanted to inform you that I'm heading back to Hope tomorrow."

Anders gave a quick run down as to what was accomplished in his absence. "Let's meet in Merritt in three weeks to give each other a further progress report."

Clint nodded in agreement.

When Clint returned to the Hope office on Monday morning, he received little fanfare. In fact, his only greeting was a huge stack of paperwork and a large stack of field notes to go over. He tried to organize a Project Managers meeting in the afternoon, but he couldn't get hold of Don. Don never checked in at the office once on Monday, and Clint was unable to reach him on the CB radio.

It's too much to hope that he's left the country, Clint thought.

Staff Sergeant Dickerson stopped in at the office the following morning.

"Hello, there, Sergeant. How's the investigation going?"

"To be honest, it's at a standstill right now, since there's very little to go by. My officers have been over the scene of the tragedy several times since it happened, but didn't find anything unusual. At this point, I'm not really sure what to look for. It seems like an open-and-shut case as far as I'm concerned. We will never know why he went crazy like that, so there's not much point in probing the site any further."

"I might have to disagree with you on that one. I know there is something out there that we have overlooked. I was thinking, why don't we go up to the site and take one more look around? I know the area very well, and I know exactly where they were surveying. At least as far as surveying goes, if anything is out of the ordinary, I can spot it a mile away. I have some free time this afternoon, so why don't you bring a couple of your constables and head up to the site with me?"

"Since you know the area so well, it might be worth taking another look with you there. Sure, we'll follow you up. We'll come back here around two o'clock."

When they all arrived at the site on Portia Bench that afternoon, Clint led them down toward where the surveyors were last working. They followed the survey markers until they came to an abrupt end.

"At this spot, they would have stopped for a break." Clint pointed to the wooded area on the right. "According to what Tom said, Farrell wandered into the woods there to take a piss, and when he returned, he was a changed man. Before that, Farrell was his normal self. Something in the woods must've caused Farrell to instantly turn into a homicidal maniac," said Clint.

"What would that be?" asked one of the RCMP constables.

"Your guess is as good as mine. That's what we're going to find out. It'll be best to try and trace the exact steps that Farrell took." He noticed some broken branches on a pine tree, and they proceeded into the forest from there. He then noticed a pattern of broken branches that led deeper into the forest.

"These branches could have been broken by an animal," Sergeant Dickerson pointed out.

"If this was done by a bear or a deer, the swath would be much wider. This could only be done by a human." Clint's theory proved to be right. He looked down at the ground, and there in a patch of mud, was a boot print. "Look over here. That was made recently. Farrell definitely headed this way. I remember hearing Tom say that Farrell had a bad habit of heading far back into the bush whenever he had to take a pee. He said that the guys on the crew would tease him about that, assuming he didn't want anyone to see his two-inch dick."

"No wonder he snapped. If I had a two-inch dick and someone made fun of it, I'd go crazy too," said Sergeant Dickerson.

After hacking their way through twenty more feet of dense bush, Clint came across two boot prints side by side. He looked forward and noticed a clump of boulders against the mountainside. All of a sudden, the Native mask appeared on the front of one of the boulders.

"Holy shit," yelled Clint.

"What is it?" yelled Sergeant Dickerson.

Clint had to think fast. He realized what he just saw, but they wouldn't believe him.

"I saw something scurry across the boulder over there, but it was just a chipmunk ... This must have been were Farrell was standing," Clint concluded after observing the angle of the boot prints. *While Farrell was urinating on the boulder, the spirit of Siaman must have somehow gotten inside his head.* But Clint kept his mouth shut on that matter. "Gentlemen, I'm afraid I've sent you all on a wild-goose chase. I thought I might have been able to find some clues that would shed some light on what happened, but nothing appears to be out of the ordinary. I didn't really know Farrell, so he must have had some hidden mental issues. I'm sorry to have brought you out here for nothing."

"That's alright, we needed an excuse to get out of the office," said Sergeant Dickerson.

After his latest sighting of the Native mask, Clint remained in total bewilderment. This was three miles west of where the previous incident happened, at the site of a completely different rockslide. He then realized that there must have been several landslides in that area at the time of the last major earthquake. *Over time, Siaman must have forgotten which rockslide was the actual one, so he now guards the entire area.*

Later that day, Clint received quite the surprise. Don actually showed up at the office. He had no knowledge that Clint returned.

As Don entered the office, he yelled out, "Hey, Johanssen, that transit you issued me is completely out of whack. I need another one."

As soon as he entered Clint's office, he was shocked to see that Clint was there.

"Clint—what are you doing here?" he exclaimed.

"I'm back, and I'm in charge of the project again."

"When did this happen? Where's Anders?"

"Anders is back in Kamloops, and for your information, I've been back here since last Monday. If you would have checked in to the office every day like you're supposed to, you would've learned about me being back much sooner. You know, you're required to check in at the office every morning before heading out to the job site. If you ever miss a Project Managers meeting again, you're history. And another thing, even though you use your own truck to travel to and from the job site, while you're on company time you are required to keep your CB radio on at all times and tuned in to the same channel as the office."

Don was obviously not pleased to see that Clint had returned—let alone receive all of this as soon as he stepped into the office. His frustration with Clint was visible.

"I want the calculations for the elevation shots of the Zopkios Ridge section on my desk first thing tomorrow morning. Now, get back to work," said Clint.

"But I need a replacement transit."

"What's wrong with it? Let me take a look at it."

Clint examined the transit that Don was using, and found a loose screw around the swivel. Once he tightened it, it worked fine.

"There, good as new. You had a screw loose, but I could have told you that," said Clint, sarcastic and smirking.

Don angrily picked up the transit and walked out with it. Clint noticed that he wasn't carrying it properly.

"Be careful with that—it's a very delicate instrument."

At the end of the workday, Clint had some other unfinished business. Cindy had not returned his calls ever since he returned to Hope.

Over the three months Clint was in Victoria, he had made the effort to travel to Hope every weekend to see Cindy, but for the past two weeks, he had been too busy with work to see her. This time, he decided to head straight over to her place instead of phoning her.

When Clint arrived at Cindy's place and rang the doorbell, a man answered the door.

"Hello, I would like to speak to Cindy," said Clint, quite surprised.

"She's busy right now," said the man.

"Who are you?" asked Clint.

"I'm Claude, her husband."

"You mean ex-husband."

"Is that what she told you? You heard it wrong. As far as I'm concerned, we're still married."

"That's not what she told me."

"Just who are you, anyway?"

"I'm Clint."

"So, you're that white-ass she's been seeing."

"What did you call me?"

"A white-ass! What's the matter, are you hard of hearing or something?"

"Listen pal, it just so happens that it's not just my ass that's white. Every other part of me is white, too, including this." Clint raised his fist.

Just then, Cindy appeared in the doorway.

"Clint, what a surprise—I wasn't expecting you," she said.

"I can see that. For your information, I have my old assignment back, so I'm back here in Hope. I've been trying to call you since last Monday. Look, Cindy, we need to talk."

"Clint, I have things to do right now. You have to leave."

Claude butted in and said, "You heard the lady, now get your ass out of here. You're trespassing on Indian land."

"You stay out of this. Cindy, you have not heard the last of me."

"Clint, please, just go."

Clint said nothing more. He merely got in his truck and headed back to his motel room.

23

SEPTEMBER 1984

Clint stewed about what went down with Cindy for the rest of the evening. He got very little sleep that night. All that kept going through his mind was, *What on earth is she thinking, letting that man back into her life? After what he did to her, the thought of taking him back should be out of the question ... a no brainer. What could he possibly have to offer her that I don't?*

Clint went to work the next day feeling half dead. As expected, he couldn't focus on his work, and he asked Linda to hold all of his calls. He kept trying to tell himself to forget about Cindy and move on, but his feelings toward her were too strong to get her out of his mind. By 10:00 a.m. he couldn't stand it any longer; he had to go to her workplace and tell her how he felt.

Cindy was at her desk at the Hope Band Administration Office when Clint arrived. Clint could tell that she sensed that he was going to show up.

"Clint, what are you doing here?" said Cindy, annoyed.

"You know damn well why I'm here."

"As far as I'm concerned, there's nothing left to talk about."

"Cindy, why are you doing this? Why are you letting that loser back into your life? Did you forget that he ran off and left you for another woman?"

"It's not that simple. After all, he is Alex's father."

"That's no excuse—he's been gone so long, she doesn't even know him anymore. Tell me something—is your father behind this? I know he doesn't like me, so he's making you reconcile with him just to spite me. Is that right?"

"No, Dad had nothing to do with it. This was my decision. Claude realized that he made a mistake, and he begged me to take him back."

"Just like that, eh? So, what's he going to do for work?"

"He's going to help out on my uncle's fishing boat."

"But that's only seasonal. What about the rest of the year?"

"I've made arrangements with one of our band members to get him a job in a logging camp in the next few months."

"Can't this guy find work on his own? Look, he has to rely on other people all the time."

"Clint, I'm very busy. Can you just please leave?"

"I believe you're making a huge mistake. I'll give you some time to come to your senses, and when you do, give me a call. You know where to reach me."

A week went by without any word from Cindy. Clint tried to remain optimistic, but deep down, he could sense that Cindy was no longer interested in him. He did his best to try and focus on his work, but it was no easy task.

By the end of the following week, Clint still hadn't heard from Cindy. Even so, he didn't want to go home until Saturday. Feeling dejected, he headed down to the Hope Hotel to drown his sorrows in a few beers.

As usual, the place was packed. A lot of the men from the various survey crews were there, so Clint spent the evening chatting with them. Then, out of the corner of his eye, he spotted Claude on the opposite side of the bar. He appeared to be having a conversation with a young blonde girl. Clint kept an eye on them, but kept his distance. He was paying particular attention to the fact that they appeared to be quite friendly with each other.

While the band was playing, Clint noticed Claude whispering something to the lead singer. Before the next song started up, the lead singer announced that someone had requested a particular romantic ballad. Right after the band began playing that song, Claude and the blonde girl got up and began slow dancing. Within seconds, they were groping each other. Clint, watching from the sidelines, began seething. His blood really began to boil. He decided that he was not going to sit back and do nothing anymore. So he waited until the band took a break and then he made his move. He got up and went over to the table where Claude and the blonde girl went back to sit.

"Claude, what a surprise. Mind if I join you?" Before Claude had a chance to answer, Clint said, "Don't mind if I do."

"I didn't say you could sit here," said Claude.

"This is a public place, so I can sit anywhere I damn well please. So, tell me something Claude, how come Cindy isn't here with you? Better yet, why are you not at home with her?"

"I have the right to come here if I want to. Now, quit sticking your nose in my business, you son of a bitch."

"You didn't answer my question. Young lady, I must inform you that this man is married. At least he tells me he's married."

"I'm warning you, you get away from my table, or I'll …"

"You'll what?"

"I'll punch your fucking lights out, that's what I'll do. But then again, you're so old, you'd probably keel over and die of a heart attack first."

"Don't you ever underestimate me. I'm in a hell of a lot better shape than you think. Why didn't you just stay away? Cindy was so much happier without you. Why did you think that you could just walk back into her life after two years and expect her to act like nothing happened?"

"Listen here, asshole, I'm not telling you again—get out of here."

Claude got to his feet, and Clint stood up seconds later. After they stared each other down for a minute, Claude took a swing, but missed. Clint gave him a right jab followed by a left hook. Claude then put Clint into a headlock. Clint somehow managed to elbow Claude in the gut and break free of the hold. He then delivered a roundhouse left followed by a right hook, which sent Claude flying into the neighbouring table. Claude grabbed a fork from the table, lunged at Clint, and drove the fork into his forehead. Clint shrieked in pain as he felt the tines of the fork penetrate deep into the flesh on his forehead. He was momentarily helpless as he was pinned down on the table. Repeated punches to Claude's stomach had no effect. Eventually, he got his knee up and nailed Claude in the crotch. With Claude momentarily stunned, Clint got a shot in, and nailed Claude in the jaw. He then got up, gave Claude a hard shove, and proceeded to give him a barrage of upper cuts. But Claude was not going down without a fight. He got in a kung-fu kick, which nailed Clint in the chest. Clint staggered backwards, and Claude went charging at him. Clint got out of the way at the last second. Then, with Clint bleeding profusely from the puncture wounds, he gave Claude a flying tackle. Claude landed on his back with Clint on top of him. At that point, Clint completely took over. It was as if years of pent-up anger and aggression were unleashed all at once. He delivered numerous right and left hooks to Claude's face as he was prone on his back. Eventually, two bouncers managed to pull Clint off him. Claude was a bloody mess, and was completely motionless.

The two bouncers escorted Clint to the exit door, and one of them physically threw him out, where he landed on the sidewalk.

"Don't you ever come back here again, you worthless piece of shit," yelled the bouncer.

Clint could see that the bouncer was Native.

"Sir, that other guy instigated the whole thing."

"That's not what I saw," said the bouncer. Clint knew that what the bouncer really meant to say was, "I saw what I wanted to see."

Clint managed to call a taxi from the Hope Hotel lobby. He went to the emergency room at Fraser Canyon Hospital. He needed five stitches to close a gash on his lower lip, and a large bandage over the puncture wounds from the fork. He also needed a tetanus shot. While Clint was in the emergency room, Claude was brought in by ambulance, still unconscious. Clint kept the curtain closed surrounding the bed he was on, so none of Claude's friends could see him. When the doctor gave Clint the green light to leave, he snuck out the back door after he called for another taxi back to his motel.

That night, Clint did not get any sleep. In addition to having a lot on his mind, the local anaesthetic around his lip wore off prematurely. His forehead was also throbbing, so he was in a lot of pain.

Clint's main concern was Cindy. He didn't want to see her get hurt again. He could tell that the same thing was going to happen again. He felt he had to warn her. So the first thing he did when he got up on Saturday morning was to head over to Cindy's place.

When Cindy answered the door, the first thing she said was, "What do you want?"

"Cindy, I need to see you. It's about Claude."

"I will have you know that I've just been to the hospital. They kept Claude there overnight, and they're not releasing him until later this morning. He told me everything about what happened last night. What is the matter with you? Do you always solve disagreements with violence? You are one sick bastard, Clint."

"Listen here, I saw him in the company of another woman. They were being very friendly with each other, and I could see where it was leading. I had to step in. I'm telling you, this guy is not faithful to you—he's done it before, and I know he's going to do it again."

"For your information, that girl is a long-time friend of ours. Claude and I have known her family for years. Her sister and I were best friends when we were growing up. Her family lives in Vancouver now, and she was just passing through here on her way to Prince George. I would have been there last night, but I wasn't feeling well."

"From what I observed, they were acting like they were more than just friends."

"Claude promised me that he's a changed man and he regrets leaving me. I agreed to give him another chance. So, for the last time, quit sticking your nose in my business, okay?"

"Cindy ... what about us? What about the special relationship we have? I thought you loved me."

"Clint, it's over between us. We're from totally different backgrounds. Our relationship will just not work out. I don't ever want to see you again." With tears streaming down her face, she said, "Now, will you please leave? Don't ever come back."

Clint said nothing more. He returned to his motel room, angrily packed his bags, and checked out. On his way out of Hope, he stopped at a Chevron station with an attached convenience store. He purchased a danish and a large cup of extra-strong coffee. He wanted to make sure he stayed awake on the drive back to Vancouver.

Clint spent the rest of the weekend catching up on his sleep and nursing his wounds. He also made a very important decision—with Cindy living in Hope, the town wasn't big enough for the both of them.

On Monday morning, Clint made a special trip to Hope and

called an impromptu Project Managers meeting. This time, Don complied and actually showed up on time. Once Don, Hugh, and Ed were all together, Clint got straight to the point.

"For the remainder of the project, I will be operating out of my office in Vancouver, and you three will hold down the fort here in Hope. I have a huge stack of paperwork on my desk back in Vancouver, and Ted is severely overworked. You will each be completely in charge of your respective sections, which includes all survey work plus all road and bridge construction. I'll come up every Wednesday morning for a Project Managers meeting when you'll each give a progress report. In addition, we'll have numerous meetings with potential contractors in the coming months. Everybody will benefit from this in the long run, and I'll be much more effective in Vancouver than here in Hope."

Clint usually concluded their meetings by asking the men if there were any remaining questions. But, this time, he avoided asking mainly because he was afraid one of them would ask him about his appearance.

Don, being his usual self, always had to get the last word in. "What's the matter, Clint? Did Pocahontas dump you? Let me guess, she found your cock too small for her liking, so she found a real man for a change." Don burst out laughing.

Clint momentarily had his back turned, so Don didn't see that he was absolutely seething. Clint quickly turned around, stood up, grabbed Don by the throat, and flung him full-force into the wall. He had Don pinned up against the wall, with his feet dangling six inches off the ground. He had him held by the throat with one hand, and was squeezing with all his might.

"I would give anything to snap your scrawny neck in half. If you ever stick your big nose in my personal life again, I'll fucking *kill* you. Do you understand what I'm saying, you useless motherfucker?"

Don was unable to breathe, and he was starting to turn purple.

Clint then grabbed him by the collar of his shirt and flung him down onto the floor. Don landed with a loud thud, and for a few minutes, he lay on the ground gasping for air, barely able to breathe. He eventually staggered to his feet, and when he regained his breath and was able to speak, he said, "I am going to have you charged with assault."

"Good luck with that. You're going to have a hard time making a case with no witnesses," said Clint.

"What the hell are you talking about?" Don looked bewildered and pointed to Hugh and Ed.

"I didn't see anything—how about you, Ed? Did you see anything?" asked Hugh.

"Nope, didn't see a thing," replied Ed.

24

Barely two days after his last visit to Hope, Clint had to make a return trip. Even though it was Wednesday, Clint was not planning another Project Manager's meeting until the following week. He had to call an emergency meeting. Since he gave the go-ahead to resume surveying on Portia Bench, no survey crew wanted anything to do with it. Since the memo was sent out, virtually all of the Crew Chiefs vowed that they would quit if they were forced to do the survey work on that section, and pretty much all of their crew members stood by them. Word had spread that the area was cursed, and they will be putting their lives at risk if they venture into that area. Clint had tried to reassure everybody that the area was perfectly safe, and their safety would not be in jeopardy. However, no one believed him. With fall approaching, winter would be just around the corner. It was vital that the surveying be completed before winter sets in, so he would have all of the necessary data available to plan the construction phase over the winter.

Clint left for Hope very early that morning, as he wanted to start the meeting right at 8:00 a.m. The night before, he had called Hugh and told him to tell the others to be there and be on time. Clint arrived at the office at 7:30 a.m. and, surprisingly, Don showed up early. But Clint quickly learned that Don's intentions were strictly to catch him alone, so he could have another confrontation with him.

As soon as he entered the office, Don stood over the desk, glared at him, and said, "I demand an apology."

Clint stood up, stared him down, and said in a snarly tone, "You're not going to get one. Now sit down and shut the fuck up."

When Hugh and Ed showed up, Clint started an open discussion as to how they could recruit a crew to complete the Portia Bench section. They all agreed that hiring a completely new crew was out of the question. At least two experienced surveyors would be necessary.

While Clint and the men were engrossed in their discussion, Henry, Greg, and Rudy came into the office to get some supplies. At first, Clint was oblivious to their presence. It was not until Henry knocked on the door that he realized he was there.

"Excuse me for interrupting, but can I …" He then stopped dead in his tracks.

"What can I do for you, Henry?" asked Clint.

Henry was momentarily speechless.

"Holy shit, what happened to you?" asked Henry.

"I don't want to talk about it. Now, what was it you wanted?" asked Clint, annoyed.

"Oh, right. I couldn't help overhear your conversation, so the boys and I talked it over, and we decided that we are not going to let no goddamn ghost stand in the way of this project. If you need a crew to do the surveying up there, we'll do it."

"Well, that's very admirable of you, Henry. I guess our problem is solved. What are you working on right now?"

"We're still taking elevation shots around Zopkios Ridge."

"How much do you have left?"

"We're on our last kilometre. We should be done by a week from Friday."

"Very well, then. We will resume surveying on the Portia Bench section one week from Monday. There is just one other concern I have, Henry. Where's that fourth person on your crew; the young fellow? I think his name was Ryan?"

"Oh, him. He has gone back to school."

"Okay, I'll see about finding your crew a fourth person. Thank you very much, Henry. You're a real life saver," said Clint, as he got up and shook Henry's hand.

"You know, back in my hometown there was a supposedly haunted house. When I was a kid, I was the only one of my friends who worked up the guts to venture inside, and when I did, I found no signs of any ghosts. If that Indian ghost wants a piece of me, he's got another thing coming," Henry concluded.

"Okay, Henry, if that's the case, you're the man. Just be careful up there, okay?"

Once Henry, Greg, and Rudy left, Don said, "Are you crazy? You're going to let that buffoon run the survey crew up there? That guy doesn't know his ass from a hole in the ground."

"What's your problem, Don? He happens to have a very good track record, and his calculations are always accurate. He knows what he's doing, so I want you to treat him with respect, or else you'll be in very deep shit. Do you understand me?" He poked Don in the chest with a pointed finger.

Don didn't answer; he just stormed out of the office in a huff once again.

25

The first order of business that Clint had to attend to when he returned to his Vancouver office was to find a fourth person for Henry's crew. He thought about it long and hard, and considering that nobody from any of the local crews wanted to take on the task until Henry had stepped up to the plate, he thought about recruiting someone from outside the region. The first person who came to mind was Matt Yablonski, the Merritt Crew Chief. The preliminary surveys on the northern section were all complete, so all that was left for the survey crews to complete was the elevation shots and cut-and-fill shots. Most of that work was being done by the Kamloops crews, and survey work on Phase Two, the section of the Coquihalla Highway between Merritt and Kamloops, was not scheduled to resume until the following springtime.

On Tuesday morning, Clint phoned Anders at his Kamloops office.

"Anders, I wanted to ask if I could borrow Matt for at least three weeks. I need someone with experience to assist my Crew Chief."

"That shouldn't be a problem; I can part with him for a little while. When he comes back to the office at four-thirty, I'll talk to him and see if he's interested."

Clint received a call from an interested yet apprehensive Matt soon afterward.

"How come you're asking me, Clint? Don't you have enough people on your own crews?"

"All of the people on my crews are very busy right now. I am trying to get as many elevation shots as possible done before the first snowfall and, up near the summit, that's not too far away. One of the members of Henry's crew went back to college, and the two other guys have little experience operating a transit; they're strictly rod-and-chain men. I'm choosing you because you have lots of experience, so you and Henry can work side by side."

"Where would I be working?"

"Up at mile fifteen in the Coquihalla River Valley, in the Bench area."

"Say, isn't that the spot where Dwight and Bud were killed?" Matt asked after a long pause.

"Yes, I'm afraid it is."

"Clint, be honest with me. Are you asking me because nobody on any of your crews wanted to work up there because they're too afraid? I have to be honest—Dwight and Bud were very good friends of mine. It would be difficult for me to work in the same spot where they met their demise, and especially in such a horrible manner."

"I see your point. But another way to look at it is this: if the project is not completed, then all of their work would be in vain. In other words, they would have died for nothing. I believe that the best way to remember them would to complete what they started. In addition, all of your accommodation and meals are on me. Come on, Matt, I really need you."

"I want to know one more thing. Am I safe up there? Isn't that area under some kind of curse or something?"

"That area is perfectly safe. It was determined that Farrell had some kind of hidden mental condition, and he never told anyone about it. It was purely an isolated incident. Don and Hugh, my Project Managers, will watch your back, and I'll travel up there from time to time to check up on how the crew is doing. I assure you, you have nothing to worry about."

"Okay, if you insist, I will take the job. When would you like me to start?"

"Next Monday, but can you make a trip up to Hope tomorrow? I want to have a meeting with everyone involved, so I can go over all the procedures. I will pay for your travel allowance. Can you be at the office at ten o'clock?"

"Yes, I'll be there."

When everyone was present for the meeting the following day, Clint outlined the procedure they will be following for the survey.

"Henry, this is Matt. I'm not sure if you two have met. You will be alternating duties between transit operator and head chainman; you will rotate each day. As for Greg and Rudy, you two will alternate between rear chainman and stake pounder. You'll start from right where the Kamloops crew left off and continue in a westerly direction. The routine will be the same; you'll start with the centre lines, followed by the twenty- and thirty-metre road allowances for both the eastbound and westbound lanes."

All throughout the remainder of the week and the weekend, all Clint could think about was Henry's crew. Deep down, he was very concerned. He eventually decided to head up to their jobsite on Monday and give them some moral support, and watch their backs in the process.

On Sunday evening, he went downstairs into his recreation room, went into his gun cabinet, and took out his .308 Remington hunting rifle. He hadn't used it in nearly ten years. The last time he fired it was when he went moose hunting near Quesnel with his neighbour. He then took ten rounds of ammunition from the shelf and loaded the magazine. The following morning, he loaded his rifle into his truck and headed up to where Henry's crew was working.

Henry and his crew began the survey precisely at the same spot where Dwight had left off. Henry mounted the transit right at the exact spot where Dwight had his. When Henry was setting up the tripod for the transit, he noticed that there were still bloodstains on the ground; there had not been any rain since the incident. They started at 8:00 a.m. and, as expected, Don was there when they started and kept observing them.

At 9:00 a.m. the crew received a welcome surprise when Clint appeared on the scene. But what had everyone even more surprised was the rifle he was carrying on his shoulder.

Don was the first one to speak up. "Clint, what are you doing here?"

"I just thought I would come up and see how everything was going."

"We're doing just fine. We don't need your help," said Don in a snarly tone.

"It just so happens that I'm in charge of this project, so I can come up here anytime I damn well please. Do you have a problem with that?" Clint cocked his rifle for good measure.

"No, I guess not."

"Good. Now, you have four other crews working for you. I suggest you go and check up on them."

Don didn't argue this time. He left without saying a word.

"Clint, what's with the rifle?" asked Matt.

"Well, I thought I would come by and watch your backs. You never know what's lurking out there."

"Wait a minute, you were the one who assured me that it's perfectly safe here, and I had nothing to worry about. So, it's not safe here after all, huh? That's a complete contradiction of what you said when you talked me into taking this job."

"Actually, it is safe to work here. I just thought I would provide some extra protection just in case."

"In case of what?"

"There are bears and cougars out here. They can pop up at any moment."

"Mr. Matheson, if you don't mind me saying so, if this is a ghost we are dealing with, a gun won't do dick," said Henry.

"Clint, you never said anything about a ghost—you weren't being up front with me at all," said Matt, annoyed.

"Now, hold on, there is no ghost around here. It is only a local Indian legend. Just go back to what you were doing, act normal, and pretend I'm not here. I will watch your backs just in case there are any wild animals."

"How can we act normal when we know our boss is standing over us holding a rifle?" said Henry.

"Are you going to be here watching our backs until we finish this project? This is going to take several weeks. Who's going to do your job?" asked Matt.

"Look, guys, stop asking questions, okay? Just carry on with what you were doing."

The crew went back to their surveying tasks, but they all appeared to be uneasy with Clint standing over them with a rifle. Clint tried not to let on that he was feeling uneasy himself. It was fairly windy, so the surrounding trees were making a lot of noise when the wind whistled through their branches. Whenever a branch made a snapping noise, Clint swung his rifle wildly in the direction of the sound. He couldn't hide his paranoia.

"Mr. Matheson, you're making me nervous. I can't concentrate on my work; I can't do this anymore. I'm sorry, but I'm afraid you're going to have to find another crew if you insist on staying here with that rifle," said Henry.

"He's right, Clint. What you're doing is completely unnecessary. We'll be all right here, I promise. Will you please just let us work here on our own?" said Matt.

"I guess you're right. Maybe I am being too paranoid. Okay, I'll let you guys work by yourselves, but there is something I want all of you to have."

Clint went back to his truck and got out a portable radio once used by the Canadian military. He had bought it at a military surplus store.

"What's that?" Henry asked.

"It's an army-issue portable radio. It's tuned to the same frequency as the other crews in the area as well as the Hope office. If you see anything that is not normal, make a call on the radio immediately and get the hell out of here right away."

"Man, this thing weighs a ton. Am I expected to wear this on my back all the time?" Henry said as he picked it up.

"No, you only need to carry it from your truck to where you are working. Besides, Greg or Rudy can have the honour of carrying it."

***

An hour after Clint left, Don drove past where the crew's truck was parked. Realizing that Clint had left, he parked his truck and walked up to where the crew was. They were taking their coffee break when Don approached them.

"Is numb-nuts gone?" asked Don.

"Are you referring to Clint?" asked Matt.

"Of course I am. Listen guys, don't listen to him, he's delusional. He shouldn't even be running this project. His problem is that he smokes too much marijuana. Did he tell you guys that you could all take a break?"

"He said that we are entitled to a break," said Henry.

"Not on my time—now, get back to work."

The crew reluctantly cut their break short and resumed their positions. The section they were currently surveying was on a twelve-degree curve to the left, and Henry was relying on Dwight's calculations, which appeared to be off by a couple degrees. After sixty metres, he stopped to take some extra calculations.

"C'mon Henry, one plus one equals two, two plus two equals four," Don yelled while Henry tried to concentrate.

"Gee, I wouldn't have known that if you hadn't told me," Henry shot back.

At the end of the workday when Don returned to the Hope office, Hugh was sitting at Clint's desk.

"Don, what's the problem?" Hugh could tell Don was angry.

"Jesus Christ, I wanted to take that transit away from that Finnegan goof in the worst way. Matheson is so goddamn stupid, hiring that moron," said Don in an angry tone.

"For your information, Don, Clint didn't hire Henry, I did. I like that he has a good work ethic, unlike some people. Frankly, I don't know what your problem is. As far as I'm concerned, Henry's doing a great job."

"What the hell do you know? You're not the one who has to work with him," said Don just before he angrily stormed out.

26

OCTOBER 1984

Henry and his crew made very good progress in their first week. Everything went smoothly without any incidents. They were off to a good start the next week, but on the Tuesday, their chain snapped. Don was with them at the time, so he called each of the other survey crews working in the area on the CB radio to see if anyone had a spare chain. Eventually he got lucky; one of Ed's crews had a spare chain. He sent Matt to near the new Nicolum River Bridge, where Ed's crew was working, to get the chain.

When Matt met up with Ed's crew, the Crew Chief, who once worked with Matt, asked him for a second opinion on some of the calculations he made for the bridge approach. Matt, always willing to lend a hand, gladly obliged. They began reviewing the calculations and lost track of time.

Meanwhile, Don began to get very impatient. He was constantly pacing and looking at his watch. He grew angrier by the minute.

"He should be back by now. Where the hell is that fucking Polack?" asked Don.

"What did you say?" asked Henry, as he gave Don a disgusted look.

"I said where the hell is that *fucking* Polack? He's taking too damn long."

"Now listen here, I don't take too kindly to what you just said."

"Why should that be of any concern to you, Finnegan?"

"You obviously don't know me, Don. I was adopted by an Irish family, and my birth mother was Polish."

"Is that so? Are you sure you weren't just left on their doorstep? That's what I would have done with you."

"No, that's not what happened."

"Let me guess. Your mom was a hooker, and your dad was a fisherman, and after being away at sea for a month, he came back, got drunk on Screech, picked up your mom, and forgot to put on a rubber."

"Hey, you take that back, you fucking beanpole!"

"Don't you talk to me like that. Don't forget, I'm still your boss—I'm just having some fun with you, that's all. No harm done. How does it feel to be the by-product of a quicky fuck?"

Henry was seething. He didn't say anything more; instead, he walked right up to Don, took a swing with his right hand, and drove his fist right into Don's jaw. Don went down hard.

"Don't you ever, *ever*, talk about my mother like that, you fucking bastard!" Henry screamed out.

Don slowly staggered to his feet, holding his jaw with his right hand. His mouth was bleeding profusely. Pointing his finger at Henry, he said angrily, "I'll see to it that you get fired for this."

The next day, Clint drove to Hope for his weekly Project Manager meeting. He was barely in the office ten minutes before Don came storming in. The first thing Clint noticed was the big bruise on Don's lower cheek.

"Gee, Don, what happened? Did you try some cheesy pick-up line on a hot looking babe and it didn't go as planned? It could be your cheap cologne, or the fact that you're butt ugly," said Clint.

"Are you finished?" snarled Don.

"Yes, I am. What can I do for you?"

"I demand that that Finnegan bastard be fired."

"Why? What did he do?"

"That son-of-a-bitch struck me for no apparent reason."

"Don't give me that. He had to have a reason, and knowing you, that could have been anything. Henry's not the type of person who would just punch somebody for no reason."

"How do you know? How can you make an assumption like that? How well do you know him?"

"I am a very good judge of character. He gets along well with everyone, except for you, of course."

"Look, I am not taking this anymore. I demand that you do something about it right now," said Don, angrily, as he slammed his fist on the desk.

"Okay, I will. As of now, you are suspended without pay for the rest of this week and all of next week," replied Clint.

Don was aghast. He could barely maintain his emotion. "What are you suspending me for? *I* am the victim here."

"Don, you obviously said something to Henry to provoke him. I wasn't born yesterday. You also say demeaning things about me behind my back, which is typical of you. You obviously don't have the balls to say it to my face, because you're nothing but a low-life chicken shit."

"This is absolute bullshit. You just have a personal vendetta against me, that's all. You just don't want to hear the facts."

"Don, one more word out of you, and I'm going to add one more week to your suspension. My decision is final. If you have a problem with it, we can go out behind the building right now and have it out." Clint proceeded to stand up, take off his watch, and flex his muscles. The two of them stared each other down for a minute, but Don eventually backed away. "You get the fuck out of this office this instant, and don't come back until I say you can."

Clint remained at the Hope office throughout the day. He held individual meetings with both Ed and Hugh, and advised them that they would need to pull in extra hours for the next week and a half while Don was under suspension. Neither of them minded. They believed that having Don out of the way was a bonus in itself. Later that afternoon, he called Henry's crew on the CB radio and Matt answered. He told Matt to tell Henry that he wanted to meet with him when they reported to the office at the end of the day.

When the crew came into the office at 4:30 p.m. Henry went into Clint's office as requested and Clint closed the door.

Henry had a very worried look on his face. "Am I in shit?"

"No, Henry, you are not in shit. Have a seat." Clint tried his best to put Henry's mind at ease. In a rational tone, he said, "Henry, can you please tell me what happened?"

Henry told him about Don making derogatory comments about his birth parents.

Clint nodded, "I understand, and I assure you that you're not in trouble. Don will not be giving you any more hassle even after he returns from his suspension." At this, he watched the relief flood over Henry's face.

"Say, Mr. Matheson, do you know where I can get some …"

"Get some what?"

"You know …"

"No, I don't know. What are you talking about, Henry?"

Henry pursed his lips, put his thumb and index finger together, and moved them back and forth from his lips in a toking motion. He then whispered, "Pot."

Clint gave Henry a look of total bewilderment. "Do you mean marijuana?"

"Yes, I was wondering if you knew where I can get some marijuana."

"Why are you asking me? Where the hell did you get the idea that I smoke pot? I will have you know that I have only tried it once in my life. I might add, as long as you want to remain on my payroll, you should know that I have no tolerance to drug use whatsoever. Now, getting back to my first question. Why do you think I know where to buy marijuana?"

"Don said that you smoke too much pot, which is why you're so delusional. His quote—not mine."

"Oh, he did, did he? I am going to have to have another little talk with Mr. Lassiter. That will be all, Henry."

Once Henry left, Clint telephoned Don at his apartment. He was surprised when Don actually answered the phone; he figured Don would be at the bar. When Don heard that it was Clint, he snarled, "What do you want?"

"Congratulations, Don, you have just added one more week to your suspension. How *dare* you even insinuate that I do drugs. You have slagged me for the last time, you hear me? One more thing—if you ever get on Henry's case again, you are history. Consider this your final warning."

27

With all of the turmoil that had been going on lately, Clint decided he needed a vacation. After talking with his local travel agent, Clint decided that New Orleans was the place to go for six days—at a reasonable price, too.

Clint booked to leave in two days for his trip, so before he left, he met with Ted and told him that he would be away next week, so he would be in charge at the Vancouver office. He then contacted Hugh and Ed in Hope, told them that he would be away, and outlined what would be expected of them over the next week. He would be in touch as soon as he arrived back.

***

In the first four days while Clint was on vacation, Henry and the crew made great progress with the surveying. They completed the centre lines for the eastbound and westbound lanes as well as all of the road allowance lines for that kilometre, and they were now starting on the next kilometre. Since Don was suspended, the atmosphere on the jobsite and the morale had improved 100 percent. They enjoyed working for Hugh much better, and as a result, their productivity improved tremendously. Another thing going for them was the weather. It had been unseasonably warm and sunny for early October, which made for perfect working conditions.

Their second day on the next kilometre started like all the other days, and at 10:00 a.m. they took their usual coffee break. For as long as they had been working together, Matt had been taking exception to Henry smoking a half a pack of cigarettes on a typical workday, but had kept his mouth shut. Matt, a health nut, finally decided to speak up today.

"Henry, those things are going to kill you some day."

"Who the hell are you, my mother? Look, I've tried to quit, but a good smoke is one of the few pleasures I get out of life," said Henry, annoyed. He proceeded to get up and head towards the forest.

"Where are you going?" asked Matt.

"Listen, since my smoking bothers you, I'll have one back in the bush."

"Henry, be careful. We haven't had any rain in nearly a month, so the ground is bone dry. A lit cigarette can easily start a forest fire."

"I'll be careful," Henry promised. "I'll look for a rock before lighting it, and will butt the cigarette out against the rock and pour coffee over it until it's extinguished, okay?" He then hacked his way through the bush until he came to a clearing. As he lit his cigarette, he thought to himself, *Good, now I can have a smoke in peace.*

Henry was in the clearing for less than a minute when he began to feel like he wasn't alone. He could feel a strange presence—it was as though there was somebody right behind him. He turned around, and there was a First Nations man standing there. He was dressed head to toe in deer hides and he looked quite young—possibly in his early twenties. Their eyes met, and Henry was totally mesmerized, as though the Native man was giving him a hypnotic glance. The native man then uttered the words, "*Kway-sh itl stawl-mihe.*" ("I grizzly warrior.") "*K unk em-e ex?*" ("Are you strong?")

"*I cen uk anuk em,*" ("I am strong,") replied Henry.

"*Kwah kwel-ek Suh-lee ah,*" ("Beware Guardian Spirit power,") said the man.

"*Pal-ahk-way t-sah,*" ("You spirit,") replied Henry.

"*Cx nem xte`stex le tena x-em,*" ("You go, do it right away,") said the man.

"*I cen uk anuk em.*" Henry repeated.

***

Henry turned and walked back to where the other men were. He walked like a zombie and repeatedly uttered the phrase, "*I cen uk anuk em.*" He was totally unaware that he had dropped his cigarette without extinguishing it. The men were still enjoying their coffee break when Henry approached them. He continued to say the same phrase over and over, and acted like he was in some kind of a trance.

Matt was the first to see that Henry was acting very strange. "Henry, are you feeling alright?"

Henry didn't respond. He proceeded to pull his penknife out of his pocket and open the blade. He glared at Rudy, who was sitting on a log. Then, without warning, he ran full speed toward Rudy, knocked him off the log, and threw himself on top of him. While sitting on top of him, Henry began slashing away at Rudy's face with the knife.

"Henry, what the fuck are you doing? Stop that!" Greg screamed.

Greg and Matt tried desperately to pull Henry off of Rudy, but Henry's enormous size was no match for them. The blade of the penknife cut into Rudy's forehead, cheeks, and chin as Henry continued to carve away. He repeatedly uttered, "*I cen uk anuk em,*" but now in a much louder tone. Rudy screamed in pain as the blade cut into his face.

Greg was worried the knife would reach Rudy's neck, where it could sever his jugular vein. In an act of sheer desperation, Greg grabbed the hatchet and, using the flat side, took a huge swing and nailed Henry in the back of the head. Henry crumpled over and landed on his back. He had knocked Henry out cold.

Matt and Greg immediately tended to Rudy, who was bleeding abundantly and screaming in agony. Greg worried that he was going into shock. Greg tore off his shirt and wrapped it around Rudy's face as a makeshift tourniquet in an effort to try and staunch the flow of blood. Greg was nearly hysterical himself, not just for Rudy but he thought he also might have just killed Henry.

"We have to get him to the hospital, quickly. Rudy, I know it hurts, but just stay calm, man," yelled Greg.

Greg guided Rudy over the snag-strewn ground towards the truck. He kept one hand on the part of his shirt that was over Rudy's forehead, so blood wouldn't run into his eyes. When they reached the truck, Greg helped him into the front seat, and Matt started to climb into the driver's seat.

"Wait a minute, we can't leave Henry behind," yelled Greg.

"What's the point in bringing him along? He's dead," replied Matt.

"No, he isn't."

"With the amount of force you used to hit him with the hatchet, you definitely killed him."

"No, he's still alive. He has to be. No matter what, we can't leave him here. There are cougars all throughout these woods, and they will feast on him."

Greg ran back toward where Henry was lying. He was still unconscious. Greg grabbed his wrist and felt for a pulse. Sure enough, there was a pulse.

"Matt, he's alive—he has a pulse. Come here—give me a hand. Get over here, quickly."

Matt grudgingly made his way to where Greg and Henry were.

"You grab his legs and I'll take him by the arms," said Greg.

"You have got to be kidding me—he must weigh over three

hundred pounds."

"That's why I need your help. I can't carry him by myself."

The two of them struggled to carry Henry over the twisted mass of twigs and stumps. When they reached the truck, they decided to place Henry in the back seat where he could lie down. It was a major job squeezing Henry into the back seat with the front seat folded down. Greg would ride up front with Rudy, where he could keep applying pressure to Rudy's face to try and stop the bleeding.

Before Matt climbed into the driver's seat, he took off his shirt, since Greg's shirt was now completely saturated with blood. The minute they took off, Matt radioed to Fraser Canyon Hospital, and informed them that he was bringing in two injured survey workers. He was just about to radio the Hope office when suddenly the man in the engineer outfit jumped out in front of the truck.

Matt yelled out, "Holy shit!" He slammed on the brakes. He squinted his eyes as he knew he was going to hit the man. When the truck came to a dead stop, he looked around, but didn't see the man anywhere. He didn't hear any kind of *thud* sound that indicated the truck hit the man. Greg, who was tending to Rudy's wounds, was completely oblivious to what just happened.

"Matt, what the fuck are you doing?" yelled Greg.

"I hit somebody! Didn't you see him?"

"I didn't see a thing."

Matt got out of the truck and looked around, but he saw no sign of the man. He even looked underneath the truck.

"Come on, Matt, we need to get going," Greg called out to Matt.

When Matt got back into the truck, he was still completely dumbfounded. "I don't know what just happened, but I know damn well what I saw."

As they made their way along the narrow stretch of road that was carved out of the mountainside high above the Coquihalla River, Matt tried to reach Hugh on the CB radio. Each try was unsuccessful, and he wondered if Hugh might be on another channel. As he repeatedly turned the dial on the CB radio, he wasn't focusing on the road, and there wasn't much room for error.

"Are you trying to get us all killed? Wait until we get off the mountain before using the CB again, okay?" said Greg.

Once the road returned to the valley bottom, Matt tried to call Hugh again. He tried repeatedly for the next five minutes, but got no response. He then called Linda at the Hope office. "Linda, Rudy and Henry were injured in a mishap on the bench. Can you try to reach Hugh on the CB radio and tell him to meet us at Fraser Canyon Hospital?"

"Okay, I'll try my best to reach him, but Hugh is most likely working in the field right now."

Once they arrived at Fraser Canyon Hospital, one of the doctors on duty was waiting for them. Rudy was immediately rushed into Emergency, and the other doctor on duty said, "You said there were two injured workers. Where is the other one?"

Matt said, "Come with me," and led him out to the truck. Henry had still not regained consciousness.

When the doctor saw Henry's size, he exclaimed, "Good God! How the hell did you guys get him in the back seat? How are we going to get him out?"

Matt called out to Greg to come over and give them a hand. Matt moved the front seat as far forward as he could, and began to ease Henry out of the back seat feet first. With Greg pushing from Henry's shoulders and Matt pulling Henry by his legs, they tried with all their might to squeeze Henry out of the back seat. But with his ample stomach, he eventually got stuck.

"Push his stomach against the folded-down front seat and twist him so that both his upper and lower parts will come out at the same time," the doctor told Greg. Greg tried this and had some success. He then gave one more tremendous heave, and Henry went flying out of the truck and landed on the ground hard with a loud thud. The three of them loaded Henry onto a stretcher, and the doctor immediately began examining him. He noted that he still had a pulse, but then he noted that his blood pressure had dropped rapidly. With that, they immediately rushed him into the emergency room.

***

It took over three hours before Linda was able to reach Hugh on the CB radio. It was when he returned to his truck to get some flagging tape that he heard Linda calling him on the radio.

"What kind of accident? What happened?"

"Matt wouldn't elaborate. He only said that he needs you to get over to the hospital right away," said Linda.

By the time Hugh reached the hospital, Rudy was out of surgery but was still under anaesthetic. The doctors had long since stabilized Henry's blood pressure, and were now checking all of his other vital signs. Matt was still in the waiting room when Hugh came in.

"Boy, am I glad to see you," said Matt, but he noticed that Hugh looked more angry than upset. "Hugh, what's wrong? Don't you want me to tell you what happened?"

"Maybe you could tell me what you were doing up there. When I was driving along that section of road across the river from where you guys were working, I saw this big column of smoke. Can you explain that?"

When Matt realized it, he was in a total state of shock.

"Oh my god—Henry's cigarette!"

"You mean to tell me that Henry was still smoking when I specifically told him not to, considering how dry it is out there?"

"I guess it was partly my fault. I made Henry feel guilty about smoking, so he went back into the bush for a smoke so he could be away from us. He must have forgotten to butt it out."

"Now I have to call the Forest Service and have them get a crew in there before it takes off, thanks to his carelessness. Tell me, what exactly happened?"

"When Henry came back from where he had his cigarette, he started acting all weird, and was talking in gibberish. It was like he was under hypnosis or something. Then, for no reason whatsoever, he took out that little penknife of his—the one he peels his apples with, ran toward Rudy, jumped on him, and began carving up his face with the penknife. Greg and I tried to pull him off of Rudy, but he wouldn't budge. So Greg grabbed the hatchet and hit Henry in the back of the head with the blunt end."

"How hard did he hit him?"

"Harder than he thought. He knocked him out cold. He never regained consciousness all the way here. The doctors are working on him right now."

"How bad was Rudy hurt?"

"He cut him up pretty bad. He lost a lot of blood on the way here. He's going to need a lot of stitches and possibly a blood transfusion."

Hugh shook his head in disbelief. "What would cause Henry to go off the deep end like that? Why would he do something like that—and to Rudy of all people? He didn't seem to be under a great deal of stress, and if he was, he wasn't showing it. Where is Greg right now?"

"I sent him home. He was traumatized by the whole thing, and there wasn't much point in both of us hanging around here. I paid for his cab ride home."

Hugh stepped out to get his jacket from his truck, and just before he locked up his truck, he called the BC Forest Service on their frequency and notified them of the fire. After he hung up, all he kept thinking was, *What is Clint going to say when he gets back?*

When Rudy was taken out of the operating room, it had taken nearly a hundred stitches to close the gashes on his face. The doctor hypothesized that the majority of the blade was within Henry's hand, so just the tip of the blade was protruding. Therefore, the blade did not penetrate the skin as much as originally anticipated. Even so, Rudy would have some prominent scars that would last the rest of his life. One of the cuts stopped just short of his jugular vein.

28

Clint returned home three days later. In that time, Henry had regained consciousness, but had no memory of what happened, and was not very aware of his surroundings. Rudy was released from the hospital after two days, and was now resting at home. As for the forest fire, it now covered over five hundred hectares. There were now over a hundred workers on the ground as well as four water bombers working around the clock to extinguish the fire, but the dry conditions and steep terrain were making all efforts difficult. All survey work in the area around Portia Bench had been suspended until further notice.

During Clint's returning flight into Canada, he could see the outline of the Fraser Valley far below. Although it was early in the evening, there was still daylight. Clint followed the course of the Fraser River as it wound its way up the Fraser Valley toward Hope, but then he noticed, to the northeast of Hope, a large column of smoke.

Man, I hope that isn't happening where my crews are working, he thought.

Once Clint was finally back inside his house, one of the first things he noticed was that his answering machine had thirty-five messages.

Aw, fuck it. I'm too tired. I'll check them in the morning.

The following morning, Clint slept through his alarm. He wasn't worried about being chastised for being late, but he knew he had a million things to catch up on, so he wanted to get into the office as early as possible. He quickly threw his clothes on and left the house without having any breakfast. In his rush, he left his answering machine unchecked.

When Clint arrived at the office, he cheerfully greeted Sandra; he wasn't sure why she seemed kind of surprised to see him in a good mood. *Maybe I really was a huge grump before I left.*

After Clint organized his notes, he went over to Ted's desk.

"Clint, you're back—what a surprise," said Ted.

"What are you talking about? I told you I would be coming back today. How has everything been going while I was away? I noticed that my answering machine had thirty-five messages, so there had to be something important. But I never had a chance to play them."

Ted said under his breath, "That explains it."

"Excuse me?"

"So, Clint, how was New Orleans?"

"Quit beating around the bush. We have business to attend to. Tell me, what's been happening this past week?"

Just then, Ted's new office assistant, Cody, approached his desk. "Ted, did you tell Clint about the forest fire?"

"I was just getting to that," said Ted, clearly annoyed.

Clint slammed his fist against a filing cabinet. "I knew something was up—that fire is near where the crews are?"

"You mean you know about it?" asked Ted.

"I could see the smoke from the goddamn plane when I was coming home last night. But I couldn't tell where it was originating.

Where is it exactly?"

"It's up around the bench area and up the Ladner Creek valley."

"You mean up on Portia Bench? But that area was logged—how did it start?"

"From what I heard, one of the crew members working up there tossed a cigarette."

"I'll bet you anything that was Henry—if it is, he is done like dinner."

"Wait a minute, there's more. Apparently, one of the crewmembers attacked another, and then got hit on the head. All I know is that two people are in the hospital. My information is quite sketchy; you're going to have to talk to Hugh."

"I don't believe this … I'm gone one week, and everything goes to hell in a fucking hand-basket. What kind of an outfit am I running around here? By the way, thank you very much for informing me, Cody. Lord only knows if Ted was going to get around to telling me," said Clint, angrily.

"I assure you, I was just about to tell you," said Ted.

"I'll bet you were."

Clint returned to his desk and immediately telephoned the Hope office. He spoke to Linda, who could only provide second-hand information, and she recommended he talk to Hugh. He informed her he'd be up there in the afternoon.

Before Clint left his office, he phoned the BC Forest Service, and they informed him that the fire was only 50 percent contained, and unless they get some rain soon, that was not expected to improve. Most of the fire was burning up the Ladner Creek Valley, and all survey crews were being kept out of the area for safety reasons. The wind could change at any time.

Clint met with Hugh that afternoon.

"Clint, I need you to know that I wasn't there when it all happened.

You should talk to Matt for a first-hand account."

"What about Greg? He was every bit involved in this, but where is he now?"

"I sent him home, and I'm having him take some time off. He's probably suffering from Post-Traumatic Stress Disorder."

"What the hell are you, a doctor? You're just assuming that. I realize he would be traumatized at first, but that was three days ago—he should be over it by now. Isn't there another crew he can help out with for the time being?"

"Clint, he thought he *killed* Henry. Not only that, he practically saved Rudy's life. Greg and Rudy have been best friends for years. To see that happen to your best friend and to have to almost kill somebody to make it stop, that's not something anyone would get over right away. Besides, none of the other crews need extra help right now."

"Okay," Clint took a deep breath. "Maybe I overreacted. Where is Matt now?"

"He's back in Merritt. I didn't have anything more for him here, and Anders had an assignment for him."

"Where's Henry?"

"He was transferred to the Neurological unit at Royal Columbian Hospital. I heard that he has emerged from his coma, but that's all I know."

"What about Rudy?"

"He was released from the hospital yesterday. He's back at his mother's place."

Before Clint left the office, he phoned the Merritt office and spoke to Anders. He made a request that Matt be in the office the following afternoon and Anders said that he could have Matt there at 2:00 p.m.

Clint then headed over to Greg's house. When he rang the doorbell, Greg's wife answered.

"Hi, could I please speak to Greg?" asked Clint.

"Sure, can I ask who you are?"

"I'm Clint Matheson. I am the one in charge of the highway project."

"Mr. Matheson, what a surprise—I'm glad to see you're back," Greg said as he entered the living room.

"Thank you, Greg. I hope you're doing okay. Do you feel up to talking about the incident?"

"Sure, well, I'll try my best. I'm still pretty shaken up, and some parts are blurrier than others. What stood out the most was the look in Henry's eyes when he emerged from the woods. It's hard to describe—it was almost as though he was looking right through everybody. I remember he seemed to be talking in some Native language ... Then, for no reason, he ran toward Rudy, jumped on him, and began stabbing him in the face. Matt and I tried to fight him off, but he was too big. All I could find that was handy was the hatchet ... I didn't mean to hit him that hard ..." Greg became emotionally distraught.

"Thank you, Greg. You don't have to say anything more. I want to assure you that when you feel well enough, your job will still be there."

After he left Greg's place, Clint headed over to Rudy's parents' place. Rudy's mother answered the door.

"Hi, I'm Clint Matheson. Rudy works for me," Clint introduced himself. "May I see Rudy?"

"He's resting right now, but I'll take you to his room anyway," Rudy's mother said as she brought Clint inside. "Rudy, your boss is here to see you."

Rudy was still covered in bandages, so all Clint could see were his eyes, nose, and mouth. "Hello, Rudy, how are you doing?"

"How do you think I'm doing? It hurts like hell, man."

"At least you're out of the hospital and back home now."

"Yeah, but I'm still in a lot of pain. Even if I try to eat, the pain is awful."

"Well, once the stitches are out, the pain should subside."

"I'll tell you something—I am going to kill that fucking fat cocksucker when I find him. When I get my hands on Finnegan, he's a dead man."

"Rudy, take it easy. I don't know what drove him to do this, but it had to be something. I haven't known him as long as you have, but you have to admit that this was totally out of character for him."

"The fact is the guy is a fucking psycho. If you see him, you tell him that I'm coming after him, and when I catch him, he's fucking dead," Rudy said sourly.

"Rudy, please don't talk like that. I don't condone what he did, but let's get to the bottom of what caused him to do this before we make any judgements. For right now, just take it easy."

As Clint headed back to Vancouver, he was at a total loss for words. When he reached the exit to New Westminster, he decided to turn off and pay a visit to Henry at the hospital.

Henry shared a ward in the Neurological Unit with three other patients. When Clint first saw him, he was sitting in a chair beside his bed reading a magazine.

"Hello, Henry, do you remember me?"

It took Henry a minute to respond. "Yes, you're Mr. Matheson. I work for you."

"Very good, Henry. So, how are you feeling?"

"I feel alright, I guess. I get dizzy a lot, so I can't stand up for very long," said Henry in a slow voice.

"Henry, do you have any memory at all of how you ended up here. Can you remember anything?"

"No, I can't remember a thing. I have no idea how I got here. The last thing I remember is standing on the deck of this boat way out in the ocean."

"Well, that's a start, I guess. But you have no recollection of being in the mountains or having a surveyor's transit in front of you?"

"No, I can't say that I have."

"But you remember people, because you know who I am. I'm sure your memory will gradually come back. I shouldn't keep you too long. You have to go down to therapy soon. I'll check back in a couple days."

29

The following day, Clint drove up to Merritt to speak to Matt. He hoped Matt could shed a little more light as to what happened. He hoped Matt would be able to think more rationally; the fact he was able to return to work was a good sign.

Matt was already in the office when Clint arrived.

"Hi, Clint. Welcome back. How was your trip?"

"My trip went all right, thank you, Matt. I just wish we were meeting under happier circumstances."

"Clint, I do feel partially responsible for what happened. After all, I was the one who made Henry feel obligated to head into the woods for a cigarette. I was getting on Henry's case for smoking. I should have realized that all I was doing was making Henry annoyed."

"Hey, don't worry about it. I've done that myself, except Henry never says anything back to me," said Clint. "Look, when Henry emerged from the woods in that hypnotic trance, do you have any idea what he was saying?"

"Yes, Henry was repeating the same phrase over and over. I couldn't make any sense of it, but I remember it clearly," said Matt.

"Oh really, what was it?"

"It was, '*I cen uk anuk em.*'"

Clint was absolutely stunned. He sat back in his chair and said in disbelief. "Good lord, this is unbelievable."

"Why, what's wrong?"

"Henry was speaking in Halkomelem."

"What in the world is Halkomelem?"

"Halkomelem is the ancient language of the Sto:lo Nation. The dialect spoken by the Sto:lo in the Upper Fraser Valley was known as Halq'eméylem. '*I cen uk anuk em,*' translated into English, means 'I am strong.'"

"Gee, Clint, you are just a wealth of information. Where did you learn about this?"

"You tend to learn about the local Native languages when you're dating the Chief's daughter," Clint said with a great deal of apprehension.

Matt seemed totally perplexed that Henry would know the local First Nations language.

"It's quite likely Henry didn't learn it."

"I don't follow you," said Matt, puzzled.

"Halq'eméylem would have been the language the local Natives were speaking three hundred years ago, right around the time Siaman was alive. In fact, '*Siaman*' is Halq'eméylem for powerful. There's a distinct possibility that the spirit of Siaman somehow got into Henry's head."

"You know what else happened? When I was heading down the road, this man jumped out in front of the truck. I couldn't stop in time, and thought I hit him. But when I got out to investigate, there was no sign of the man at all. It was like he completely vanished."

"Was he wearing grey and black striped overalls with a matching cap?" asked Clint.

"Wait a minute, you know about him too? Who the hell is he? Why didn't you tell me about any of this crap before? You lied to me."

Clint knew he had to be honest. He owed at least that much to Matt. "I've had several encounters with that man since the project started, but it wasn't until after I saw the wreckage of the locomotive that had crashed on the bench in 1926 that I realized that man must be the ghost of the engineer."

"Clint, I asked you if that area is cursed, and you told me it wasn't … You told me that I had nothing to worry about. I should have realized that you were feeding me nothing but bullshit. What happened to Henry was the exact same thing that happened to Farrell, but you tried to tarnish his image just to cover your own ass. Farrell was a good friend of mine, and I will *not* have him thought of as some crazed lunatic who outright killed his coworkers. I've got news for you—you can forget about me ever working near that place again. I don't give a damn what you do—you can fire me, for all I care," said Matt, angrily.

"Matt, you're officially working under Anders, so it's not up to me to determine your employment status. I completely understand how you feel … I admit that I wasn't being totally upfront with you. I respect your decision to resign from Portia Bench."

"Well, thank God for that. And one more thing—may I suggest they change the name of the Coquihalla Highway to the 'Poltergeist Highway'?"

Losing Matt was the least of Clint's worries for the next week, as the Forestry crews were still having a difficult time battling the forest fire, despite two days of rain. None of the survey crews could get within ten miles of the fire zone until they got the "all clear" from the BC Forest Service. It was two more weeks before the fire was extinguished enough to allow the survey crews back into the area. It took a week of steady rain to assist the fire crews with battling the blaze.

Before any of the crews returned, Clint arranged a tour of the area affected by the fire with a willing staff member of the Hope fire department. His main concern was the area where the surveying was taking place on Portia Bench, right around where the fire originated. When they arrived up on Portia Bench, they immediately headed over to where Henry's crew had been working. Anything that was made of wood in the fire's path had been destroyed, which included nearly two kilometres of survey stakes. There was nothing left but little charred sticks. Clint had the sickening feeling that over three weeks of work was completely destroyed. The end of October was fast approaching, and winter started much earlier in the higher elevations. The surveying was going to have to resume on the double before the first snowfall arrived.

Clint called Hugh on the CB radio and requested that they have an emergency meeting. With Henry incapacitated and Matt defected, they had to determine which crews were available to fill the void. Clint wasn't sure if he wanted to bring Rudy back or not. Physically, he had fully recovered from Henry's attack; all of his stitches had been removed and the wounds were healing well on their own. However, he heard that Rudy had hired a lawyer and planned to lay formal criminal charges of aggravated assault and attempted murder against Henry. If he was successful, Henry could face up to ten years in prison. No judge in the world would ever accept the defence that Henry was possessed by a spirit. That would never stand up in court.

When Clint arrived back at the Hope office, Hugh was there waiting for him.

"Clint, I am stretched to the limit in manpower. I'm racing against the clock myself to try to get in as many elevation shots as possible before the first snowfall," Hugh stressed.

"Then you'll be happy to know that I've thought of a solution as to what to do about a Crew Chief, and all it will take is one phone call." The person he telephoned was none other than Don.

"What is this about?" asked Don when he answered the phone.

"Well, I have some good news and some bad news. The good news is that you are reinstated," said Clint.

"And the bad news?"

"Congratulations, Don, you have just been demoted to Crew Chief."

Don, obviously not too pleased, went into a non-stop tirade.

"Don, you don't have any other options other than something called 'Unemployment Insurance'."

"Alright, fine," Don reluctantly accepted the offer.

"Well, I have to get back to work," Hugh said.

"That's fine, I'll figure something out with this staffing situation." He then gave Rudy a call. "Rudy, would you be able to come down to the office?"

"What's this about, Clint?" Rudy was obviously wary.

"I just need to talk to you."

When Rudy arrived at the office, Clint saw that he looked a lot better than the last time he saw him. Over time, there would be very little evidence of what Henry did.

"Hi, Rudy. Thanks for coming down. Listen, I want you to think twice about charging Henry. He really went out of his way to provide work for you and Greg ever since he was appointed Crew Chief, you know. He always put in a good word for you guys, and he has proven to me that he genuinely cares for your well being. At one point he even offered to be laid off so that you would remain employed. You've got to realize that some external force got into Henry's head … It was as if he was possessed."

"Don't tell me you believe in all that ghost bullshit. Let me guess, that Chief's daughter had you convinced that there was a spirit of some Indian guy running around up there. C'mon, man, that was just her pussy talking," said Rudy.

"I beg your pardon?"

"I know you were fucking her—it's all over town."

"Ah, the joy of small-town living, where everybody has nothing better to do than to talk about everyone else's personal life … where it is impossible to keep a secret. Maybe the big city isn't so bad after all."

"For your information, I had a crush on Cindy all through high school—right up until she married that Claude bastard. But no, she never noticed me. I should have realized that she would never go for a joe-boy like me."

"Oh, so that's it—you're *jealous* of me? Look, our relationship just happened to come about, but it's over now, so just forget about it. Now, do you want to come back to work for me or not?"

"You must think I'm crazy. There's no way I'm coming back to work for you, man. As far as this job is concerned, I quit. Oh, and I'm going to stick with my plans. I'm going to nail that fat fuck's ass to the wall, and he's going to get what he fucking deserves." With that, Rudy stormed out of the office.

Clint wanted to find out from Ted why his workload was so excessive that he would have needed to hire Cody to assist him, and wanted to know if he could get by without him for a while. When Clint returned to the Vancouver office, he called Ted and Cody into his office.

"Ted, I'm thinking we should give Cody some hands-on experience working in the field. One of the survey crews working on the new highway needs an extra person, so it would be a great opportunity for Cody to learn what it's like to work on a survey crew."

"That should not be a problem; I can handle my workload on my own."

"That sounds good to me, Mr. Matheson. I'd like to accept the challenge."

"That's good to hear. We meet at the Hope office at eight o'clock in the morning the day after tomorrow. We will provide you an accommodation allowance." With that settled, Clint then outlined to

Cody the task he would be performing. "You'll be writing information on the survey stakes using a greased marker known as a keel, and then you'll pound each stake into the ground using the back side of a hatchet. The head chainman will tell you what to write on the stake and exactly where to pound it."

Clint spent the remainder of the afternoon looking over the stack of job applications. Judging by the size of the stack, there was quite a wide range of applicants, indicating that there were still a great many people looking for work. He paid particular attention to the application of Kevin Rycroft. Clint gave him a call and asked him to come in for an interview the next morning at 9:00 a.m.

At the interview, Clint told Kevin the position would be for a rod-and-chain man, and would be located in Hope. One of the main characteristics Clint liked about Kevin was that he was single, and therefore would have no trouble relocating. Kevin was okay with the location, so Clint hired him on the spot. He told him to meet at the Hope office the following morning at 8:00 a.m.

With the Project Manager duties placed squarely on Hugh and Ed, Clint knew he had to provide them extra support, and the only way he was going to be able to do that was to work out of the Hope office. But this time, things would be different. As long as he was in Hope, he would try to keep as low a profile as possible. He would not make any public appearances except at the office. He didn't want to risk running into Edwin, Cindy, or even worse, Claude. He was definitely going to stay away from the pubs in Hope.

At the meeting the next morning, Clint introduced Kevin and Cody to Don and Greg. The arrangement was for Greg to be the head chainman and for Kevin to bring up the rear. Using the topographical map on an overhead projector, Clint outlined the area to be surveyed, giving specific instructions to Don on which coordinates to use. "Well, what are we waiting for? Let's boogie," said Clint as he concluded the meeting.

"Are you coming up to the jobsite anytime today?" asked Don.

"No, Don, I plan to do nothing but sit in my office and smoke pot all day. Of course I am coming up to the jobsite—don't ask stupid questions like that. When I do come up is for me to know and for you to find out," said Clint.

For the next three weeks, the crew made marginal progress. The constant rain, combined with parts of the ground covered in ash, made the ground very muddy. The crewmembers had to be very careful where they walked; otherwise, they would end up becoming stuck in the mud. It was also difficult to place the transit on solid footing. The transit would often start to sink into the ground when left in the same spot for several minutes.

By early November, they were periodically encountering wet snow, but it wasn't sticking. That slowed their progress even further. Right after Remembrance Day, they received their first heavy snowfall. That day, the bench area received over three feet of snow, and all surveying on Portia Bench had to cease. It continued to snow for four more days, and by then, it was over seven feet deep. By the time the first major snowfall hit, they still had not completed two road allowance lines on their second kilometre. They still had a long way to go and little time to complete it.

A month after Clint last visited Henry, he decided to pay him another visit. But before he went into his room, he met with Henry's physiotherapist. Clint was pleased to learn that Henry had made excellent progress in the past month. He was now walking without the aid of a walker and had regained most of his memory. However, the physiotherapist didn't elaborate as to what he can and can't remember. What Henry didn't know was that he would face charges once he was out of the hospital.

"Hello, Henry, how is everything going?"

"Not too bad—I'm up and around a lot more. I'm not getting as many headaches and dizzy spells as I did before. I'm getting pretty anxious to get the hell out of here and get back to work."

Clint pulled up a chair and said in a sombre tone, "Henry, there're some things we need to talk about. I need to ask you some questions. The first thing I need to know is how much you can remember from the last day you were at the jobsite until you were brought here."

"I remember going back into the woods to have a cigarette. Matt kept raggin' about me smoking, so I went there for a smoke to get away from him. The next thing I know, I'm here."

"So, you still have no memory of going back to where the other guys were?"

"Nope, none at all."

"When you were in the wooded area, did you see anybody else there, or did you hear any voices?"

"No, there was just me there. I didn't hear anybody else. Why do you ask?"

"Henry, do you know any Halq'eméylem?"

"What the hell is that?"

"That was the language once spoken by the local Natives before the white men came along. Are you sure you never learned any of it in the time you lived here?"

"No, I never heard of it. What's this all about?"

"So, you have no idea what '*I cen uk anuk em*' means?"

"No, not a clue ... Why?"

"Henry, did anybody tell you how you received that bump on the back of your head?"

"No, nobody tells me a damn thing around here. How did it happen?"

"Okay, I have to be totally honest with you. Greg hit you with the backside of the hatchet. He was trying to protect Rudy; you attacked Rudy and carved up his face with your penknife. While you were attacking him, you kept repeating the words, '*I cen uk anuk em*,' which means, 'I am strong' in Halq'eméylem. Rudy needed a hundred stitches in his face."

Henry was completely beside himself. "I swear to God, Mr. Matheson, I have no memory whatsoever of that happening. I really like Rudy—I would never do something like that."

"I understand. And I believe it wasn't your fault. From what Matt and Greg described, you appeared to be in some kind of trance just prior to attacking Rudy. My theory is that the spirit of Siaman got inside your head, and possessed you to say those words and attack Rudy. Siaman is sending a message to all of us that we are disturbing ground that is sacred to him, and he was doing it through you. I know it sounds farfetched, but this seems to be the most likely scenario."

"I don't know what you're talking about. Who is this 'Siaman' person?"

"I guess I never really talked about it with you before. He was a young warrior who was going to be the Chief of the Hope Band around three hundred years ago. His fiancée was killed by a rockslide somewhere that we're surveying, and he now regards the place as sacred. According to a local Native legend, his spirit still guards the area. Do you remember when we both saw that image of a Native mask? And the sound of Native drumming? It just appeared and then disappeared. That was Siaman's way of making his presence known."

"Yeah, but why would he want to get inside my head?"

"That was Siaman getting his point across that our presence is not welcome there. He might have thought you looked gullible or something."

Henry appeared to be very worried. "How is Rudy doing? Is he mad at me?"

"Rudy is doing quite well; he had all the stitches removed. He will have some permanent scarring, but it was less severe than originally thought. As for him being mad at you … that's an understatement. He's planning to lay criminal charges against you, claiming you were trying to kill him."

"Oh my god, what's going to happen to me? Am I going to end up in jail?"

"I don't know. I haven't had any luck with talking any sense into Rudy so far, and I don't expect that to change. I'll have a talk with the Government Legal Advisor, and see what course of action we can take. But for right now, I wouldn't worry about it. You just focus on getting better, because I want you to come back to work for me once the snow melts next spring. We will work something out, I assure you."

PART 2

30

MARCH 1985

The winter of 1984–1985 proved to be one of the most severe on record. It snowed relentlessly all throughout December and January. At one point, there was twenty-five feet of snow near the summit of Hope Pass. Back in Vancouver, Clint had been receiving a significant amount of criticism over the Coquihalla Highway project, mostly from the media. Critics were saying that it would be impossible to keep the highway open throughout the winter, and that people and workers would have to put their lives at risk travelling over it and maintaining it. Clint tried his best to reassure the public that with today's heavy-duty snowploughs and sand trucks, keeping the highway open throughout the winter should not be a problem.

As for Henry, he was released from hospital in early December. As soon as he came home, he was arrested and charged with aggravated assault and attempted murder. Clint immediately posted his bail, and the trial was set for 21 August 1985. He then contacted Salvatore Bertelli, a senior partner in the law firm that includes the Provincial

Government legal advisors. Salvatore's specialty was criminal law. When Clint met with him, Salvatore was willing to take on the case, but admitted he was doubtful Henry would be successful with an insanity plea.

Clint also went to bat for Henry with the Worker's Compensation Board. He made a case for Henry that his injury was work related. With Greg backing him up, they made the claim that Henry tripped, fell backward, and hit his head on a protruding branch of a fallen log. In the end, Henry received full compensation, which he lived on throughout the winter.

Over the course of the winter, Clint dealt with the remaining tenders for construction of the highway. Due to the sheer magnitude of the project, more than one construction company would be required. By the time the bidding process was completed, seven different construction companies were successful bidders. The project would be divided into sections, with each highway construction company assigned a particular section.

The company that would handle the highway construction from the Ladner Creek Bridge to Zopkios Ridge, including Portia Bench, was Kurt Onerheim Construction. Clint and Kurt went way back, but he had since retired and turned control of the Company to his son, Oscar.

By the end of March, the weather had warmed up considerably, and most of the snow had melted. It was time to resume surveying, and not a moment too soon. For the past several weeks, Henry had been repeatedly phoning the office and asking when he could come back to work. He had nothing to do but sit around his apartment all day, and he was bored out of his mind. Henry was ecstatic when Clint phoned him and told him that the surveying was going to resume and they needed his services as a Crew Chief again.

Henry wasn't the only one delighted at the thought of being back. Don was also glad to have him back, so he could have his job as Project Manager back. Clint reluctantly reinstated Don as Project Manager, but still told him to watch his step. Now that Clint was staying in Hope again, he would keep a close eye on him.

On the day that surveying was to resume on Portia Bench, Clint called everyone into his office for a meeting. This was the first time Henry had seen Greg since that fateful day last fall. Clint anticipated there would be some animosity between the two of them, but that was not the case.

"Henry, it's good to see you. Man, I'm so sorry I hit you over the head so hard with that hatchet."

"It's okay, Greg. You were just trying to protect Rudy," Henry accepted his apology. "I would have done the same thing if someone was attacking my best friend with a knife. I have no hard feelings, but I admit I still have no memory whatsoever of the incident. I only wish that someone could talk some sense into Rudy."

Henry had also never met Kevin or Cody, so he was introduced to them.

"Alright, this little love-in is over. Let's get down to business," growled Don.

"Don, who is running this meeting, me or you? If I'm not mistaken, I believe I am. I say when the meeting starts—not you," said Clint. He then outlined to Henry where they had left off when winter set in. "There are still two road allowance lines that need to be completed on the kilometre you'll be working on before proceeding to the next kilometre." He gave Henry a list of coordinates and then adjourned the meeting.

Due to his heavy workload, it was two days before Clint was able to head up to Portia Bench and check on Henry's progress. According to Henry, the crew was proceeding really well, except for having to dig through six inches of snow before pounding in a stake.

Henry's crew seemed oblivious to Clint's arrival, which explained the fact that nobody was wearing their hard hats.

"Mr. Matheson, what a surprise—I wasn't expecting you," said Henry.

"I can see that. In case you guys are unaware, hard hats are a requirement for this job. I better not catch any of you not wearing them again—or else."

Clint observed the line they were surveying, and something didn't look right. He noticed that a number of the stakes appeared to be out of alignment. He knelt down and bent over until he was eye level with the top of the stakes. Sure enough, there were stakes out of alignment both to the right and to the left, some as much as three inches; and this was supposed to be a straight line.

"What the hell is going on here?" said Clint. "Henry, get over here *now*."

"What's the problem, Mr. Matheson?" Henry asked.

Clint pointed to the line of stakes that appeared to be going every which way. "Look at this line you guys surveyed. Does that look like a proper tangent alignment to you? It looks more like a goddamn dog's breakfast. Get down on your knees, bend over, and look at the line of survey stakes from ground level. Now, does that look like a straight line to you?"

Henry gave a puzzled look and scratched his head in disbelief.

"You know damn well that survey lines must be accurate to within five millimetres. These markers are out a hell of a lot further than that."

"I don't understand it ... When I looked through the transit scope, I called it out to mark the spot when the rod was right on the centre line," said Henry.

"Bullshit—you must have been looking at something other than the centre line, because that's not what the results are," said Clint. "Listen, everyone, man your positions. I want you to survey another thirty metres of baseline. But this time, I want to observe."

Greg proceeded forward, and when he walked thirty metres, he pulled the chain tight. He then held the rod perfectly perpendicular, and Henry called out to go either right or left. When the rod was in perfect alignment with the centre line of the scope, Henry called out, "mark," and Greg planted the end of the rod into the ground.

Clint was standing right behind Greg. "Henry, move away from the transit. Greg, stand right where you are." He looked through the transit scope, and much to his horror, the rod was at least six centimetres off to the right. "Henry, that the rod is off-centre by a long-shot. You need to take another look."

Henry looked through the scope, and said that the rod was dead-centre.

"Like hell it is. Get away from that transit. Henry, is there something wrong with your vision?" asked Clint, angrily.

"No, I can see you clearly."

"What about Greg? Can you see him clearly?"

"Yes, I can see him no problem."

Clint stood in front of Henry about three feet away, stretched out his arms, and pointed inward with both index fingers. He told Henry to look him straight in the eye, and he then slowly brought both index fingers towards his eyes simultaneously, moving them in a "V" formation. He noticed that the pupil in Henry's right eye was not moving.

"Henry, can you see my left index finger?"

Henry didn't answer.

Clint then took his left index finger and moved it back and forth in front of Henry's eyes. Again, he noticed that the pupil in Henry's right eye didn't move.

"Henry, there's definitely something wrong with your peripheral vision. You are going to have to see an ophthalmologist."

"What's an ophthalmologist?"

"An eye doctor, for God's sake. I believe that the bump on your head did something to your peripheral vision."

"Oh no, how am I going to work if there's something wrong with my sight? I mean, surveying is my life ... Am I going to lose my job?"

"Don't jump to conclusions. We will get your eyes examined and go from there. Hopefully this is something that can be corrected. Make an appointment with your doctor, and he'll get you a referral. But in the meantime, you are not working here until your eyes are examined." Clint shifted his attention to the rest of the crew. "Okay, Cody, remove all the survey stakes from the baseline you guys have surveyed over the past two days. You're going to have to start all over again right from where you started yesterday. I have a couple of hours to spare, so I will man the transit. Henry, you can wait in the truck. By the way, have you seen any sign of Don?"

"No, I have not seen hide nor hair of him all day," replied Henry.

"I don't believe this. Hugh said that he hasn't seen him all day either. Where the hell is he? I'll skin him alive when I find him."

After helping the crew for two hours, Clint said that he had to get back to the Hope office. The funny thing was, with Clint manning the transit, they surveyed as much baseline in two hours as had been managed the previous day entirely. This made Clint start to question Henry's leadership skills as well as his vision.

"Alright, guys. You can all leave early today, but be prepared to work extra hours tomorrow. I'll sort out what to do about a temporary Crew Chief this afternoon."

Just as they were packing to leave for the day, Don finally showed up. He looked surprised to see Clint there.

"Don, where the hell have you been? I've been trying to reach you all morning and all day yesterday."

"Uhh, I had to recheck some elevation shots ..." Don trailed off, obviously making it up as usual.

"Well, for your information, I've been up here for the last two hours fixing Henry's screw-up."

"Henry screwed up? Why, I oughta ..."

"You what? Yes, Henry made a screw-up, but it went unnoticed for two days. You were supposed to check on them on a regular basis. By not doing so, you are just as much at fault as he is. By the way, the only reason Henry made a mistake was because he is having problems with his vision, but you didn't notice that either. Why—because you were not here like you were supposed to be." Clint also noticed a distinct smell of liquor on Don's breath. "Have you been drinking?"

"I had a little drink of scotch, but that's it," replied Don.

"Oh, I bet it was more than that. Don, I want to see you in my office this afternoon."

It was 3:00 p.m. when Don finally showed up. When he entered Clint's office, Clint told him to shut the door.

"Don, this is obviously not working out with you as Project Manager. You're never available when I call you, you never get any work done, and you don't supervise the crews properly. Henry is going back on medical leave, so I'm putting you back in charge of the crew working up on the bench while he's gone. Case closed. One more thing—don't ever let me catch you drinking on the job again. This is a very important job, so you have to be one hundred percent focused all the time. If you wish to drink, do it on your own time."

Clint expected Don to launch into a tirade, but instead, he paused for a few moments and then said calmly, "Okay, whatever you say, college boy."

"Oh so that's it? You're jealous I'm educated? Listen, I have no regrets about the career path I took. The fact that you dropped out of high school is not my fault—it has nothing to do with me. You chose to take that career path, and I must say, you have actually done quite well—so far. But don't push your luck. I want you in this office by eight o'clock tomorrow morning to pick up the crew, understand?"

Don said nothing. He just got up and left in a huff.

Once Don had vacated the office, Clint picked up a roll of surveyor's chain wound on a spool and walked over to Linda's desk. Holding a length of chain in one hand and the spool handle in the other, he said to Linda, "You know something, I would really like to take this chain, wrap it around Don's neck, and pull both ends until I have squeezed the life out of him."

31

The return of Don to Crew Chief duties meant that Clint had to make trips up to the site on a regular basis. Clint's main concern was that the other crewmembers would band together and form a lynch mob against Don. The wealth of experience that Don had in the field of surveying could never make up for his lack in people skills. The crew was always glad to see Clint when he made his daily visits, since whenever he was around, Don had to behave himself.

As an alternative to being off work completely, Clint offered Henry Cody's job as Ted's office assistant at least for the time being. He promised that it wouldn't be permanent—only until it could be determined if the problem with his vision could be corrected. In the end, Henry said that it was better than nothing.

The first week with Don as Crew Chief passed by without incident. They also made fairly good headway with resurveying the baseline lost to the forest fire. Even so, Clint still planned to make his regular daily visits.

On one particular day in week two, Clint met up with the crew early in the afternoon, as per usual. This time, though, Don actually seemed excited about seeing Clint.

"Hey, Clint, you'll never believe what I saw over there," he pointed east, "this morning—an elephant."

"Oh, really? An elephant, you say?"

"Hey, you may think I'm just pulling your leg. But I know what I saw."

"Actually, Don, you're right. I don't believe you. Did any of the others see it too?"

"No, it was there for only a couple seconds. When I saw it, I pointed it out to the other guys. But when they turned to look, it was gone. It must have run away."

"Don, we are not in Africa or India. This is not a native habitat for elephants."

"Well, I'm telling you that it was indeed an elephant. I'll stand by it any day."

"Okay, but if you see it again, you better try to corral it. I would suggest you bring along a huge bag of peanuts." After he left, Clint kept thinking that maybe Don really did see an elephant. It seemed like such a strange coincidence that it was the third case where he heard about someone sighting an elephant, and every one of the sightings was in the same general area. *If it is an elephant, how would it survive out here? Where did it come from? Did it belong to somebody at one time?*

Two days later, Clint made his usual visit to where Don's crew was working. Clint was taking notes when Don picked up the transit to move it to the next position. Before he proceeded forward, he momentarily looked behind him. There, standing in the clearing, was the elephant.

"Look everybody, over there!" yelled Don, pointing to where the elephant was standing.

"Well, I'll be," exclaimed Clint.

"You see, I told you I saw an elephant, but you didn't believe me, did you? There, see for yourself," exclaimed Don.

Clint raised his hand and said, "Shhh, be quiet. You're going to scare it."

The elephant just stood there in the clearing, oblivious to the men's presence. Then it turned and started walking away from them, heading eastward.

"C'mon, let's follow it," said Clint.

They tried to follow it as close as possible, yet keep enough distance so that they wouldn't startle it. The elephant crossed the Pipeline Road and headed into the forest, still heading in an eastward direction. Clint told everyone to try and not lose sight of it, but after going nearly a half a mile through the dense forest, it eventually disappeared from sight.

"I think we've lost him," said Clint. He then noticed something very unusual. There were still two inches of snow on the ground, yet there were no signs of elephant footprints anywhere. Also, despite the denseness of the forest, there was not one sign of any freshly broken branches.

"Look, over there!" yelled Greg.

There, in the distance, propped up against a tree, was an old railcar. It had obviously rolled down the mountainside from the KCR line. It had landed on its roof, as the wheels were dangling in the air on top. It had sustained heavy damage after leaving the tracks and was nothing more than a mass of broken wood and twisted metal. Right beside it was another boxcar. This one landed on its side. Just beyond that one was a third boxcar, and that one appeared to have been split in two.

"A train must have derailed, and these freight cars rolled down the mountainside as a result," Clint speculated.

The railway grade was at least two hundred feet above where they are standing, which would explain the amount of damage.

They peered inside the boxcar that was upside-down, as the door was missing. There was nothing inside. Greg climbed up onto the boxcar that was lying on its side.

"Be careful," Clint warned. It looked to be severely rotted, so he could risk falling through.

Greg cleared the snow away, and noticed that there appeared to be some kind of writing on the side. There was a heavy accumulation of moss, and the letters themselves were severely faded. He meticulously cleaned away the moss, scraping his pocketknife in a sideways motion. He saw that the letters were arranged in a semi-circular pattern. Eventually, he made out the word "ring", but then saw more letters. He soon uncovered an "L", then an "I", then an "N", and after that, a "G". That was followed by a space.

"Are you uncovering anything?" Clint asked.

"I found the word 'Ringling'," Greg answered.

Clint thought about it for a few seconds, then it dawned on him. "Ringling—as in Ringling Brothers Barnum & Bailey Circus! That's it—that's where that elephant came from. This was part of a circus train. This must have been the boxcar the elephant was riding in." He pointed to the mangled upside-down boxcar. "When it crashed, the door broke off, and he escaped, and has been here ever since."

Greg scraped some more moss off the side of the boxcar and uncovered the word "Brothers", thereby confirming Clint's theory. Cody surveyed the damage of the third boxcar, and noticed on the side a very faded drawing of what appeared to be a clown.

"Look at how badly these railcars were damaged—and you say these would have fallen at least two hundred feet? How the hell could that elephant have survived? It doesn't look like anything could have survived a crash like that," said Don.

"That's a good point. Yet it somehow came out of this alive. Someone must have been looking out for him," said Clint.

One other item that perplexed Clint was the fact that the last train ran over the rail line in 1959. That was twenty-six years ago. But judging by the accumulation of moss, the amount of rust, and how rotted the wood parts were, this accident most likely happened much earlier. He noted that elephants have a life span of sixty to seventy years, so it was possible that even if the accident occurred forty years ago, the elephant could still be alive. *But how could it survive in this area with its harsh winters and lack of vegetation?*

Kevin saw that further up the mountain, there were remains of another railcar. This one was a passenger car, and was lying perpendicular on its side. The crew climbed up to investigate. One end was resting against the trunk of a large tree, preventing it from sliding further down the mountain. One third of the end was imbedded into the ground. Greg and Kevin both climbed onto the side in the air, which was now the roof. All of the seats were still in place, and only a few of the windows on the side facing the sky were broken. There was a strong musty smell, and there was also a noticeable smell of bear dung. Bears had been using this railcar as a shelter over the years.

Greg noticed that there was writing on the side, and this time it was clearly legible. Sure enough, it read "Ringling Brothers Circus."

"In the early days, the circus travelled by train," Clint had to explain to Greg, Cody, and Kevin, who were too young to remember. "Nowadays, circuses are transported by large trucks and buses. This passenger car is a real old-timer, likely dating from the thirties."

That weekend, Clint travelled to Penticton. On Saturday morning, he paid a visit to the museum.

"Clint, how nice to see you again. To what do I owe the pleasure of your visit this time?" Barbara greeted Clint.

"My crew and I came across the wreckage of another train accident, and this time, we discovered that it was from a circus train. I was wondering if you would have some information on that."

"Oh, you mean the Ringling Brothers train accident of 1944. Yes, indeed, I have the whole story," said Barbara. "The timing of that accident couldn't have been worse. It happened less than a month after that tragic fire in Hartford, Connecticut. That was the one where the entire big-top caught fire and burned right to the ground, and 139 people were killed."

"Yes, I remember when that happened. I was five years old at that time."

"That fire had a devastating effect on the Ringling Brothers Circus as a whole, especially as many of the victims were children. The accident here made things even worse, mainly due to the fact that it was the result of negligence on the part of the Kootenay Central Railway The main purpose for the circus to go on regular touring schedules at that time was to boost morale on the home front and keep people's minds off World War Two. For the children, it was difficult for them to have their fathers overseas fighting in the war, and it was equally difficult for the wives as well. The circus provided a means to help cheer them up. Then to have not one but two tragedies happen within a month was a very bitter pill to swallow."

"What do you mean when you say that it was negligence on the part of the KCR?"

"We have some information about that accident. I'll get it for you—it will provide better detail than I can. Hang on for a minute, I'll look through our files for it." Barbara returned a couple minutes later with a file folder full of newspaper clippings and old photographs. "The most comprehensive account of the accident is this article from the August 2nd, 1944 edition of the *Vancouver Sun*. This was written the day after the accident. The headline read, 'Train carrying touring troupe of the Ringling Brothers Barnum & Bailey Circus returning to Vancouver collides with westbound freight train at Iago Station in the Coquihalla Pass—second tragedy to hit Ringling Brothers Circus within a month.'"

Clint started reading the article. "This particular touring troupe for the Ringling Brothers Circus was on tour through the Okanagan and Kootenay regions and through to Vancouver. When the train left Penticton, a new crew was assigned. When the train reached Brookmere, it would fill up on water and take on a load of coal. From there, they had clearance on the main track right through to Hope, as eastbound Extra 4112 would pull onto the siding at Iago to let them pass.

"When the train was scheduled to leave Brookmere, the Engineer and Brakeman were nowhere to be found. After waiting ten minutes, Brookmere Station Agent Hubert Turley went to the locomotive, climbed aboard, and began blowing the whistle repeatedly. He assumed that they were at the hotel having a drink at the bar. It would be five more minutes before the Engineer and Brakeman emerged from the nearby woods and climbed aboard the locomotive. Turley opened the switch and gave them the 'all clear' signal.

"The crew of the circus train must have realized that they were running behind schedule. According to a statement made by Coquihalla Station Agent Bill Adams, when the circus train passed Coquihalla Station, it was travelling at a high speed.

"At Iago, Section Foreman Andrew Rossington was sitting on the station porch as Extra 4112 pulled onto the siding. One-third of the train was still on the main track when he saw a train heading west round a curve in the distance.

"Realizing that it was the circus train and it was on a collision course, Rossington immediately jumped up and began waving his arms in the air wildly in order to signal the crew to stop, but it was too late. When the locomotive reached the west switch, it collided with the remaining cars on the main track. The force of the collision caused the locomotive to jump the tracks, and sent eight of the ten cars hurtling down the mountain into the river valley far below. Only the last two cars, which were used as living quarters for the roustabouts, remained on the tracks. Rossington described hearing a sickening crunching sound of metal on wood, which was deafening. There was a massive cloud of dust, but no explosion.

When Rossington surveyed the damage, it was a scene of total devastation. Four of the seven cars of the eastbound train that were still on the main track were smashed beyond recognition. The locomotive ended up on its side twenty feet down the embankment; the front end smashed in. The Engineer and Brakeman were thrown from the cab and were killed instantly, two people in the passenger car were killed, and sixteen others were critically injured. Three elephants, three Siberian tigers, and four horses were also killed in the mishap."

The number one item Clint noticed in the article was that three elephants were killed. "There was no mention about the one elephant that did survive," he commented to Barbara.

"What are you talking about? There were only three elephants travelling with the troupe, and all of them were killed," said Barbara.

"None of them survived?"

"You said that you saw firsthand the remains of the boxcars. How in the world could anything survive a crash of that magnitude? Besides, if one did survive, it would never survive the harsh winters they have up there."

"Now that you mention it, when I was looking through one of the boxcars, I saw something that looked like bone fragments, but I didn't give it a second thought." Clint had the uneasy feeling that the elephant he and the crew saw was actually a ghost. He wasn't sure how to inform the crew about this. "I'm also surprised to find out that only two people in the passenger car were killed."

"Of the two people killed, only one died as a result of the crash itself. A man who worked as a clown was thrown from his seat and hit his head on the front wall. He was killed instantly. The other fatality was a woman who performed as 'the fat lady'. After the crash, she climbed out of the car and tried to climb up the mountainside toward the railway, but she suffered a massive heart attack in the process."

"Why does that not surprise me?"

"All of the circus performers travelled together in the passenger car. This included the Ringmaster, the clowns, the acrobats, the lion tamer, the midgets, and an assortment of people with deformities who were classified as 'side show freaks' … which, if you ask me, is pretty disturbing that back then people found it perfectly normal to pay money to see people with deformities put on display."

It's too bad that Don didn't try out for the circus side show back then. He could easily be classed as 'the man with no brain', Clint thought.

"And, of the circus performers who were injured, some of them were injured so severely that they could never perform again. A good example was the tightrope walker, who had to have a leg amputated. As well, the ringmaster himself suffered permanent brain damage, and was unable to talk properly again. And as for the clown, he claimed that his grandfather was a Lieutenant in the US Calvary, and fought alongside General Custer in the Battle of Little Bighorn."

After hearing this, Clint had one of his own questions answered. At first, he wondered why there were no reported sightings of a ghost of a clown up there, but then he realized that with the spirit of Siaman guarding the region, the clown would be competing for space in the afterlife up there.

32

"Thank you, Barbara, for providing me with more information once again."

"Whoa, wait a minute, there's more. You haven't heard the rest of the story," said Barbara. "We're just getting started. You haven't heard the juicy part yet."

"I don't follow," said Clint, rather puzzled.

"When the bodies of the Engineer Roland and Brakeman Peter were removed from the wreckage of the locomotive, they were immediately taken to the coroner, and included in the autopsies were toxicology tests. It was determined that both men had blood-alcohol levels of 2.0, which is more than double the legal limit of an impaired driver. The police officers that were investigating the accident searched the wooded area behind the roundhouse in Brookmere and found an empty bottle of whiskey with both men's fingerprints all over it."

Clint shook his head in amazement and commented, "To think that not only were they endangering their lives, but the lives of the people in the circus as well. There's definitely no doubt that the KCR was negligent."

"But wait, there's still more."

"You really like keeping me in suspense, don't you?"

Barbara pointed to one paragraph in particular and asked Clint to read it back to her.

"During examination of the bodies of Roland Carruthers and Peter Biery, the coroner discovered traces of semen in both men's posteriors, indicating that they had a double sexual encounter shortly before the accident. A subsequent further investigation revealed that both men had been leading a double life for the past five years. Despite both of them being married and having families, the two men were lovers. The combination of excessive alcohol consumption and their state of romantic bliss led to their complete lapse of judgement, which was the reason they were travelling at an excessive speed and ignored both red signal lights." Clint looked up at Barbara. "Holy shit, they actually printed this? Man, oh man, this kind of material would be considered taboo even now. This would have really caused a stir in 1944."

"That reporter ended up in very deep shit for writing that article. I believe he was even fired for it. The newspaper itself was even threatened with obscenity charges, and their business license was nearly revoked. That article had a devastating impact on the families of both men. Peter's wife took their three children and returned to England, but in the case of Roland's wife, that took an even more bizarre turn."

"Oh really, what happened?"

"Roland's wife Edna was seen boarding a westbound passenger train, but she didn't have any luggage. She told the people on the platform who knew her that she was going to Vancouver. She was wearing a long, white dress. It didn't really look like a wedding dress, but it was the dress she wore when she and Roland were married nine years earlier. That would have been during the Depression, so she wouldn't have been able to afford anything fancy.

"When the passenger train reached Iago, it pulled up to the station and stopped. Iago was not a regular passenger stop—passengers wishing to disembark there had to request ahead of time. Edna got off the train there. Andrew Rossington was clearing a culvert a mile east of Iago, so he never saw her. Andrew's wife Sadie was upstairs in the Section House when she noticed Edna getting off the train, but didn't give it much thought. After the train left, Edna walked down the tracks to where the siding ended at the west switch. Then she reached into a hidden pocket in her dress and pulled out a .38 calibre revolver, which had belonged to Roland. She then stuck the barrel in her mouth and pulled the trigger. Sadie heard the gunshot, and ran out to investigate. She saw Edna lying on the ground by the west switch, and it was then she realized what happened."

Clint was in a state of utter disbelief. *That woman I saw at the site of Iago was Edna. That would explain the long white dress and the blood coming from her mouth.*

Barbara went on, "In the years following Edna's suicide, a number of people have reported seeing her standing by the west switch. Even after the rails were removed in 1962, a few of the pipeline maintenance workers have reported seeing her while driving past the site of Iago."

Clint tried to be coy about it by not letting on that he had seen her himself. "What did she look like?" asked Clint.

"I don't know; I don't have a picture of her. When Edna shot herself, there was an article about it in the *Penticton Herald*. In fact, it made the front page, and her picture was included. I'll find it for you." Barbara went into her archives and brought back the 15 August 1944 issue of the newspaper. The headline read, "Wife of engineer killed in circus train mishap shoots herself at Iago."

The second Clint looked at the photograph, he recognized Edna. That instant, he knew it was her. Clint sat there, absolutely stunned. If he didn't believe in ghosts before, he certainly did now.

He was completely speechless.

After a moment of silence, Barbara said softly, "You saw her, didn't you?"

Clint didn't answer. He didn't know what to say.

"Don't worry, you're not going crazy. It's okay to admit you saw her. Many other people admitted seeing her, so it's perfectly okay. I guess she wants to look over that place for eternity. Why she wants to is beyond me."

Clint decided at that point he had seen enough. "Thank you, Barbara. I think that's enough for me today."

"You know something, I wish I knew a medium, then we could tell that chick that there's no point in her staying there, now that the railway is gone. After all, the new highway is going through there, right?"

"Actually, the new highway will be bypassing Iago completely. It turns northward three miles west of Iago."

"Even so, there's no reason for her to be there."

33

The minute Clint returned to Vancouver, he had to get right down to business with the construction contractors, as the highway construction was about to get into full swing. With a great deal of apprehension, he met with Oscar Onerheim. In addition to being the President of Kurt Onerheim Construction, he also ran the road construction crew. Ever since Oscar took over the company, the quality of workmanship diminished drastically. Originally, Clint didn't want Kurt Onerheim Construction to be part of the bidding process, but he felt he owed it to his old friend Kurt to give his old company a try, even if it was under his son's control now.

Nevertheless, Oscar didn't have the same amount of expertise in road construction his father had, even though he seemed to think he did. Oscar also refused to accept Clint's expertise, which had resulted in many run-ins over the years. It seemed like the guy was 99 percent ego and one percent brains. He couldn't believe how much Oscar and Don were alike. He didn't think it was possible that God could make the same mistake twice.

Over the course of the meeting, there was an aura of tension building between Clint and Oscar already. Oscar was constantly putting in his two-cent's worth as to how he wanted the construction to be carried out.

In the end, Clint got in Oscar's face and said, "I want everything done exactly to my specifications—no compromises. This will be followed to the letter, or else."

The next day, Clint headed up to the Hope office. Later in the afternoon, Greg, Kevin, and Cody returned from the jobsite. Their boots were all caked in mud as a result of the torrential rain.

"Hi, everyone. How's the job going?" Clint asked.

"The absolute shits," said Greg in a snarly tone.

"Alright, where is Don?"

"Don takes his own truck to and from the jobsite. He doesn't want to be seen with us peons, as he thinks he's so high and mighty. He probably takes his own vehicle so that he can hide bottles of booze, so he can get drunk after work," said Cody.

"I don't know where Don is, and frankly, I don't give a fuck. For all I know, he went somewhere to whack-off his little two-incher," said Greg, angrily.

"Easy, Greg," though Clint couldn't help but smirk.

A few minutes later, Don pulled up and parked in front of the office.

The moment Don entered, Clint yelled out, "Don, Greg, into my office, now."

When Don and Greg entered Clint's office, he invited them to have a seat. As they sat down, he slammed the door and gave them both a death glare. There was momentary silence, and Greg began to feel uneasy. Both of them had a good idea what this was about.

"Gentlemen, as you are well aware, I am the District Engineer. What you don't seem to be aware of is that I'm not your goddamn babysitter. The two of you are adults, all grown up and on your own—physically, that is. Mentally, I am not so sure about. I have certain expectations of my employees; the most important one being that they achieve the goals I set out for them and do so in a professional manner. When I set out tasks, I want to ensure that those tasks can be completed problem-free without my constant supervision. Greg, I am going to start with you. You must accept the fact that Don is your Crew Chief now. Therefore, he is in charge and he calls the shots."

"Wait a minute, who's side are you on here?" asked Greg, surprised.

"I'm on nobody's side. Now, don't you ever talk out of turn again," said Clint. Clint noticed Don out of the corner of his eye, and he had his typical cocky smirk on his face. "Okay Don, you can stop patting yourself on the back now. I have known you for many years. I'll give you credit; you are a capable surveyor. But ever since I first knew you, your people skills have not improved one bit. You have to start showing more respect toward your workers. Greg, for example, has five years experience as a rod-and-chain man. He knows what he is doing. Greg, what is the main source of your disagreements with Don?"

"For one thing, it's speed. Don always says that we are working too slow. In addition, he insists that using the plumb bob is unnecessary on a straight line."

Clint could understand why Greg would be mad at Don for that. In all the years he had been associated with surveying, he knew that the plumb bob was an important device for preliminary surveys.

"Do you think plumb bobs are just a decoration? There is a reason why we carry them in our equipment boxes. Why don't you want to use one?" Clint asked Don.

"When you're holding the chain, you're no more than two feet above the ground. You can easily eyeball it from that level. Using a plumb bob takes too much extra time."

"I have to disagree with you, Don. In preliminary surveys, you have to be accurate within five millimetres. A plumb bob is a vital tool that ensures the measurement is exactly ninety degrees above the ground. If I find that any of the baselines you surveyed are out of alignment, I will have them done over again at your expense. Greg is right; I want a plumb bob used at all times when surveying baselines. Secondly, even though we're under a tight deadline, I cannot stress enough that accuracy is far more important than speed. I don't mind if it takes a little longer than planned, as long as it is one hundred percent accurate. I know that we have had a lot of rain lately, so that makes for poor ground conditions. In this case, I advise you to cut the crew some slack. When the weather improves, we can pick up the pace. Now, Don, if you respect your workers, they will respect you back in return. Yelling at people will not make them work faster; it will only make them mad and want to put in less effort. Okay, guys, I do not want to have this conversation with you again."

As usual, Don said nothing in the end. He merely got up and left.

"I'm telling you, I am going to kill that bloody bastard," said Greg, still visibly angry.

"Greg, don't talk like that. Just calm down, okay? Don can be very strange at times; sometimes he can be a really nice guy, and other times, he can be the meanest son of a bitch on the face of the earth. It all depends on whether or not he has been drinking. The only times he is nice is when he has had a few drinks, but if he's sober, watch out."

"How about before we start work every morning, I offer Don a double scotch, then," Greg suggested.

"Absolutely not. The person operating the transit needs to be one-hundred-percent focused. Otherwise, when he looks through the scope, he might see at least three poles, so which one would be the right one? Greg, just do your best and don't worry about Don. If Don continues to give you problems, let me know, and if I'm out of town, let Hugh know. Either Hugh or I will take care of Don."

A few days later, the rain finally stopped. It was now sunny and warm, so now Don's crew could make up for lost time. Clint didn't spend very much time in the office; he wanted to head up to the jobsites and check on the progress of the crews.

Don's crew must have been very engrossed in their work; they didn't even notice Clint appear on the scene. As usual, Don was berating Kevin for not pulling the chain tight enough. Clint noticed that none of the other men on the crew were smiling.

"Good day, gentlemen. How is everything going?"

"Clint, I didn't know you were here," said Don.

"Obviously not. Well, I see you guys have really gained some ground. Good work, Greg; good work, Kevin; good work, Cody." Clint looked over at Don, who looked rather annoyed. He then noticed that Don's truck was parked right at the edge of the furthest road allowance line. "Don, why did you have to park your truck so close to where they're working? You're risking getting stuck and knocking over survey markers."

"My truck is a sturdy four-wheel-drive; you don't have to worry about it getting stuck. I can go well outside of the road allowance lines. I also carry extra supplies in my truck, so if we need them I can get them without walking all the way back to the company truck."

"What do you mean, extra supplies?" asked Clint.

"You know, extra stakes and keels. But mainly, I have an extra chain, and a good one at that. Not this cheap piece of shit you issued us. This one is so brittle, it could break any minute."

After this, Clint headed up the Boston Bar Creek valley to where the other crews were working. With the improvement in the weather, the crews working up there were able to make up for lost time as well. The entire ten-mile section west of the summit was now ready for the grading phase. Clint had a chat with Hugh, and after receiving a satisfactory report on the progress, was ready to head back to the Hope office.

Since it was only 11:30 a.m. and he had no meetings scheduled until the next day, Clint decided to take a detour onto the Pipeline Road and drive as far as the concrete snow-shed one mile east of Iago Station. The current road bypassed the old snow-shed, so there was a spot in front of the east portal where he could pull over. He parked his truck and ate his lunch there.

Ever since he passed Iago earlier, all Clint could think about was Edna, and what she must have gone through after learning her marriage was a fraud. He decided to attempt to make peace with her; to make her understand that it is time to let go and spend the rest of her eternity in heaven. He wasn't sure if he would be able to communicate with the dead, but it was worth a shot.

When Clint reached Iago on the return trip, he pulled up and parked in front of the old section house. He then walked up to the approximate spot where the west switch was. He looked around to see if Edna would appear, but didn't see any sign of her.

"Edna—Edna Carruthers! I know you're out here; I know you can hear me. I just want to tell you, Roland didn't mean to hurt you. I understand that he lied to you for all those years, and I don't condone what he did. He was just trying to protect you by not telling you. You may not believe me, but Roland really did love you, and if he was here now, he would tell you he is sorry. The time has come for you to put it all to rest. God has been waiting for you for forty-one years. Come on, Edna, it's time to let go. You don't want to keep the big guy waiting any longer. Now you and Roland can be reunited."

All the while Clint was speaking, he was unaware that Edna was right behind him. But then, he felt like there was some kind of presence behind him. He quickly turned around, but Edna was gone. He looked up, and the wind suddenly picked up in the treetops.

He smiled and said, "Goodbye Edna."

He then looked down and saw a shiny object partially imbedded in the ground. He reached down, pulled the object out from the ground, cleaned off the dirt, and realized that it was a diamond-cluster ring. This must have been Edna's wedding ring.

"I'll hang on to this until my next trip to the Penticton museum, where it will have a permanent home."

34

Don and his crew stopped for lunch at noon. Greg, Kevin, and Cody had their lunches in the company truck while Don had his lunch alone in his truck as usual. As the others left, Don asked Greg to see him in private.

"What is this about?" asked Greg.

"What do you think? This is a new type of aluminum alloy; it's ten times sturdier than the metal on the chain you're using. This will last practically forever," Don said as he showed him the new roll of survey chain.

Don handed the spool over to Greg. He examined and felt it, but didn't notice any difference.

"Greg, this curve we're working on is only eight degrees, yet every time you move to the next thirty-metre mark, you go way too far to the right. Why do you keep doing that?"

"I'm trying to make it easier for you and to stay within the range of your viewfinder. I didn't think I was moving to the right that much."

"You say that you have five years experience as a rod-and-chain man, then you should be able to use your own judgement on determining an eight-degree curve; it's second nature. One more thing—you missed one of my hand signals again. That's the second time in less than a week that you missed a hand signal. If that happens again, you're going to sit in the truck for the rest of the day."

"You're moving your arms too damn fast. You flail your arms like you're being attacked by a swarm of mosquitoes. In addition, if you would move the transit closer more often, I would be able to see you better."

"Don't you tell me when to move the transit. You're not the boss here, I am. If you have trouble seeing me, then get glasses. But for now, you pay more attention to what you are doing, understand?"

Greg didn't respond; instead, he angrily made his way down to where the others were having lunch.

"What did Don want to talk to you about?" Kevin asked him once he had met up with them again.

"Same old bullshit. I swear to God, I am going to kill him," said Greg, angrily.

A few minutes later, Hugh pulled up alongside their truck and joined the men for lunch. He stayed and chatted with the men for twenty minutes before he had to leave.

***

Back at his truck, Don was having his customary lunch, which consisted of a thermos of coffee with a shot of rum. He had a twenty-six-ounce bottle of rum hidden underneath the seat. He brought a sandwich and some crackers, but wasn't hungry. He brought along the latest edition of *Playboy* for something to read. After twenty minutes, he decided to stretch his legs. After he stepped outside of his truck, he heard the sound of tree branches rustling and twigs snapping. He took a quick look around, but saw nothing.

He reached into the cab and took out the spool of surveyor's chain. He held it in such a way that he would hold a weapon and said, "Who's there?" No response.

The rustling sound stopped momentarily, but then started again. Don was concerned that it might be a bear or a cougar, but couldn't see anything. He noticed that there was a stiff wind blowing in the treetops. Just then, the image of a First Nations mask flew by. Don was shocked by what he saw and dropped the spool of surveyor's chain on the ground. He tried to see where the mask flew to, but it seemed to just disappear. He then began to feel some kind of presence behind him. He turned around, and there was the spool of surveyor's chain, suspended in mid-air.

Don uttered, "What the hell?" as the chain slowly unravelled from the spool by itself.

As Don tried to approach it, the spool began to spin around him at eye level, still letting out more length of chain. Then the chain started to wrap itself around Don's neck. After it was wrapped around his neck six times, it tightened with full force. Don gasped for air. He tried to yell for help, but with the chain wrapped around his larynx, he could barely squeak anything out. He grabbed at the chain and fought valiantly to try to pull it off, but the force that was pulling it was so strong it wouldn't budge. His face turned red, and then turned purple. He fell to his knees, still gasping for air and unable to breathe. He began foaming at the mouth, and his eyes were nearly bulging out of his head. Eventually, gurgling sounds emanated from his mouth as blood began pouring out. A few seconds later, he finally collapsed, and breathed his last.

***

Meanwhile, the other men on the crew continued on with their lunch break. They had parked their truck on the side of the Pipeline Road, slightly downhill from the bench. Therefore, they were completely out of sight of Don's truck. When it got to 12:35 p.m. Greg looked at his watch.

"Hey, guys, we better head back; otherwise, numb-nuts will wonder where we are," said Greg.

"It's a wonder he hasn't started yelling for us to get our asses back. He always knows when the half-hour is up," said Kevin.

When they made their way up the hill, they could see Don's truck in the distance, but no sign of Don. They saw that the driver's side door was open. At first, they didn't think anything was out of the ordinary. But as they got closer, they saw a person lying on the ground. They soon realized it was Don, but at first, everyone assumed Don had had too much to drink and had passed out. Greg, however, began to suspect that something wasn't right, so he went over to investigate. He saw the surveyor's chain spool on the ground about ten feet from Don, and noticed that the chain was completely unwound. He followed the chain until it reached Don's neck, and saw that it was wrapped tightly around his neck at least six times. Don was lying face down, and wasn't moving at all. He wasn't breathing.

"Oh my God, Don's dead!" yelled Greg.

The others rushed over, and Kevin asked Greg if he was sure. Greg pointed to where the chain was wrapped tightly around Don's neck.

"Look at that, he's been strangled. He's not breathing. We need to call for help—don't any of you touch him."

Greg tried to use the CB radio in Don's truck, but soon found out it wasn't starting up. He ran down to the company truck, and called Hugh on the CB radio.

Hugh was just crossing the Coquihalla River Bridge coming into Hope when he got the call. When he realized it was Greg, he picked up the receiver and said, "Yes, Greg, what can I do for you?"

"Hugh, it's Don—he's dead—"

"Greg, what are you talking about?"

"Don's been murdered. When we were having lunch, somebody strangled Don with the chain …"

"You mean the surveyor's chain?"

"Yes, the surveyor's chain. Can you please call the police and get them up here?"

"Yes, I will. I'll call them right away. In fact, I'm heading back up to where you are right now."

***

After Clint concluded his side-trip on the Pipeline Road, he thought he would check on Don's crew one more time before heading back to the office. He wanted to see their progress since this morning. But when he came upon the spot where the company truck was parked, he was surprised to see a Chevrolet Suburban with the RCMP logo stamped on the side parked right beside it.

What the hell are the police doing here? he wondered. *Maybe Don has finally pushed Greg over the edge, and he snapped.*

He parked his truck behind the police car and went over to investigate. Greg was talking to one of the police officers and the other officer was guarding the body, which was covered by a tarp, when Clint approached. He asked Kevin and Cody what was going on.

"It's Don—he's been murdered," said Kevin.

Clint was in a state of shock, but not in a total state of disbelief, as he sensed that something like this was possible. He approached Constable Friesen, who was guarding the body, and asked to see it up close.

"I'm sorry, Mr. Matheson, but this is a police investigation," said Constable Friesen.

"I understand that. But you may remember him from our first meeting, you know, at this same location. We can both confirm his identity."

"Right, I thought he looked vaguely familiar. Okay, suit yourself," said Constable Friesen, as he removed the cover.

The surveyor's chain was still wrapped around Don's neck. The first thing Clint noticed was how tightly it was wound. If it were any tighter, it would have severed his head clean off his body. Clint was completely bewildered, as he knew that it was almost impossible to bend aluminium alloy to that extent, and not just once, but six times.

"What's his full name, how old is he, and what else can you tell me about him?" asked Constable Friesen.

"His name is Donald Lassiter, fifty-five years old, divorced, one daughter, and he has been with the BC Department of Highways for ten years."

"Do you have any idea who would want Don dead?" asked Constable Friesen.

"Where would you like me to start? I don't think he had a friend in the world. To put it quite simply, if murder was legal, he would have been dead ages ago. Anyone who has ever worked with him and for him will vouch for that."

"Okay, perhaps you can answer me this question. If this guy was so disliked, and you say that you're in charge of this project, then how come you didn't fire him?"

"Alright, the one thing I did like about him was that he was a top-notch surveyor. He had many years of experience, and knew all the ins and outs of every aspect of surveying. His only drawback was that he got a swelled head about it," replied Clint.

After Greg finished talking to the other Constable, Clint then asked him to give his version of what happened.

"When we broke for lunch, Don wanted to see me in private. We were running a curve, and I guess I over-estimated the degree of the curve, as I've been moving too far to the right when we advance. As expected, he got after me for it. Then he got on my case for missing a hand signal. I told him that he moves his arms too fast, and he flipped out on me. In the end, I just left. But I swear to God, he was still alive when I left."

Just then, Hugh appeared on the scene.

"I would have been here sooner, but just after you radioed me, Greg, I realized I was just about out of gas, so I had to go and fill up at the gas station near Kawkawa Lake. So, can anyone fill me in?" Hugh asked.

"I will make it simple. Don has been murdered," said Clint.

"It must have happened when we were all down at the truck having lunch; likely at the time you were talking to us. Don was just fine when I left him," said Greg.

"I don't understand any of this business of him being strangled by the surveyor's chain. How is it possible to strangle someone with that kind of chain?" asked Hugh.

"Come with me, and find out for yourself," said Clint.

Clint led Hugh over to where Constable Friesen was guarding the body. He replaced the tarp over Don's body. Clint asked him once again to remove the tarp.

"What is it for this time?" asked Constable Friesen, looking annoyed.

"This is Hugh. He is the Project Manager for this particular section. He's Don's immediate supervisor."

"Good grief, your outfit seems to have a case of too many Chiefs and not enough Indians."

"On the contrary," replied Clint. "In this case, I believe we are dealing with one Indian too many."

Constable Friesen removed the tarp once again. Hugh took a close-up look at where the surveyor's chain was wrapped around Don's neck.

"Good lord, how can anyone bend the chain that much? To be able to pull it that tight, you'd have to be built like Hercules," said Hugh.

"It didn't appear as though Don put up much of a struggle. The ground doesn't appear to be very disturbed, meaning that he didn't do any kicking or jumping," said Clint.

"Do you have any idea who could have done this?" asked Hugh.

"I don't think it's a matter of who—more like a matter of what," replied Clint.

"I don't follow you."

"I'm beginning to suspect that our Native spirit friend Siaman is behind this. There doesn't seem to be any other explanation. I really don't think any of the men on the crew are responsible."

"Come on, Clint, you don't believe any of that Indian legend bullshit. That Chief was just trying to instil fear into you because he didn't want this highway built. I'm starting to think that maybe more than one person was involved."

"Well then, go ahead and play amateur sleuth. I am going to stick to my theory."

"This immediate area is now a crime scene, so all work here is suspended until further notice. Everyone who was working directly with Don will need to come down to the RCMP detachment and answer some questions. The body will be taken to the coroner's office as soon as the ambulance arrives," said Constable Friesen.

Clint and Hugh couldn't help but overhear the conversation between Greg, Kevin, and Cody, which centered around the comment Greg had made when he joined them for lunch, and the fact that he was alone with Don for at least five minutes.

"Greg, is there something you're not telling me?" asked Clint.

"When Don got on my case for missing a hand signal, I guess I overreacted. I was pissed off when I joined everyone for lunch. I made a comment that I wanted to kill him, but that's all it was—a comment. I didn't mean it literally. When Don and I were alone, all we did was talk. I never laid one hand on him but, believe me, I was tempted. Mr. Matheson, I realize that I said it to you, too, but I was just speaking in the heat of the moment. I didn't really mean what I said. Now all of you are thinking that I'm the one who killed him …"

"No, nobody is pointing the finger at anyone, and nobody will be accusing anyone. Just let the police handle this for now," said Clint.

"Think about it—if I did kill Don, why would I say that I want to kill him? That would be incriminating myself right there. And why would I return to the jobsite if I knew he was dead? Wouldn't I try to cover it up? I'm not that stupid," said Greg.

"Like I said, let the police handle this investigation. To be honest, every single one of us is just as much a suspect. I myself would have a motive, so I could even be a suspect. But there is not enough evidence to incriminate any one of us, so in the end, we are all going to be cleared. For right now, I want everyone to meet at the Hope office. Just because this particular job is suspended, it doesn't mean we can all sit around. There is still a lot of work to be done. Hugh and I will decide where each of you will be temporarily reassigned."

Clint and Hugh decided to send Cody back to the Vancouver office, where he would resume his position as Ted's office assistant. As for Henry, they determined that the problem with his eyesight should not affect his ability to hold up the rod while taking elevation shots. Therefore, he and Greg would assist the Vancouver-based crew on the Box Canyon section. Kevin would work with the other Vancouver-based crew taking elevation shots near the site of Lear Station.

When Clint phoned Ted and told him that Cody was coming back and Henry was heading back into the field, he thought Ted was going to pass out from sheer excitement. He could almost hear Ted turning handsprings in the background. Apparently, ever since Henry began working in the office, Ted had never had one moment's peace between Henry constantly asking how to work the computer programs and talking non-stop about anything and everything.

35

APRIL 1985

It was less than forty-eight hours later when Clint saw Constable Friesen in the foyer of the Hope office.

"Hello again, Mr. Matheson. I'm here to see Greg Draayer," Constable Friesen said when Clint ventured outside his office and acknowledged his presence.

"He's working in the field on the new highway project at the moment."

"Will you please contact him and have him return to the office immediately?"

Clint had to collect his thoughts for a moment. Even though he had a gut feeling about Greg's possible involvement, he could tell that Greg was telling the truth.

"What's all this about? Don't you need a warrant for the arrest of Greg if he actually murdered Don? There has to be some kind of mistake."

"No, there is no mistake. The Crown Prosecutor has compiled enough evidence to warrant an arrest," said Constable Friesen.

"Oh really?" replied Clint. "What evidence would that be?"

"We are not at liberty to discuss this, but we can tell you this much. When the surveyor's chain and the spool were examined at the forensics lab, Greg's fingerprints were found all over them. The only other person's fingerprints found were Don's," said Constable Friesen.

Clint reluctantly gave in, and called Greg on the CB radio. At first, Greg didn't answer.

"If you aren't able to get Greg to come to the office, I'll go out to the jobsite and bring him in myself."

"I assure you that won't be necessary. Just bear with me and I will keep trying." He made another call on the CB radio, and this time, Greg answered. "Greg, you need to come up to the office immediately."

"What is this about?" asked Greg.

"I can't talk about it now, I just need to see you immediately. Stop what you're doing, tell your Crew Chief that I called you into the office, and get over here right away," replied Clint.

Twenty minutes later, Greg pulled up in front of the office. Constable Friesen emerged from the back room.

"Gregory Draayer, I'm placing you under arrest for the murder of Donald Lassiter," said Constable Friesen before reading him his rights.

"Greg, I promise I'll find you a good lawyer," Clint said as Constable Friesen led Greg away.

Once Greg was gone, Clint immediately made a phone call to Salvatore Bertelli.

"Salvatore, it's Clint. Is it was possible to acquire your services once again? One of my surveyors has been charged with murder."

"Clint, I already have my hands full with Henry's case, and there are some other cases I'm working on as well. Also, if I was to represent two people who work for the same company and in the same division, that could cause a possible conflict of interest," replied Salvatore.

"Very well, then. Thanks, anyway."

Clint then decided to call Herman Jacob's office. Herman was the lawyer who represented him during his divorce proceedings. He owed it to Herman that he was still living in his house, even though his ex-wife had custody the kids. If she had had her way, she would have received the house and both vehicles as well as the kids. In addition to handling family law, Herman was also a top-notch defence attorney.

When Clint phoned Herman's office, he reached Herman's receptionist. "Hi, Mr. Matheson. Herman actually retired last year. His senior partner, Margaret Lawson, has taken over the practice. She is an expert in criminal law, so she would be your best bet."

Clint agreed and made an appointment to see Margaret the next day. *Gee, I didn't realize Herman was near retirement age. He didn't appear that old.*

With his mind preoccupied with Greg's predicament, Clint couldn't focus on work. After lunch, he drove over to the Hope RCMP Detachment.

Once there, Clint asked to see Staff Sergeant Dickerson. When he was led to Sergeant Dickerson's office, Clint brought up the subject of other possible suspects.

"You know, Sergeant, Don had many enemies, and a large percentage of them were working in the same general area."

"I'm glad you brought that up. This brings me to a question I want to ask you," said Sergeant Dickerson.

"Oh really, what's that?"

"Where were you at the time Don was murdered? Nobody I have talked to can account for your whereabouts around that time. The men on Don's crew say that they last saw you around ten o'clock, and Hugh and his crew say that they last saw you around eleven-thirty. You were not seen again until you returned to where Don's crew was, and that was one-thirty in the afternoon. That's quite a gap. Can you explain it?"

"Yes, I went for a drive up the Pipeline Road."

"Don't you realize that whole area is private property? Pacific Coast Gas Trunk Lines owns all the land up there, and they have a strict no trespassing rule."

"Are you friends with Simon Dale or something?"

"I know of him, but I don't know him personally. Now, back to my question. Can anyone vouch for you travelling up the Pipeline Road?"

"I went up there by myself."

"So, I am taking you entirely at your word. For all I know, you could have travelled on foot through the woods to where Don was, snuck up behind him, wrapped the chain around his neck, and strangled him, all the while wearing gloves so you would not leave any fingerprints."

"That is an interesting theory, but it is completely false."

"I wonder about that. I was talking to your secretary yesterday, and she told me about a comment you made about Don not too long ago. You described what you would like to do to him, and your description is exactly word-for-word what actually happened to him. You went so far as to hold up the exact same type of instrument that was used to kill him. Is that just a mere coincidence, or is there something you are not telling me?"

Clint remembered what he said that day, and realized that it did match what had happened.

"Look, it was just a coincidence. Don was pissed off at me for demoting him to Crew Chief, and disrespected my authority. I was speaking in the heat of the moment; I didn't mean it literally. If I really wanted to kill Don, would I do it in the exact same manner that I described it to another person? Am I that stupid? Besides, why would I want to frame Greg? I like him, and would have nothing to gain by framing him."

Back at the office, Clint confronted Linda. "Gee, thanks a lot, Linda, for relaying my off-the-cuff commentary to Sergeant Dickerson. I'll be sure and send you a postcard from Millhaven."

"Clint, I had to be honest with him. I was afraid that if I didn't tell him everything I knew, I could be charged with perjury."

The next day, Clint had his meeting with Margaret. The sign on her office door read "Margaret Lawson, QC", so Clint figured that if there was a "QC" beside her name, she must be good.

"Hi, there." A look of recognition came upon Margaret's face as she looked up from her desk to greet him. "I knew I remembered the name 'Clint Matheson' from somewhere. I remember you from my university. You were on the football team, weren't you?"

Clint nodded, surprised.

"Small world. I was always in the cheering section. Well, how can I help you now?"

"I'm here on behalf Greg Draayer, who has been charged with murder. Greg is unable to be here, as he is being held at the Hope lock-up. Bail has not been approved yet."

Margaret carefully looked over all of the arguments for both the Defence and the Prosecution. As a strategy for the Defence, Clint decided to go with the theory that somebody was hiding in the woods until Greg left, and then snuck up on Don from behind, wrapped the surveyor's chain around his neck, and strangled him. He vowed to keep his mouth shut about Siaman. If he brought up the idea that this act was performed by the spirit of a Native man who had been dead for three hundred years, Margaret would think he was a total head-case and drop the case like a hot potato.

"There are two important factors that will be necessary in order to prove Greg's innocence. The most important factor is a timeline. If the exact moment of Don's death can be determined, and it occurred after Greg had left, then we have it made. The second most important factor is other suspects. Is there anybody else who would want to kill Don?"

"Well, practically everybody who has worked with him."

"Gee, that sure narrows it down. I take it he was quite the prick," said Margaret, looking rather astonished.

"In all the years Don was in any supervisory position, he had the highest staff turnover rate of anyone in the department. Many of his workers quit in disgust or were fired, and a large percentage of them still harbour bad feelings toward him. I have run into a number of Don's former employees over the years, and every one of them gave a graphic description of what they would like to do with him if the opportunity arose. None of the descriptions were pretty."

"Splendid. We are starting off on the right track here. From now until the trial date is set, I need you to help me with the investigating and to line up some witnesses for the Defence. I will head up to Hope and meet with Greg. I will have to check my schedule; it will be tomorrow at the soonest," said Margaret.

36

Back at the Vancouver office, Clint telephoned the coroner, Dennis. According to Margaret, determining the exact time of death was of utmost priority, so he hoped that Dennis could provide the answer.

"Hi, Clint. I've actually been trying to reach you since yesterday, but kept missing you. I need to see you at the lab as soon as possible. We need to talk. Things are not adding up—again. It's the same situation as the previous incidents that occurred on that highway project of yours. I'm telling you, Clint, this is happening far too often."

"I'll be there later this afternoon," Clint reluctantly agreed.

Dennis's coroner lab was becoming an all-too familiar site to Clint since the start of the highway project.

"Clint, Clint, Clint, I'm starting to sound like a broken record. Just when I thought I'd seen everything, this project of yours brings me more casualties, and each one more bizarre than the previous. This really has to stop."

"Trust me, Dennis. None of these incidents were ever intended to happen. But there's one thing you must realize—shit happens."

"Yes, I fully understand that shit happens ... That's why I have this job. What I don't understand is why it keeps happening on your damn highway project."

"I don't know either. Now, what was it you wanted to see me about this time?"

Dennis proceeded to show Clint what he termed "Exhibit A"—the surveyor's chain and the spool.

"I had the unenviable task of meticulously removing this from Don's neck. I had to unwind a total of six metres."

He then showed the exact places where Greg's fingerprints were found. One set of fingerprints were on the handle of the spool, another set were at the other end of the chain, and another set were right by the two-metre line—there were only two fingerprints here. The position of Greg's fingerprints in relation to where each end of the chain and spool were found at the time Don was murdered meant that Greg would have to have arms that were three metres long. He pointed out the exact locations on the chain where Greg would have had to grip in order to pull the chain as tight as it was pulled.

Dennis re-enacted the wrapping of the chain around Don's neck, using a Styrofoam floatation noodle to simulate his neck. He wrapped the chain around the noodle six times, and tried to pull with gripping just the chain with each hand. His hands were unable to get a grip on the chain, and therefore he was unable to pull the chain tight. He then put on a pair of work gloves, and tried to pull the chain tight again, but to no avail. As a last resort, he wrapped the chain once around each hand and kinked it at the edge of each fist. This time, he was able to maintain a grip, but was unable to pull it as taut as it was around Don's neck. If this was how it was done, then the chain would have been twisted all out of shape, and there would be two distinct kinks. None of this was the case.

"If the assailant had indeed pulled the chain the way I just demonstrated, he would have to be built like Hercules to pull it to the extent that it was when it was wrapped around Don's neck. The diameter of his neck at its narrowest point is less than three inches. Considering how flexible the metal of the chain is, it would be next to impossible to pull it that taut. You should give it a try both with and without wearing gloves so you can see what I'm talking about," said Dennis.

Clint gave a mighty pull, but was unable to pull the chain really tight around the noodle. He then put on the pair of gloves and gave another strong tug on the chain, but was still unable to squeeze the noodle enough to make the diameter half of what it was originally.

"This will make an excellent case for Greg's defence," said Clint.

Dennis wanted Clint to gain a better understanding of what he was trying to demonstrate, so he led him into the room where the corpses were kept in climate-controlled drawers. Clint was surprised that the body of Don was still there.

Seeing the surprise on Clint's face, Dennis said, "All corpses must remain here until they are identified by a family member. So far, nobody has been able to locate Don's ex-wife or his daughter."

"I can't say that I blame them for not wanting to claim him. Would *you* want to admit it if you were related to him?"

"Clint, I know you and Don didn't like each other, but at least show some respect for the dead."

Opening the drawer containing Don's lifeless body, Dennis showed Clint how close Don came to being completely decapitated.

"The indentations where the chain was wrapped around his neck are still clearly visible. His windpipe was completely crushed, and his jugular vein was severed. If strangulation hadn't been the cause of death, he would have bled to death, anyway. I can't figure out why Don did not put up more of a struggle. He might have had a chance of putting up a fight after it was wrapped around his neck once, but giving the killer the opportunity to wrap the chain around his neck six times doesn't make any sense."

"The killer must have been very quick with his hands, never

allowing Don a chance to break free after it was wrapped around his neck once … especially if he was able to sneak up on him from behind," Clint theorized. "Oh, by the way, did you examine his rectum?"

"No, why the hell would I need to examine his rectum?"

"Don't all coroners have to follow some set of guidelines and procedures? When a deceased person is brought in here, don't you have to examine every part of his or her body?"

"The job of the coroner is to determine the cause of death and the estimated time of death. In Don's case, it was very obvious. You don't have to be a rocket scientist to determine that he died by strangulation. I could tell the minute I saw what was left of his neck exactly how he died. There was no need to examine any other part of him."

"So, in other words, you didn't check his rectum?"

"Of course not. Why are you asking me this?"

"Oh, right, it's a long story. When my crew and I found the wreckage of a circus train that collided with a train going in the opposite direction, I decided to do some research on the accident. This accident happened back in 1944, and was the result of negligence on the part of the engineer and brakeman on the circus train. They were both killed in the accident, and their bodies were taken to the coroner. When he examined them, he found traces of the other man's semen in each of their rectums. I was hoping you could tell me why that coroner would examine their anuses in the first place."

"How would I know? Every coroner is different. I don't know if they did things differently in 1944. All I know is that the standard procedure when bodies are brought in is that they are always lying on their backs. The coroner first checks the area around the frontal lobes unless the injury that caused the death is very obvious. From the head, the neck is then examined, and every part downward after that. Once the front part is examined, the body is then turned over onto its stomach. In the case of the train drivers, when the first body was turned over, the coroner likely noticed a wet spot—or dried-up stain—on his rear end. That would have warranted a further investigation, and would be realized later that it was from the other guy's sperm dribbling out of his ass."

Dennis saw the obviously squeamish look on Clint's face.

"Hey, you started this line of conversation—not me."

"Okay, okay, you've made your point," said Clint.

"You know something, when you kept asking me if I checked Don's ass, you had me wondering. The two of you are both divorced, you both work out in a remote area, and it's probable that neither of you have gotten it lately, so I was thinking that maybe you and him went back in the bush and had a little romantic encounter?"

"For the love of God, no! There is no way I would ever get *that* desperate. Don and I could be stranded alone on a deserted island for forty years and my dick would never get within one mile of his ass."

Dennis placed Don's body back into the cabinet and closed the door.

"Well, Clint, this conversation has been very enlightening; you've really made my day. I can now go home to my wife and tell her over dinner that Clint Matheson from the Department of Highways came over to the lab, and we had a frank discussion about anal intercourse between men. She'll be pleased to hear that."

"I'm glad. Say, before I leave, I was wondering if you're able to determine the exact time that Don died. I need this information to help provide an alibi for Greg."

"Based on the analysis I performed at the time Don's body was brought in, I determined that the death occurred between twelve-fifteen and twelve-thirty that day. I'll have to run some more extensive tests to pinpoint the exact time. Even after two days, the exact time of death can still be determined."

"In that case, please perform all of the necessary tests, and let me know the results. Dennis, I really need you to testify on behalf of Greg when his trial comes up. The evidence you have brought before me here will be vital for his defence. Would you be willing to testify? What you have shown me will prove beyond the shadow of a doubt that Greg did not kill Don. Without your testimony, an innocent man could be sent to prison for life. Greg has a wife and two children … I don't want to see that happen. I am begging you—please do the right thing and testify on Greg's behalf."

"Okay Clint, have Greg's lawyer contact me and give me all the details for when the trial will be. I'll start running those tests to determine when Don died."

"Thank you, Dennis. You have been a tremendous help."

"There's one more thing I want to add, Clint. When this project of yours is finished and the highway is open to traffic, it will be a cold day in Hell before I ever drive on it or let anybody in my family travel on it. If I ever travel up-country, I want to make sure I get to my destination alive."

"Dennis, I assure you, you have nothing to worry about. The highway will be perfectly safe."

"Not from what I've seen. The highway is only in the construction phase, and already it has claimed a high mortality rate."

"I promise you, this will be the last incident. You have my word that nothing bad will ever happen again to anyone working on the highway project."

"I'll believe that when I see it."

The next morning, Margaret paid a visit to Clint's office. She told him all about her visit with Greg at the Hope lock-up the previous day. "Greg's first court appearance will be Wednesday of next week at ten o'clock. In addition to presenting the opening arguments, I'll also be making an application for bail."

"Great. Dennis will be preparing a written report that will be sent to your office, and Dennis will also be willing to testify on Greg's defence." Clint went over the details of his most recent visit with the coroner.

"Fantastic. We are really getting off to a good start. By the way, you should go up to Hope and visit Greg some time soon. You haven't been going up there lately—why is that?"

"With the survey work on Portia Bench currently under suspension, there's not much point in spending any time there; I can get more work done here. Besides, my two Project Managers can run the show just fine. To be honest, I don't really like to be in Hope unless I absolutely have to. I'm paranoid I'll run into my ex-girlfriend."

"Oh, I'm sorry to hear that. Was the break up mutual?"

"No, she got back together with her ex-husband."

"I'm divorced myself, and I might add that there is no chance of that ever happening with me. I guess that's her loss. Anyway, I will see you a week from Wednesday. If you obtain any more information, give me a call."

Right after Margaret left, Clint phoned Bill Plotnikoff in Victoria to follow up on a request he made a long time ago.

"Clint, great to hear from you. How is everything going?" asked Bill.

"Well, I'm managing, but things could be better. Listen, did you or Stan ever get information on where to locate a person or group that eradicates evil spirits?"

"Oh, right, I completely forgot about it, and I never told Stan about it."

"Well, something needs to be done, and fast. Our Native spirit friend is still causing havoc, and the engineer of that runaway train doesn't know when to call it quits and head to the great beyond where he belongs."

37

MAY 1985

When Greg made his first court appearance, both the Prosecution and the Defence made their opening arguments, but the main issue was whether or not to grant bail. In the end, the Judge granted bail in the sum of $50,000. The trial date was set for August 25th.

"Mr. Matheson, thank you so much for providing the bail money. I feel bad that you had to use your Registered Retirement Savings Plan."

"Don't worry about it. It's for a cause that I believe strongly in, which is your innocence."

"I promise I won't skip town."

"I trust you. Just be back at work next Monday, okay?"

The next day, Clint met with Margaret, and gave an update of his own investigative work.

"Did you come up with anything new and exciting?" asked Margaret.

"Most definitely. Less than two weeks before Don was murdered, a news crew from CBC News was doing a story about the construction of the Coquihalla Highway, and Don was interviewed when they were up at the jobsite. During the interview, Don divulged the exact location of where he and his crew were surveying. This news feature was seen on every CBC affiliate station in BC, including up north. A large number of Don's former survey assistants live in Dawson Creek and Prince George—two places where Don was both a Crew Chief and a Project Manager. He had his share of enemies here in the Lower Mainland as well. When he gave that interview, he basically gave away his position to everybody in BC. He even mentioned that the area was very remote."

"I will get in touch with the CBC and ask for a transcript of the interview; it will be a useful tool for the Defence. Can you also provide the names of Don's former workers?" said Margaret.

"Sure, no problem."

"Can we meet again next week?"

"We sure can. Same time, same place."

The following day, back at the Vancouver office, Clint received a call from Hugh. He sounded upset.

"Clint, I've just returned from Zopkios Ridge, and realized that the crew from Onerheim Construction made a much larger than planned cut in the roadway for nearly 400 metres. When you view it from the side, it looks like one massive dip in the road. When I confronted one of the earth-mover drivers, he said that he was just following instructions from Oscar. I then went to their site office to have it out with Oscar, but the man in the office told me that Oscar was not in today."

Upon hearing this, Clint was furious. This was another case of Oscar deliberately defying Clint's authority. He wanted nothing more than to have it out with Oscar himself, but he was tied up in meetings all afternoon.

"Hugh, I'll come up to Hope tomorrow morning and will meet you in the office at nine o'clock."

During their meeting, Hugh unrolled the blueprints for that section onto the desk and went over all of the calculations for both the elevation shots and the cut-and-fill shots.

"I gave Oscar the precise specifications and expected him to adhere to them. I can't figure out why Oscar would get it wrong. I wonder if they thought the marker posts for the cut-and-fill shots were just there for decorations."

"The guy obviously has shit for brains. Come on, let's head up there and take a look for ourselves," said Clint.

"I need you all to stop what you're doing," Clint immediately ordered to the equipment operators once they reached the section in question. He then took out the level and set it up on a tripod. He handed the measuring rod and a roll of surveyor's tape over to Hugh. "Stop and hold the rod upright every ten metres." Adjusting the viewfinder on the level to a 6-percent gradient, he calculated the elevation change every ten metres. When Hugh reached a distance of 100 metres, the tape ran out, but by then it was painfully obvious that the cut was way too deep. The measuring rod was three metres too low.

When Hugh returned to where Clint was standing, he showed Clint. "See? The flaw is obvious when looking straight ahead."

"Yes, I noticed that right away. It looks like a gigantic dip in the road. Since the road is on a 6-percent gradient at this point, if a car is travelling downhill at normal speed and enters the dip, it could easily go out of control."

Clint and Hugh then made their way over to the other side of Boston Bar Creek, where they viewed the dip from the side. Even from the side, it was obvious.

"What was he thinking? You don't have to be a genius to tell that the cut was too deep," said Hugh.

"This is Oscar you're dealing with here. He is anything but a genius," said Clint. He then turned to address Oscar's equipment operators. "All of your work is suspended for the day."

Clint and Hugh then headed over to the site office.

When they stepped inside, Clint asked the young man at the desk, "Okay, where is that useless fuck-head leader of yours?"

"Oh, you mean Mr. Onerheim?" said the young man in a very polite tone.

"Of course I mean Mr. Onerheim. Where the hell is he?" said Clint, angrily.

"I don't know, he hasn't been by for the last couple days."

"Well, you better find out where he is. He has some serious explaining to do. Are you sure he is not at the Headquarters building?"

"No, I called there about an hour ago, and they said that he's not in today."

"The next time you see him, you tell him that if he makes one more screw-up, your entire company will be terminated from this project. Do you follow me?"

The next morning, Clint phoned Onerheim Construction first thing, and managed to reach Oscar in his office.

"Where the fuck have you been these last few days?"

"I had some family matters to attend to. What's your problem?"

"Your crew cut out too much on a four-hundred metre section near Zopkios Ridge. I'll be coming over to your office shortly, and will be bringing all of the blueprints and field notes on where the screw-up took place. I expect immediate action to take place, meaning I want the entire section filled to the exact specifications. There will be absolutely no deviations whatsoever. Your company is on very thin ice."

In an effort to aid in Greg's defence, Clint had been spending part of his spare time trying to dig up some dirt on Don to prove that there were many other potential suspects in his murder investigation. In the process, he learned that Don's body was finally claimed by his brother, who had it transported to his home town of Quill Lake, Saskatchewan. There was a funeral for him there, attended by his brother's family along with some of Don's childhood friends.

"I've managed to locate Don's ex-wife," Clint informed Margaret on his next visit to her law office. "She is now living in the village of Lund, which is fourteen miles north of Powell River on the Sunshine Coast. She lives with a commercial fisherman, but isn't working herself. Apparently, they took out a life insurance policy together when they were still married, and never cancelled it when they got divorced. Therefore, she would receive benefits upon his death. As for their daughter, she is supposedly living somewhere in Southern Ontario, but I'm not sure where. Neither one of them attended his funeral."

"Thank you, Clint. I've been doing some investigation work of my own. Through the RCMP, I've obtained a search warrant of Don's apartment. I found a series of IOU notes, indicating that Don had a bunch of gambling debts with some loan sharks. Apparently, he liked to bet on the horses, but he wasn't a very good handicapper."

"That's a very good clue, but don't forget, if a loan shark were to kill Don, he would never get his money back. He can't pay the loan back if he's dead," said Clint.

"I thought of that, but there's also the theory that he did pay him back, and threatened to expose him. Another theory could be that one loan shark is trying to frame another loan shark in order to have him put away, so he could move in on his territory."

"Either way you look at it, it proves that other people had motive to want Don dead—not just Greg. Man, you and I make a great team, don't we?"

"We sure do. Listen, Clint, I want to ask you something. The Mayor's annual Charity Ball is this Saturday. I'm planning to attend, but I don't have anyone to go with. Would you like to go with me?"

"Are you asking me on a date?"

"Yes, you could consider this a date."

"I would be most delighted. In fact, I would like to make the evening my treat."

"Thank you, Clint; you don't really have to do that. I would still like to make a contribution, though. All of the proceeds go to charity. Incidentally, it is a black-tie affair. You do have a formal outfit, do you?"

"Yes, and it still fits me."

Margaret gave Clint her address for him to pick her up at 5:30 p.m. on Saturday. "Cocktails are at six o'clock, and dinner is at seven. It's being held at the grand Ballroom at the Hotel Vancouver."

38

Clint arrived at the front door of Margaret's apartment building precisely at 5:30 p.m. on Saturday. Although Hotel Vancouver was only a short distance away, he thought it might take a while to find a parking spot. He wanted to make sure he arrived in time so he could have a few drinks before dinner.

Margaret's apartment was on the twenty-second floor, so it was a long elevator ride. When Margaret opened her door, Clint's eyes completely bugged out. Margaret was all decked out in an elegant sequined evening gown, but what he noticed most was the plunging neckline almost down to her navel. He thought to himself, *Man, I hope she doesn't bend over.*

"Clint, you're right on time. I like a man who's punctual. Make yourself right at home, and I'll get my coat," said Margaret.

There were numerous dignitaries and local celebrities present at the ball. Premier Davenport was even there. Clint knew that Bill would not be attending. Being a Doukhobor, he was a devout vegetarian, and the two featured items on the menu were Prime Rib and Chicken Kiev.

When Premier Davenport approached Clint and Margaret, he

said, "Clint, what a pleasant surprise. And Margaret, how nice to see you again."

"You two know each other?" said Clint and Margaret, simultaneously.

"Yes, Bill Plotnikoff introduced me to Clint; he says that Clint's the one who will push the Coquihalla Highway through in time for Expo. If there's anybody who can put a highway through any kind of terrain, Clint's the man. Margaret here has helped me with my campaign in the last three elections. I'm telling you, I don't know what I would have done without her. Did the two of you come here together?" said Premier Davenport.

"Yes, I'm her date for the evening," replied Clint.

"Well, I hope the two of you have a wonderful evening. Clint, Bill and I are going to come up and have a look at the progress on your highway some time soon. I'll be in touch."

After the dinner and the speeches, a live orchestra came out and started playing. Clint and Margaret danced the night away.

After the gala ended, Margaret invited Clint back up to her apartment. Once inside, she made martinis for both of them. Clint immediately noticed that his was heavy on the vodka and light on the vermouth. Margaret then proceeded to give a demonstration of her new stereo system, which included the latest in sound technology—the compact disc. She put on a disc of jazz music.

"Can you notice the improvement in sound quality?"

"It does sound much clearer." She insisted that they continue dancing. "I thought the ball ended way too early."

They weren't dancing very long before they began to kiss passionately.

"I could tell that you couldn't take your eyes off me all evening. You liked my choice of an evening gown? It's a Bob Mackie original," said Margaret.

"Indeed, a very wise choice. This is what I like best about it," replied Clint.

He proceeded to reach in and caress her breast. She offered no resistance whatsoever. Eventually, she led him into her bedroom.

After they were able to catch their breaths, Margaret said, "Wow, it's been ages since a man has been able to make me orgasm. I've forgotten what it felt like. You know what, all those reports I read that state that men reach their sexual peak in their teens—I think that's all a bunch of bullshit. Do you agree?"

"I don't know—I have never read any of those reports," replied Clint, a smirk on his face.

"Good, because you are proof positive that whoever wrote those articles was dead wrong.

After they cooled off, they fell asleep in each other's arms.

When Clint woke up the next morning, he looked at the clock and saw it was 9:30 a.m. He still felt groggy from the night before, so he was quite slow to get up. He could hear Margaret in the kitchen, and a few minutes later, she came into the bedroom and brought him a coffee. She was wearing a nightshirt, and it was obvious that she was wearing nothing underneath.

"I made your coffee with cream and sugar. I hope you like Eggs Benedict."

Margaret went into her closet and brought out a bathrobe, and handed it to Clint for him to wear since he didn't bring any clothes other than his suit. After breakfast, Margaret got up from the table and removed her nightshirt directly in front of him. She invited him to make love to her one more time. Clint complied.

"Consider this an honour; I normally don't sleep with my clients," Margaret said playfully.

"I'm not your client; I am your client's employer," replied Clint.

"That's right. I guess I can consider this a loophole. We can do this again some time without feeling guilty."

"Of course, but how about you come over to my place next? There's enough space between the houses so the neighbours won't hear us."

39

Ever since Clint saw Oscar, he had an uneasy feeling that something was going to go wrong again, but after two weeks, everything appeared to be going well. According to Hugh's report, the heavy equipment operators completely repaired the dip in the roadway.

Around the spot where the new highway entered the Coquihalla River Valley, there was a major obstacle in the way. Where the old KCR line crossed Boston Bar Creek, there is a massive earthen fill and a concrete abutment at the western approach to the old trestle. Originally, this was all trestlework until the fill was made in 1946. Oscar decided to use dynamite as a quicker means of removing the obstacle.

The explosives expert for Oscar's crew was Kyle. In the days leading up to the blast, he calculated the amount of dynamite that would be needed, and also put in an order for blocks of C-4, blasting caps, and detonator cord. He then gave the requisition order to Oscar, who in turn placed the order at the C-I-L Explosives Division. In all, he ordered two hundred pounds of TNT equivalent.

Three days before the blast, Kyle began drilling holes into the fill. Using a large pneumatic drill, he drilled holes horizontally three feet inside the fill. He made holes at four different levels on both sides of the fill, and packed each hole with dynamite and C-4. He then packed a generous amount of C-4 along the base and the sides of the concrete abutment. Neither Hugh nor Clint was informed that a blast was going to take place.

On the morning of the planned blast, Hugh passed by this spot around 9:00 a.m. on his way up to Zopkios Ridge. He saw Kyle stringing cords and wires all over the fill on both sides. He thought to himself, *What the hell is that guy doing?* Even then, he still hadn't heard a peep from anybody with Onerheim Construction.

When Kyle finished connecting all of the charges, he rolled the wires all the way to the site office, where he connected them to the plunger mechanism that would set off the charge.

***

Oscar was at the site office, so he went outside to check on how Kyle was doing. He told Oscar that everything was set to go, so Oscar radioed every one of his crewmembers to stay clear of the blast area, but nobody else.

"Okay, let's giv'er," said Oscar.

Oscar counted backward from ten, and once he said, "Three, two, one, *fire*," Kyle pushed the plunger handle down. A thunderous explosion of immense proportions followed. Rocks, wood, and concrete flew nearly a thousand feet into the air. The blast propelled debris outward as well.

"Quick, behind the trailer!" yelled Oscar.

Kyle and Oscar scrambled to take cover behind the site office trailer as the rocks whizzed by them. A few seconds later, Oscar happened to look up, and saw that the rocks that were propelled into the sky from the blast were now coming down, right where they were crouched.

"Get underneath the trailer, *now*," Oscar ordered to Kyle. They made it underneath just in the nick of time, as rocks and other debris began to rain down all around them.

***

Up near Zopkios Ridge, Hugh was assisting one of the crews with cut-and-fill shots alongside the Onerheim equipment crew. Hugh was manning the level with a measuring rod when all of a sudden he heard a massive blast. The blast knocked him off his feet, and his hard-hat fell off in the process. The force of the blast knocked the level over, putting a crack in the lens. A few seconds after the blast, he heard a tremendous thundering sound, like a freight train was heading right for him. *What the hell was that?*

He looked to the south and saw a huge black mushroom cloud rise into the sky. This was followed by a massive cloud of dust. Hugh's first thought was that the road crew working down the way ruptured a natural gas pipeline, but then he remembered that the pipelines run up the Coquihalla River valley, not the Boston Bar Creek valley. He knew it had to be something else.

One of the earth-mover operators from Oscar's crew climbed out of the cab of his machine and walked over to Hugh.

"Are you all right?" the operator asked Hugh. "Wow, that blowed up real good."

"You know about that? What was it?" asked Hugh, perplexed.

"That's our explosives expert, Kyle. He just blew up what's left of that old railway bridge."

"This is the first I have heard of it—nobody from your company said a goddamn thing to any of us."

"That's strange; Oscar told us all about it."

"Not only that, but what about the signs? You are supposed to have signs posted by the side of the road warning people that blasting will be taking place. Anybody coming up this way will have no idea that there will be blasting."

Just then, a scary thought came to mind. Hugh remembered that it was Wednesday, which was the usual day that Clint made his weekly trips to Hope. He knew that Clint was a die-hard morning person, so he began to wonder if Clint was on his way to see him. When he had left the office at 8:00 a.m. Clint still hadn't arrived. Hugh looked at his watch and saw that it was now 9:40 a.m. He thought about calling the Hope office on the CB radio but decided to check out the site of the blast first. Hugh got into his truck and headed down to where the blast occurred.

When Hugh arrived on the scene of the blast, the area looked like a war zone. There were boulders, smaller rocks, and broken pieces of wood scattered all over the place. One side of the Onerheim site office was pockmarked by flying rocks, and all of the windows were smashed. But by far the most significant effect of the blast was also the reason for that loud thundering sound. The blast had dislodged rock outcropping 300 feet above, causing a huge rockslide. There was a massive pile of rocks, mud, and trees over fifty feet high directly in front of him, covering the proposed roadway and obliterating all of the survey markers. It also blocked the existing road, so Hugh and everyone else up there were stranded. The far edge of the slide covered the channel of Boston Bar Creek to a depth of ten feet, creating a small lake. Oscar and Kyle, standing near the site office, both appeared completely dazed.

Hugh got out of his truck and went over to Oscar and Kyle. "What the hell happened here?"

Oscar was still in a state of shock, so he didn't say anything.

"I think I used too much dynamite," said Kyle, dumbfounded.

"What the hell were you thinking—blowing down that old railway bridge approach with dynamite? You only needed a small amount for the part that's made of concrete. The rest of the approach was made of gravel, so it could have easily been removed with a backhoe.

You could have blown everyone around here to rat shit."

Hugh went to his truck and called the Hope office on the CB radio. He hoped that Clint was in the office.

"Hugh calling Hope office—mayday, mayday."

"Clint here. What's up now?"

"Clint! Man, am I glad to hear your voice. It's a good thing you're still in the office."

"Hugh, what's going on? What is the problem?"

"The Onerheim explosives guy just blew up the approach to that old railway bridge, and he used too much dynamite. It caused a huge rockslide, and now it's all piled up over the road. It even dammed part of Boston Bar Creek."

"Whoa, back up there—I didn't know that they were going to blow up that approach. In fact, I didn't know that Onerheim even had an explosives expert at all. Were there any warning signs posted?"

"No, there were none. I had no idea there was even going to be a blast. Look, we need extra equipment up here, and fast. All of our vehicles are stranded up here."

"I'm heading up there right now. I will check out the situation for myself."

***

Clint had arrived in the Hope office only five minutes before he received Hugh's call. The night before, he had invited Margaret over to his place for dinner, and they ended up spending the night together. Needless to say, he didn't get much sleep that night. He groggily muttered a few choice swear words before leaving the office and making his way up to the site.

The minute he turned onto the Boston Bar Creek logging road, Clint saw rocks scattered all over the road. By the time he was within a hundred yards of the old trestle, the rocks strewn all over the road were scraping the undercarriage of his truck, even though it had high ground clearance. He decided to park there and walk the rest of the way. Then he reached the fifty-foot high rockslide blocking the road. *Holy shit.*

Clint realized that if he had stuck to his original schedule, he would likely have passed by this spot around the time of the blast without knowing about it. He had been planning to check on the construction progress on Zopkios Ridge as a first priority that morning.

He got to thinking about all of the articles he had read over the years regarding the benefits of sex—that now took on a whole new meaning. It had potentially saved his life. He scrambled up the side of the slide, which was not easy. There were huge boulders as well as small rocks, all loosely packed. Every time he tried to get a foothold, at least one rock would dislodge. It took him nearly a half an hour to climb up and over the slide, and all that was going through his mind was, *Somebody is going to pay for this.*

Once he was on the other side, Clint made his way up to the Onerheim site office. He could see Hugh's truck in the distance heading toward him. Behind him were two of Onerheim's bulldozers. When Hugh met up with Clint, he explained what happened, and they entered the site office together. Oscar and Kyle were both sitting at the desk.

"Alright, Oscar, I *demand* an explanation," Clint growled.

"I thought it would be easier to remove that old rail bridge with dynamite." said Oscar simply.

"Oscar, you know the rules. No blasting is to be performed without my approval, and if I do approve it, the surrounding area must be completely secured. None of these rules were followed." Clint pointed at Kyle. "Is this your demolitions expert?"

"Indeed he is."

"How much dynamite did you use?"

"Two hundred pounds."

"Two hundred pounds? Are you out of your fucking mind? That's enough to level a three-storey building. You only needed a quarter of that amount, tops. Where did you learn to use explosives?"

"I first learned about explosives when I was in the Military Engineers, and when I worked for Hudson Bay Mining at their mine in Flin Flon, I was the one who did the blasting," replied Kyle.

"Which unit were you in for the Military Engineers?"

"I belonged to 1 Combat Engineer Regiment at CFB Chilliwack."

"Do you have a Demolitions Certificate?"

"Yes, I earned my certificate when I worked for the mine in Flin Flon."

"Alright, you earned your certificate when you were in Manitoba, but what about here in BC? You must be certified here at the provincial level as well before you can handle explosives."

"Kyle here showed me his BC Certificate when I hired him, and everything is good. I have it in my office if you ever want to look at it. Now, will you please stop giving him the third degree?" said Oscar.

"Listen here, Oscar—I have every right to ask these questions. My workers pass by that spot on a regular basis. One or more of my men could have been killed. This amounts to nothing more than outright negligence. I want every piece of your equipment and every one of your workers to stop what they're doing right now and get to work removing that slide. Until that slide is cleared, nobody is going anywhere."

He then scrambled back over the rockslide toward his truck and used the CB radio to call the other crews on duty. He requested they stop what they're working on right now and bring every person and every piece of equipment over to the first mile of Boston Bar Creek Road. He then backed his truck down the road to the intersection with the Coquihalla Road so it wouldn't be in the way of the equipment. He went back to the site of the rockslide and re-joined the others.

It didn't take long before the cavalry arrived. Clint figured that the best plan of action would be to shovel downward from the top of the slide in order to allow easier access for the scooper of the backhoe. Fortunately, there were very few large boulders at the top of the slide; it was mostly small rocks and dirt, so that made the going easier.

By 3:00 p.m. Clint was completely exhausted. It was a combination of a lack of hard, physical work over the years as well as a lack of sleep. He decided to call it a day at that point. The entire crew had made some progress by then, but they still had a long way to go.

Clint offered a ride into Hope to Hugh and the survey crews working east of the slide area since their vehicles were stranded. One of the Crew Chiefs said that he had lots of room in his van, so some of the surveyors travelled back with him.

"Hugh, I'm going back to Vancouver as soon as we return to the office. I'd like you to organize a meeting with everybody once we get there, and tell Ed to be there as well. Until the slide is cleared, all survey work east of the slide area is suspended, so it must be determined if any of the other survey crews need extra help over the next day or two. Otherwise, some of the surveyors will have the day off tomorrow."

"Hey, what about us? When can we go home?" said Oscar.

"I cannot—for the life of me—believe you would ask such a question. This whole slide was the result of your fuck-up. We at the Department of Highways have a policy, which is that if you fuck it up you must fix it up. I don't give a shit if you guys are here all fucking night—I want this slide cleared, and you're not going home until that's finished. Do you understand me?" As he made his way down toward his truck, Clint said to Hugh, "As God is my witness, that Onerheim guy is history."

40

On the journey home, Clint tried his best to not fall asleep at the wheel. He just wanted to get home and go straight to bed, but Margaret wanted to return the favour by inviting him over to her place for dinner.

"You look like you've had a rough day," Margaret said to him over dinner.

"You don't know the half of it. I'm having problems with one of my construction companies, Onerheim Construction. I'm completely at my wits' end."

"Wait a minute, did you say Onerheim Construction? The one run by Oscar Onerheim?"

"That's the one. You know him?"

"Of course I know him. I represented him on two different occasions in class-action lawsuits. Believe me, those were not stellar moments in my illustrious career."

"Why does that not surprise me?"

The next morning, he packed his suitcase to stay over in Hope that night. On the way up to Hope, he took a detour over to CFB

Chilliwack, and paid a visit to Major Stillwell at the headquarters for 1 Combat Engineer Regiment. Little did Kyle know that Clint had a long association with the regiment. For all the years Clint had been with the Department of Highways, the regiment had helped out on numerous occasions, building Bailey bridges whenever Provincial highway bridges were washed out as a result of flooding. As a result, Clint got to know the Commanding Officer, Major Morley Stillwell, very well.

"Mr. Matheson, what a surprise it is to see you here. You must know that records of all Military personnel are kept confidential, so I won't be able to provide any information on anyone's track record. All I could do is say when Kyle Redekopp was in the service. However, we don't have records of anyone with the name 'Redekopp' ever serving in the Regiment. What does the guy look like?"

"Well, he's big and fat, fairly mean looking, and has long red hair. He looks quite young, like he's in his twenties," replied Clint.

"Then he would be in our recent files, which is not the case. If he is that young, he would have been in the unit recently, and I would remember him. Why are you asking about him?"

"He works for this construction company that is building the new highway east of Hope, and he claims to be an expert on demolitions. He told me that he first learned to use explosives while serving in your unit."

"If he told you he learned about explosives while serving in my unit, he's feeding you a crock of shit. Our Demolitions Training course is very intensive, and only a select few pass. I don't know who this guy is, but you better find out before he kills somebody."

"Don't worry, sir, I will definitely find out. Thanks for your time."

When Clint arrived at the Hope office, he decided to do some more research on this so-called "demolition expert". He phoned long-distance information, and asked for the number of Hudson Bay Mining Company mine in Flin Flon, Manitoba. Once he obtained the number, he phoned them and asked to speak to the Human Resources Manager.

"Yes, I would like some information on a former employee of yours—Kyle Redekopp. He is applying for a position as an Explosives Expert with my company, and is using your company as a reference."

After a moment's silence, the HR Director said, "I'm sorry, sir, but there is no record of anybody by that name ever working for this company. As for anybody working with explosives here, we have had the same people for at least ten years."

"Very well, then. Sorry to bother you."

After he hung up the phone, Clint wanted to strangle Oscar. He decided at this point that this was the final straw. He headed up to the site of the rockslide. After scrambling up to the top, he spotted Oscar and the Onerheim crew manning the shovels. Clint summoned Oscar into the site office, and Hugh followed.

"That so-called demolition expert of yours is a phoney. When you hired him, you never even checked his references. I had to do that for you, and do you want to know what I found out? He never worked for any of the places he mentioned. He doesn't know a goddamn thing about explosives and he forged his demolitions certificate. Do you even know if Kyle Redekopp is his real name? He could be a bloody terrorist for all we know. You were supposed to follow up and make sure this guy was qualified for the job, considering its nature. He could very well do that again, and next time, when you bring him the dynamite, he could disappear. He could then blow up a military installation or a landmark."

"Wait a minute—I admit I was a little over-trusting of the guy, but if it makes you happy, I fired him yesterday," said Oscar.

"That won't make any difference. You should never have hired him in the first place. You have made many mistakes over the years, and it has cost the Highways Ministry thousands of extra dollars as well as major delays. You and your company are terminated from this project. If you try to sue me for breach of contract, you won't have a hope in Hell of winning. I want all of your men and equipment off this project, effective immediately."

"I'm telling you, you're going to pay for this. Mark my words," said Oscar, as he stormed out the door.

"What did he mean by that?" asked Hugh, sounding concerned.

"I wouldn't worry about it, Hugh. We've seen the last of him," replied Clint.

41

JUNE 1985

One week later, Clint received a surprise visit from Bill at the Hope office.

"Good to see you, Bill. Listen, I was hoping we could touch base on what we talked about a while back."

"I know. That's what I came to discuss. Can we talk about it over lunch?"

"Sure, let's head over to the Kootenay Central Restaurant."

"I'll be honest, Clint. We're not having any luck finding any person or group who eradicates evil spirits. Stan looked through the library at the Legislature, and I looked in the library at the university. I looked under the headings for Paranormal Activity, Psychic Phenomena, and even Ghost Encounters. When I asked the librarian if they had any information on evil spirits, she looked at me like I was some kind of weirdo."

"Maybe she knew who you were and she supports the opposition party."

"Very funny."

Throughout their conversation, they were oblivious to the fact that Edwin Baptiste was having coffee in the booth next to them. It was at this point that Edwin made his presence known.

"Hello, gentlemen, how's everything going? Not so well, from what I hear."

"Look, Chief, if you're going to rub our noses into it and tell us 'I told you so', then you can zip it, okay? We don't need this right now," said Clint.

"You really want this highway project to go through, don't you?" asked Edwin.

"What do you think? Construction has already started, and most of the surveying has been completed. It's too late to turn back now," said Clint.

"Listen, I can help you guys out." Edwin sat down in their booth.

"What—*you* help us out?" asked Clint, astonished.

"Meet me at my office. We can talk about it," said Edwin as he put some change on the table to cover his tab.

As Edwin left, Clint and Bill gave each other blank stares. After some deliberation, they agreed to see how Edwin thought he could help.

"First of all, Chief, why the change of heart?" Clint asked, once he and Bill had arrived at Edwin's Band office later that afternoon.

"Look, I've come to realize that maybe this highway isn't so bad after all. One thing is for sure—it will take a lot of the traffic off the Fraser Canyon, and we can then have easier access to our fishing grounds. And like you said, it will boost tourism in the area."

"That's what I've been trying to tell you all along. So, what do you have in mind?"

"When I was younger, I was taught a ceremonial dance that drives away evil spirits. My people have performed this dance for many generations with great success. If you were to get someone from outside our tribe, Siaman wouldn't understand them. I speak fluent Halq'eméylem, so he'll get my message. I still remember how to do the ceremonial dance, and I'll do it for you if you want."

"Well, that's very admirable of you, Chief. Sure, go for it. You name the time and place."

"Whoa—not so fast. I'm not going to do this for free. I want to get paid."

"Alright, what's your asking price?" asked Clint.

"Wait a minute. If there's money involved, we have to get approval from the Premier," interrupted Bill. "Chief, would you like to come to Victoria and meet with Premier Davenport along with myself and my assistant Stan Fisher?"

"That's fine with me; I'd love to come to Victoria."

"We can even travel there together," said Clint.

"No, I would rather go there on my own. I have an old friend of mine who lives on the Cowichan Reserve. I haven't seen him in ages; it'll be nice to visit him."

"I'll pay for your round-trip fare on the ferry, Chief," said Bill.

"Since you're in such a generous mood, Mr. Highways Minister, how about throwing in afternoon tea at the Empress Hotel?"

"Alright, if you insist."

Three days later, Bill phoned Clint at the Hope office. They arranged a meeting for next Saturday afternoon at 1:00 p.m. with Premier Davenport. Clint then phoned Edwin and passed the information along.

Everyone arrived right on time for the meeting on Saturday. Edwin arrived all decked out in a three-piece suit. Clint looked quite surprised.

"Chief, why are you all dressed up?"

"When you're having tea at the Empress, you have to look your best. You should know that, Clint."

"Chief Baptiste, it is my understanding that you can perform a ceremonial dance and ritual that can get rid of evil spirits. Is that correct?" asked Premier Davenport.

"Yes, that is correct."

"What makes you think that performing this dance will make this so-called ghost disappear?" asked Premier Davenport.

"Our people of the In-Sha-Tla'tkw have an understanding of each other, and we always have a deep respect for the wishes of others. Since we speak the same language, we have an easier time communicating. This dance was performed long before Siaman was around, so he will get the message that it is time for him to travel to the great beyond."

"Do you believe this will have an influence on the other so-called ghosts that have been sighted in the area?" asked Premier Davenport.

"Most definitely. Once Siaman is cast off, any other spirits in the immediate area will realize their presence is no longer welcome, so they will follow suit."

"Just imagine, once he's in heaven, Siaman will have his own pet circus elephant," said Clint, sarcastic.

"Okay, Chief, if you're convinced this ceremonial dance will work, what's your asking price?"

"Glad you asked that, Mr. Premier. I'm asking fifty thousand dollars."

"Fifty thousand dollars? Are you out of your mind?"

"Take it or leave it."

"What do you need that much for?"

"Normally, Indian Affairs is a Federal jurisdiction, but with all of the budget cutbacks they've been making lately, my Reserve has not been getting as much funding lately. Since your Government likes to spend copious amounts of money on this new highway, it shouldn't make that much difference spending a little bit extra, which will benefit my people in the long run."

"Well, I got news for you—you can kiss my ass. Forget it."

"Now wait a minute, Mike. Let's not make any quick decisions here. Chief Baptiste may be our only hope. I suggest we talk it over first," said Bill.

"I realize it may sound like a lot, but you need to ask yourselves what's more important. I'll let you gentlemen think it over. But my offer stands. I must go now. I want to enjoy some tea courtesy of our distinguished Highways Minister."

After Edwin left, Premier Davenport looked like he was ready to explode.

"Who the hell does that guy think he is? How do we know he's not just trying to pull a fast one?"

"Mike, let's not jump to conclusions. I'm sure he knows what he's doing," said Bill.

"He seems legitimate," said Stan.

"We also have another problem. My recently appointed Finance Minister is really into cutting expenses."

"Well, I believe this is none of my concern; I'm merely along for the ride. But I will tell you this much: I saw first-hand what this Siaman dude is capable of. Believe me, this isn't Casper we're dealing with. If there is anyone who can send him to the great beyond where he belongs, Edwin's the man. Anyway, I better head back to the mainland," said Clint.

"This meeting is officially adjourned," said Premier Davenport.

As Clint prepared to leave, Premier Davenport asked to speak to him in private.

"What did you want to see me about, Mr. Premier?"

"Well Clint, I really must congratulate you. Tell me something, you fancy yourself as quite the ladies man, don't you?"

"I'm afraid I don't follow," said Clint with a puzzled look.

"Don't play coy with me, Matheson. I'm talking about Margaret. I saw how she was all over you that night. So, how was it? Was she a good lay? What's your secret? Do you have a fourteen-inch cock or something?"

Clint was absolutely aghast that he would ask such a question.

"Sir, I really beg to differ, but what goes on between Margaret and me is strictly between us. Why is this any concern of yours?"

"Do you realize how many years I have been trying to get inside her pants? I've had no success, but you—you score with her right from the start."

"Mr. Premier—you're married!" Clint was horrified.

"Hey, that hasn't stopped me before."

On his way back to Vancouver, Clint continuously shook his head in disbelief at the thought of the BC Premier actually being jealous of him. As if that weren't enough, there was also the fact that he admitted to him that he is unfaithful to his wife. Clint wondered how in the world he would ever be able to face Mrs. Davenport again, knowing this secret. But then, he realized that she rarely appears in public; whenever the Premier attends a function, it is always on his own. *Maybe their marriage is strained already. Who knows?*

It was two weeks before Bill got back to Clint. In that time, Clint wondered if Bill and Stan would be unable to convince the Premier that Edwin was the best way to go. But then, he received the phone call he had been waiting for while he was at his Vancouver office.

"I'm sorry I didn't get back to you sooner; I've been very busy with the Legislature," said Bill.

"Don't worry about it. So, what's the story?"

"It's all approved. Stan and I managed to convince Mike to give the ritual a try. He approved it under one condition—that he will be present when the ritual is performed. As for our finances guy, I was able to successfully bullshit my way into having the fifty grand approved. I made up this story about an unexpected rise in the cost of construction materials, and he fell for it hook, line, and sinker.

That guy is so gullible."

"Okay, so when will you guys be heading up to Hope?"

"We're planning to leave here tomorrow morning. Will that work for you?"

"Sure, let's all meet at the Hope office tomorrow afternoon."

"Now, I want to make this very clear; this must be kept in complete secrecy. Do not utter a word about this to anyone, including any family members," said Bill.

"Hey, my lips are sealed."

Clint then phoned Edwin at the Band office.

"Chief, I've got some good news. The ceremony is a go. I promise that Bill will bring along a bank draft. You are to perform the ceremony tomorrow night."

"That will work out just fine. Be sure and bring along lots of firewood, as we will need to build a big bonfire. I'm going to bring along my sons Terry and Leon, along with Cindy, to play the drums," said Edwin.

"Whoa, back up there—you never said that Cindy would be part of the performance. What the hell do you need her there for?"

"Her drumming ability, along with her dancing, will play an integral role. You're not still mad at her, are you?"

"What do you think? She dumped me for that bastard."

"I'll have you know that she has since split up with Claude for good. She tells me quite often that she misses you."

"Chief, there's an old saying: where you make your own bed, you sleep in it. I will have you know, I have a new lady friend in my life, so if she has any thoughts about us getting back together, she is shit out of luck," Clint said sourly.

Clint then phoned Hugh at the Hope office and explained what would be happening tomorrow.

"Now, Hugh, you must not tell anyone, including Ed. Please tell Ed that his weekly meeting with the Project Managers will be postponed until the following day, so there will be no need for him to go to the Hope office at the end of the work day tomorrow. You should bring your sleeping bag and tell your wife that you will be staying overnight up at the site.

The next day, everyone arrived at the Hope office by 4:30 p.m. Premier Davenport was incognito, wearing a baseball cap and large sunglasses. As expected, he gave Clint a rather chilly reception. When Cindy entered the office, she was cordial.

"Hello, Clint, how are you doing?"
"I'm getting by all right. How's everything going with you?"
"I'm coping the best I can. I still think about you a lot."
"Oh, I bet you do."

Everyone agreed to have dinner then, so Clint ordered six large pizzas and had them delivered to the office.

On their way out, Bill showed Clint his new mobile phone, which the Premier had issued to all of his Cabinet Ministers. When the antenna was fully extended, it was nearly two feet long.

"The Premier can now contact me from anywhere as long as it's within a hundred-and-twenty-mile radius of Victoria."

"Wow, what will they think of next," Clint commented.

When everyone arrived up on Portia Bench, Edwin, Terry, Leon, and Cindy all changed into their ceremonial regalia. Cindy's outfit did not leave much to the imagination, bringing back memories of Clint's intimate evenings with her. This was something that Clint had long since tried to put out of his mind—to no avail, evidently.

They had trouble finding level ground where they could pitch their tents, so the tents all looked lopsided once they were up. By that time, the sun was going down. Clint got the bonfire started, and by the time it was completely dark, it was going really well—its flames even reached over six feet in height.

"Okay, let's get the festivities started," said Bill.

Premier Davenport, Bill, Stan, Hugh, and Clint all sat together on a log. Terry, Leon, and Cindy began beating their drums and chanting, while Edwin began what must have been the ceremonial dance. Every few minutes Edwin would pause, look up into the heavens, and say some words in Halq'eméylem in a loud tone while waving a stick in the air. This process continued with little variation for nearly an hour. Clint noticed that Stan, who was sitting next to him, had his eyes completely fixated on Cindy.

"Clint, check her out. Man, she is one hot-looking babe."

"I ought to know. I used to go out with her."

"You used to go out with her? Jeez, Clint, how did you let her slip through your fingers?" asked Stan.

"Look, she dumped me, okay? Now, if you don't mind, I don't want to talk about it."

"But she's so gorgeous—"

"Stan, I'm not telling you again. Put a sock in it, will you?"

Premier Davenport, who by now was getting somewhat annoyed, said, "What the hell does he think this is, *Dance Fever*? Are you sure this crackpot knows what he's doing?"

"Mr. Premier, remember that saying about ye who has little faith? Just trust him, okay?" said Clint.

"If word ever gets out that we spent fifty thousand dollars of taxpayer's money to bring this asshole here, we will be completely fucked. If this ritual of his doesn't work, it will be all for nothing," said Premier Davenport.

"Mike, will you calm down? Lay off Clint. I was the one who talked you into it, so I will take responsibility. Don't worry about anybody finding out; we are the only ones up here," said Bill.

After ten more minutes of dancing and chanting, Edwin once more raised his arms high in the air, holding the stick in his left hand, when all of a sudden, there was a massive clap of thunder so loud that the ground shook. The men looked up, but there wasn't a cloud in the sky. This was followed by a blood-curdling scream, which was distinctively a male voice.

Bill pointed upward and shouted out, "Look, up there!"

Clint and Hugh looked up to see the Native ceremonial mask levitating in the air thirty feet above them. It then shot up into the sky and fizzled.

"Goodbye, Siaman," said Clint in a sombre tone.

Now that Stan had a focal point other than Cindy's body, he was obviously frightened by the whole spectacle. He was holding on to Clint for dear life.

"Uh, Stan, you can let go of me now? I strongly advise you to save the intimacy for when you get home to your wife."

"Do you think it worked?" asked Stan.

"I guess we'll find out in due time," replied Clint. "Let's give a round of applause to Edwin. You did an excellent job. This calls for a celebration."

Clint reached into his backpack and pulled out a flask filled with whiskey. He also took out six shot glasses, and offered a drink to anyone who was interested. The only ones who took him up on his offer were Premier Davenport, Stan, and Hugh; Edwin, Terry, Leon, and Cindy declined. He didn't expect Bill to take up the offer, since he knew that Doukhobors didn't drink. When Stan took a big gulp from the shot glass, he nearly gagged. Clint figured that Stan didn't drink very much.

"Stan, you have to drink it in moderation; it's pretty potent stuff," said Clint.

Hugh and Clint agreed to share the same tent. Before everyone bedded down for the night, Clint asked if anyone was interested in having their drinks topped up.

When everyone declined, Clint muttered to himself, "Okay, screw you guys. I'm going to get loaded." He proceeded to polish off the flask while he sat on the log and watched the fire die down.

It took him fifteen minutes to stagger from the log to the tent.

The following morning, Clint awoke at 5:00 a.m. He ended up sleeping on a hard, uneven patch of ground, so when he woke up, his back was killing him. Not only that, but his head was also throbbing wildly, and his mouth felt as dry as a wool sweater. Being unable to go back to sleep, he decided to get up and extinguish the bonfire from last night. The only piece of equipment he had to work with was a hatchet, since nobody thought to bring along a shovel. By 6:00 a.m. the fire was completely out. It was at this time that he woke everybody else up.

"Gee, Clint, do you feel well enough to work today?" asked Bill.

"Sorry, Bill, I just felt like celebrating last night. I assure you, I feel up to working today."

"That's good to hear, because I'm coming back up here in three days to see how the job is going, and I plan to stay for a few days."

"Super, I look forward to seeing you then."

Back at the Hope office, Clint made a pot of strong coffee in the hopes it would help cure his hangover. He had just sat down at his desk when Ed came bursting through the front door, yelling out, "Clint, where the hell have you been? I've been trying to get a hold of you all last evening. I tried your Vancouver office, the office here, and even your house. Where were you?"

To Clint, Ed's voice seemed ten times louder than it really was. "Ed, you work for me, so it's none of your damn business where I was last night," Clint shot back.

Ed saw Clint's dishevelled appearance as well as the distinct smell of alcohol on his breath.

"Jeez, man, you look like shit. You must have had quite the wild night. Who was she?" asked Ed.

Clint glared at Ed, pounded his fist on the desk, and said, "For the last time, Ed, what I do in my off hours is my business. Now, what was it you wanted to see me about?"

"It's the new construction company. Talks between management and their union broke off last night, so they're going on strike."

"Oh, is that all? Tell their union leader that if they go on strike, it will be a cold day in Hell before they ever get a Government contract again. Those morons should be thankful they have a bloody job, considering how the economy is. Give them a week; they'll come to their senses. That will be all, Ed. Good day."

42
JULY 1985

A backlog of paperwork at the Vancouver office meant that Clint was unable to resume surveying on Portia Bench until the following Monday. When the day finally came, Clint and Hugh had to figure out what to do about a new Crew Chief, since Don was dead. Eventually, Clint decided that it had been years since he had any hands-on experience with manning a transit, so there was no better time than the present to brush up on his transit skills.

Hugh seemed rather surprised by Clint's decision. "But, Clint, what about all your other work?"

"I am pretty much caught up on everything else. Basically, my only role now is to get progress reports from you and Ed and do follow-up reports with the construction companies. I need an excuse to get out of the office and into the field again. Besides, I will find out first-hand if my field note calculations were accurate. If not, we are definitely up shit creek without a paddle."

Their next priority was to round up the members of the crew who were scattered among different crews after surveying on the bench was suspended. Clint called Greg and Kevin into his office.

"Gentlemen, surveying on Portia Bench will resume, and I will be your new Crew Chief." Clint paused for dramatic effect. "I can tell from the look on your faces that you were not expecting this. Don't think of me as the 'big boss' on the jobsite, okay? I'm just one of the boys. By the way, I'll take care of the fourth person."

Clint then phoned the Vancouver office and informed Ted that he required the services of Cody for the remainder of the surveying. "Tell him to pack his bags and be here in Hope tomorrow morning."

Once they were up at the jobsite, Clint set up the transit at the exact spot where the last survey post was pounded into the ground. He decided to carry on with the centre baseline for the westbound lane until it connected with the survey marker for the same baseline at the other end. He was anxious to find out if his calculations were correct.

The going was very slow that day. The ground was still soggy as a result of a torrential downpour the previous night. By the end of the day, they completed the second-last kilometre. There was only one kilometre to go before one baseline was completed from one end to the other.

The most important thing Clint noticed that day was that neither he nor any other of the men on the crew saw or heard anything out of the ordinary. There were no sounds of Native drums, no Native masks flying through the air, no elephants, and most importantly, no man in the grey-and-white striped overalls. So far, so good.

The next day, the soggy conditions were not any better. It poured buckets all morning, and the ground was an absolute quagmire. At one point, Clint considered packing it in for the day. But, by noon, the rain stopped and the sun came out.

At around 1:00 p.m. they were down to their last thirty metres of baseline. It was the moment of truth. Greg, as head chainman, proceeded forward, and when Kevin, as rear chainman, yelled, "Stop," indicating that thirty metres had been reached, Greg saw that he was directly over the survey stake for the other end. He removed the stake, took out the plumb bob, pulled the chain tight, and held the plumb bob string right over the thirty-metre mark. Even though he was directly over the hole where the stake was, if they were out even a couple millimetres, there would be a major problem. When the plumb bob stopped swinging like a pendulum, he nervously called out, "Mark ... mark ... mark," and let it fall with its own weight to the ground. It landed squarely where the stake used to be—a perfect alignment. Greg was overjoyed, and let out a resounding, "Alright—yeehaw!"

Clint left his post at the transit and ran over to where Greg was.

"Look—the plumb bob landed squarely in the hole where the stake is."

Clint noted the position of the plumb bob, and then looked at the calculations he made in his field notebook.

"Excellent, my calculations were bang-on, Damn, I'm good," said Clint.

The crew spent a few moments congratulating each other, but then Clint brought them back down to reality.

"Gentlemen, I hate to burst your bubbles, but we have thirteen more baselines to run at two kilometres each. After that, we have to take all the elevation shots. This all has to be completed before the end of summer. We still have a long ways to go. We'll have to save the celebrating until after this project is completed."

When they returned to the Hope office at the end of the work day, Bill was there waiting for them.

"Bill, I'm surprised to see you here," said Clint.

"I said that I wanted to see how the project was coming along, remember? So here I am."

Bill was staying at the same motel as Clint, and was only four doors down from him.

"Why don't you come over for dinner tonight, Clint? We have a lot to talk about."

"Sounds good. What are you making for dinner?"

"Chinese ... takeout, that is."

That evening, Clint told Bill the news they had both been hoping for.

"Well, Bill, Edwin's ceremonial dance appears to be working. There haven't been any incidents, and nobody has seen anything out of the ordinary."

Bill was delighted. "That's great news. Perhaps that outrageous expense was actually worth it ... I just hope that it always remains a secret."

43

Bill visited Clint and his crew up at the jobsite the next morning. He was pleased to see the progress that the crew made, and was even more pleased when Clint informed him that all the survey work would be completed within the next couple months. Bill then left to visit with the other survey crews working in different locations on the project. Later in the afternoon, he returned to where Clint and his crew were working, and when their work for the day was completed, Bill followed behind Clint's truck when they returned to Hope.

***

When they arrived at the Hope office, Linda caught Clint's attention.

"Clint, some man had been phoning the office all day asking to speak to you. He wouldn't give his name, but he kept repeating that he *had* to speak to Clint Matheson, and that it was important. I wasn't able to give him an exact time that you would be returning to the office, since it varies from day to day."

"Alright, Linda. Well, thanks for letting me know. Maybe he'll call back."

Clint spent the next half hour entering his calculations into the computer. All the while he was there, this man of mystery never called back. Clint was getting hungry by then, so he didn't feel like sticking around any longer.

Linda was getting ready to leave as well, so Clint said to her, "Whoever this guy was, it couldn't have been that important. I'll tell you what. If he phones anytime tomorrow, tell him that I will be back here before five, so he can call me right at five o'clock." He turned to Bill. "Bill, do you fancy Italian tonight?"

That sounds great, but I didn't think there was an Italian restaurant in Hope."

"Technically, there isn't, but the restaurant in Silver Creek makes superb spaghetti and meat balls."

The next day, Bill spent most of the day observing the construction of the Dry Gulch Bridge. Later in the day, he revisited Clint and his crew, and stayed there until they were finished for the day. They all returned to Hope together, and when they arrived back at the office, it was 4:50 p.m. Sure enough, at 5:00 p.m. the phone rang.

When Clint answered the phone, the voice at the other end said, "Clint, long time, no see." It was Oscar.

"Oscar, you were the one who has been phoning here asking for me? What's this all about? There is no way your construction company is coming back here."

"No, that's okay. I accept full responsibility for my mistakes."

"Alright, what is it you wanted to talk to me about?"

"Since you dumped me from the project, I've been having trouble finding new contracts."

"That doesn't surprise me one bit."

"Not to worry, I've decided to expand my horizons. That's the reason for my call. I have a business proposition for you."

"Me doing business with you? Fat chance."

"Come on, Clint, don't jump to conclusions. I realize we have had our differences, but I want to make it up to you. I have something you'll be very interested in, so I strongly advise you to come over to my place and take a look at it. You can make a decision from there."

"Oscar, I don't believe there could possibly be anything of yours I would ever be interested in."

"Like I said, Clint, don't be so judgemental. All I ask is you come over and take a look at what I have for you, and if you're not interested, that's perfectly fine with me."

"Alright, you win. I'll come over and take a look at whatever it is you have."

"Splendid. I am at the Fraser Canyon Motel, Room 108. Come by in fifteen minutes. Oh by the way, bring the fucking commie with you."

"Commie? Who are you talking about?"

"Plotnikoff, you idiot. There's something in it for him, too." He hung up.

"Who was that on the phone?" asked Hugh.

"That was Oscar Onerheim, that useless tit who runs Onerheim Construction. He's the one who always managed to fuck up everything he did. He says he has something he wants to show me and wants me to meet him at the Fraser Canyon Motel in fifteen minutes."

"I don't know about this. It might be a trap," said Hugh, concerned.

"Not only that—he wants Bill to come with me," said Clint.

"Me? What does he want me for?" said Bill, sounding very surprised.

"Well, I guess we're going to have to go over there and find out."

"Clint, be careful. I don't trust this guy," said Hugh.

"Don't worry, Hugh. I know how to handle him. We'll be all right. Come on, Bill, let's see what this asshole has for us."

Clint and Bill made their way over to the Fraser Canyon Motel, and when they arrived there, Clint knocked on the door of Room 108. Oscar answered the door, and was in a very jovial mood.

"Clint, how nice to see you. Come on in. No hard feelings, eh? Mr. Plotnikoff, this is indeed a pleasure. I have never met a Provincial Cabinet Minister face-to-face before," said Oscar.

One of the first things Clint noticed in Oscar's room was the Panasonic VHS player situated on the counter beside the television set, with all of the cables connected into the back of the set. He had never seen a VCR in a motel room before.

Oscar saw Clint eyeing the VCR. "That VCR unit, it's mine. It doesn't belong to the motel. Check it out, guys. The VHS is the latest in video technology. It will soon make the Betamax Machine obsolete. It's a good thing this motel has new TV sets. The outlets are compatible with the cable connections."

Clint was just about to ask Oscar what he wanted to show him when there was a knock at the door.

Oscar said, "Excuse me," and proceeded to answer the door. It was Kyle. He was wearing a large trench coat with a sinister expression on his face to match.

"Clint, you remember Kyle," said Oscar.

Kyle never said any type of greeting. He just reached into the inside pocket of the trench coat, and pull out a .38 calibre handgun. He pointed the gun at Clint and Bill, and ordered them to sit on the couch.

"Whoa, now, take it easy," Clint was both horrified, as was Bill. All Clint kept thinking was, *Hugh was right—this* is *a trap.*

"Gentlemen, there is no need to fear anything. Just do as I tell you, and nobody will get hurt. Now, as I said over the phone, I have branched out my business endeavours. I have now become a documentary filmmaker. I invited the two of you over to view my latest film project. I hope that if you like the film you will purchase it," said Oscar, calmly.

Oscar turned on the television and the VCR. He then took out a videocassette and put it into the VCR. He spent the next several minutes muttering to himself, trying to figure out which remote does which function. Eventually, he got it going.

"Okay, gentlemen, sit back, relax, and enjoy the show."

"How the hell can we relax with him pointing a gun at us?" said Clint, nervously.

"Oh, right. Kyle, it's okay, put the gun down."

When the video started, the first image the men saw was a large bonfire at nighttime. They could clearly see Premier Davenport, Bill, Stan, Clint, and Hugh sitting on a log near the fire. As Edwin began the dance, Clint came to the sad realization that while the ritual was going on, Oscar had been hiding in the nearby grove of trees that escaped the forest fire, and filmed the entire thing.

Fifteen minutes into the video, Oscar commented, "You can see how these latest models of camcorders have superior picture and sound quality, and they can pick up every word anyone says."

This was especially notable when Premier Davenport uttered the line, "If word ever gets out that we spent fifty thousand dollars of taxpayer's money to bring this asshole here, we will be completely fucked."

"You're telling me you paid that fucking moron fifty grand to dance around and wave a stick in the air for an hour? I could have done that," Oscar said in disgust. He then made his offer to Bill and Clint. "This tape is the only copy of the video I have, and it can be yours if you want it. But it comes with a price."

"How much are you asking?" asked Bill.

"Glad you asked that, Mr. Highways Minister. Since you had no problem paying that clown fifty thousand dollars, this tape will cost you double."

"A hundred thousand dollars? That's outrageous," said Bill.

"Outrageous? You think this is outrageous, but paying that guy fifty grand wasn't? As far as I'm concerned, there's no difference. I'll tell you what—I will be fair. I'll give you two weeks to decide what you want to do. If, after two weeks, you don't have the money or don't want to buy it, that's perfectly okay with me … but I know of another party who would be very interested in seeing this video: the media. They would love to see a classic example of their elected officials squandering their hard-earned tax dollars."

Oscar removed the tape from the VCR and handed it to Kyle. He then brought up another item of interest.

"Plotnikoff, I have something else here, which might be of interest to you. You heard that old saying that it pays to have friends in high places? Well, as it turns out, a good friend of mine works for the *Nelson Daily News*, and he came across some very interesting pictures in the archives. During the fifties, there was this staff member of the *Daily News* who regularly took pictures whenever there was a Doukhobor uprising. God bless him for having that foresight. In 1957, one of the Doukhobor leaders was on trial for blowing up a KCR bridge, and a group of his fellow 'Freedomites' decided to stage a protest in front of the Nelson Courthouse. You know that type of protest where everybody strips naked?"

Kyle reached into the other inside pocket of his trench coat, pulled out a black-and-white photograph, and handed it to Oscar. Oscar then showed the photograph to Bill. The photo was of a group of "Sons of Freedom" Doukhobors staging a protest in front of the Nelson Courthouse. Nobody in the photograph was wearing clothes.

"Isn't that your dad? Your mom? And your grandmother, right? I must say, your mama sure had a nice rack on her. Well, at least she did back then. Your grandma sure had a bad case of sagging tits; I would actually pay her to put her clothes on. Tell me something, was your dad's nickname Needle Dick?" Oscar sneered as he ran his finger across the photograph.

Bill glared at Oscar and looked like he wanted to take a run at him. Kyle pointed the gun at him and cocked it.

"Don't get any ideas. Don't even think about trying to take the tape. Kyle will be watching my back all the time. There's one more thing I want to add—no cops. If you get the police involved, the tape goes straight to the media. Besides, it's your word against ours, and without the tape, there's not a shred of evidence to prove your case. Now, Kyle will show you guys to the door. When you're ready to deal, you know where to find me."

"Alright you two, get out. Don't come back until you are ready to make a deal," said Kyle as he pointed the gun at them again.

On the way back to the motel, Bill and Clint didn't say one word to each other.

When they arrived there and entered Clint's unit, Bill completely lost it. "How the hell did this happen? How did he know about it?"

"How the hell should I know? I never told anybody about it."

"Oh man, what are we going to do now?"

"I don't know, but I know one thing for sure. We are not going to give in to him. As far as I'm concerned, that is out-and-out blackmail."

"But if that video is released to the media, both my career and Stan's are over, and so is Mike's. This could bring down the Government altogether."

"Look, we have two weeks. Hopefully we can devise a plan to get that video without paying that asshole one cent."

Clint didn't get one wink of sleep that night. When he went over to Bill's unit, he could tell that Bill didn't sleep either. They decided to go over to the restaurant next door for breakfast, but they both ended up only having coffee. Clint suggested to Bill that he take an extra large cup of coffee with him on the trip to the ferry terminal so he could stay awake.

As usual, Clint was the first one to arrive at the Hope office. He wondered if he would be able to function at work. He could barely see straight, which would be a problem if he were to run the transit. At least it was Friday.

"Gee, Clint, you look like shit," said Hugh as he arrived at the office.

"I couldn't sleep last night, and I'm not feeling well. Listen, what's on your agenda for today?"

"I'm adding up the construction costs so far for the section between Lear and Deneau Creek, and I'm doing a cost projection for the next week."

"You know what, that can wait until Monday. I was wondering if you could lead the crew today."

"Sure, I can do that."

"Thanks, Hugh. I know I can always count on you. By the way, we have a problem."

"A problem? What is it?"

"It's very serious, but I don't want to talk about it here. We can talk about it on Monday in private."

"You have good timing. My wife has a meeting on Monday night, so I'm on my own for dinner. You can come over to my place."

44

Once Clint arrived at his own house that day, he went straight to bed. At 2:00 p.m. the telephone ringing rudely interrupted his sleep. When he answered the phone, it was Bill.

"Clint, I tried to reach you at the Hope office, and also at the Vancouver office. What the hell are you doing at home?"

"Bill, don't start in on me, okay? I have been putting in ten- or twelve-hour days all this week, and considering what we went through last night and the fact that I never slept, you should cut me some slack."

"The reason I am calling is that Mike wants to see you in his office."

"Oh God, I don't need this right now." He sighed. "Okay, I'll come over there tomorrow."

"Can't you come over today?"

"Bill, it's Friday afternoon, and it's the first weekend of summer. The ferry terminal is going to be a fucking madhouse. I don't feel like sitting in the ferry line-up for four hours, especially now, since I feel like shit. If you will just let me get some bloody sleep, I'll catch the early ferry tomorrow morning."

After Clint got off the phone with Bill, he unplugged both of his phones and went back to sleep. He slept until early evening.

The following morning, Clint caught the ferry to Victoria, and he prepared to face the wrath of Premier Davenport.

As expected, Premier Davenport was in a foul mood when Clint arrived at his office. Bill was in there as well. Once Clint was inside, Premier Davenport got right down to business.

"Can you explain to me how the hell this happened?" asked Premier Davenport.

"As I said to Bill, I have absolutely no idea. I never said a word about it to anyone," replied Clint.

"Well, someone must have told him. Otherwise, how would he have known we were up there at that time and knew what we were doing?"

"For the last time, I don't know how he found out. If I knew anything, I would tell you."

Premier Davenport still didn't seem convinced that Clint.

"Could you have inadvertently blurted out something to someone?"

"No." Clint vehemently denied telling anything to anyone.

"Why don't you come out and say 'I'm a goddamn liar, Mr. Premier'? Are you sure you didn't let out a little hint to—let's say—Margaret? Are you sure something didn't slip out while you were fucking her brains out?"

They stared each other down for a moment, and then Bill stepped in and said, "Gentlemen, please. This is not going to solve anything."

It took a few minutes for cooler heads to prevail.

"Our best strategy is to confront Oscar when he is alone. Kyle can't be in there twenty-four hours a day seven days a week. One of them has to step out to get provisions, and Kyle is the most likely person to do that, since he's working for Oscar. The trick is knowing exactly when Kyle leaves the motel. If Oscar is in the room by himself, we can force our way into the room and steal the tape. The trouble is that the only other person in Hope who knows about the ceremony is Hugh. I haven't discussed Oscar's blackmail with Hugh yet; I plan to do so on Monday. Bill, if you can come up to Hope in the next couple days, we could all work as a tag team."

"The Legislature is winding down for the summer, so I could come up there in a few days," said Bill.

"The sooner the better, since we don't have much time," said Clint.

After their meeting, Clint headed straight for the Swartz Bay Ferry Terminal. He had a big date with Margaret that night. He didn't dare say anything to Premier Davenport about it; he was afraid he would go into a fit of jealousy again. Clint figured this would be a great way to get his mind off everything that was going on.

That evening, Clint and Margaret attended a live theatre production at the Arts Club Theatre on Granville Island. That was followed by a late-night dinner at the nearby Keg Restaurant. Afterward, they went over to Margaret's place. It was mid-morning the next day before they woke up.

"You may find this hard to believe, but Premier Davenport admits that he is insanely jealous of me for the fact that I am seeing you," said Clint.

When Margaret heard this, she laughed uncontrollably for a couple of minutes. "Clint, if it makes you feel any better, it wouldn't make any difference if Mike was single. I wouldn't fuck him for all the tea in China," said Margaret, after she regained her composure.

The following Monday, Clint went over to Hugh's place after work. Over dinner, Clint explained everything, including how Oscar somehow learned about the ceremony and filmed the whole thing.

"Clint, I'll do whatever I can to help take the video away from Oscar. Do you have any ideas?"

"Well, Oscar has his supposed 'explosives expert' Kyle assisting him, and he has a gun. That's the main problem. To start with, try to do as much of your work as possible from the office; don't go up to the jobsites unless you absolutely have to. Then, every few hours, step out and drive past the Fraser Canyon Motel. Don't do it too often; you don't want to look conspicuous. Leave at least a three-hour gap between trips. I'm not sure if Oscar is familiar with your car. Kyle has a metallic-black Corvette, which is impossible to miss. When you drive past the motel, if you don't see the Corvette parked there, come back to the office and get me, and we will pay Oscar a little visit," said Clint. "In order to be available to pay a surprise visit to Oscar, I have to be in the office myself, and not out in the field. Therefore, I won't be able to lead the crew up on Portia Bench. I'll have to get a replacement for myself on the crew."

"What do you suggest?" asked Hugh.

"Greg has experience with running the transit, and he knows all of the coordinates. I was wondering if I could get Henry back on board for the time being."

"Probably, but what can Henry do with his vision problem?"

"He can still be a head chainman. Greg will tell him where to stand with the rod, and the plumb bob is controlled by weight, so it does all the work."

When all of the surveyors assembled in the office the next morning, Hugh called Greg and Henry into Clint's office.

"What is this all about?" asked Henry.

"Gentlemen, I have a lot of work to do here in the office, so I will be tied up here for at least a week. Therefore, I won't be able to run the crew. That's where you come in, Henry. I need you to fill in for me, but there will be some other changes as well. Greg, you will be running the transit; Henry, you will be head chainman. Kevin will be the rear chainman, and Cody will pound in the stakes. Any questions?" Clint then gave Greg the list of coordinates and told him which baseline to start on once he completed the baseline he was currently running.

Throughout the day, Hugh made three trips past the Fraser Canyon Motel, and each time, Kyle's Corvette was parked out front. The last trip he made was at 4:00 p.m. At the end of the day, Clint suggested that they drown their sorrows at the Silver Chalice Pub.

Clint and Hugh were in the Silver Chalice barely ten minutes before Oscar and Kyle joined them, catching them both by surprise.

"Clint, mind if I join you? Hugh, long time, no see."

"What do you want, Oscar?" asked Clint.

"Well, I was hoping you would take me up on my offer. Let's not forget, it's only on for a limited time, and there isn't much time left."

"It's not up to me. The Premier and Bill have the final say about it. It's their careers that are on the line."

"You have to realize, Clint, that your reputation will be tarnished as well. You can be seen in the video just as clearly as the others."

Clint wanted desperately to make a move on Oscar, but then he heard the faint sound of a gun being cocked. Kyle must have had the gun concealed under the table and likely had the gun pointed right at him, so he kept his hands on the table and said nothing.

"Bill and I will give it serious consideration, and we will be in touch soon." Clint drank his beer quickly and suggested to Hugh that they leave.

"I don't believe it. It was as if they knew we were going to be there," said Hugh.

"I know. How did they know we were going to be there at that particular moment? Maybe one of them is watching us," replied Clint.

***

All throughout Wednesday, Kyle never left the motel room; his car was always there whenever Hugh drove past the motel.

On Thursday afternoon, Hugh finally saw what he had been hoping to see all along. When he passed the Fraser Canyon Motel, Kyle's Corvette was not in the parking lot.

He hurried back to the office, burst through the front door, and yelled out, "Kyle's car is not there!"

"Hot diggety dog! Oscar is all ours," said Clint, enthusiastically.

As they made their way up Third Avenue, approaching the CNR crossing, the signals started and the gates came down across the road. Seconds later, three locomotives whizzed by, followed by the rest of the train.

"Turn into the alley that goes behind the motel," Clint told Hugh once the train finally passed by.

Hugh parked the car at the far end of the motel building. They tiptoed through the breezeway that divided the two halves of the motel.

"Are you good at disguising your voice?" Clint asked.

"I can try, but what do I say?"

"Just say that you are the maintenance man, and you're here to check the air conditioner. I want you to knock on the door, since Oscar knows my voice."

When they got to the door of Oscar's room, Hugh was just about to knock when they heard a voice say, "You looking for somebody?"

Clint and Hugh turned around and there was Oscar, standing forty feet away. Partly concealed with his jacket, he had the handgun pointed at them. He approached them with the gun drawn.

"What did I tell you about trying anything funny? I gave specific instructions to not try anything. Let me make this clear to both of you. I will always be one step ahead of you, and I mean business. So, for the last time, don't come back here until you are ready to make a deal. My offer still stands. Now, get the hell out of here."

Neither of them said one word on their way back to the office. Once they were inside, Clint immediately began ransacking the place. He started by ripping all of the pictures off the wall. He turned all of the chairs upside down, pushed all of the items off of the tables, and even moved the filing cabinet.

"Clint—calm down—what are you doing?" asked Hugh.

"Oscar and Kyle somehow must have broken into here and planted a microphone. How else would he know our every move?"

"How would they break into here?"

"Well, do we have an alarm system in here?"

"No, we don't. There isn't anything in here that is worth stealing. There is the computer, but that is three years old. All of the survey equipment is locked in the storage room. How could anybody possibly break in here? Both the front and back doors have deadbolts."

"On the back door, the lower lock can be jimmied, and Kyle likely found a way to pick the lock on the deadbolt. They covered their tracks by locking the door when they left."

"How would they be able to lock the deadbolt without a key?"

"I guess you're right. Another possibility is that a member of one of the survey crews is a spy for them. Any one of our surveyors has access to the office when it is open. Someone could have planted a microphone in here when we weren't looking."

"I don't know, Clint. I think you're living in a fantasy world."

"Then you tell me, how does that scumbag know our every move?"

Hugh did not provide an answer.

Clint continued to turn every item in the office upside down and explore every nook and cranny. He even looked down the heat register. He then went into the foyer and began rifling through Linda's desk.

"Clint, do you mind?" said Linda, looking very annoyed.

"Linda, we are dealing with a breach of security issue here. I must leave no stone unturned."

Clint proceeded to explore every crack and crevice on the underside of Linda's desk. When he finally gave up and got back on his feet, Linda said angrily, "Are you finished?"

"Yes, I couldn't find anything out of the ordinary."

***

At that point, Clint decided to give up the search and call it a day. He packed his briefcase and headed back to his motel room, realizing that both Hugh and Linda probably thought that he was losing it. He knew that he had to steal the tape from Oscar, but he needed a new strategy.

After another night with little sleep, Clint was in the office early the next morning. Hugh arrived shortly afterward.

"Let's head up to the jobsite," said Clint.

As they made their way up the Coquihalla road, Clint never said a word. His paranoia had him believing that Oscar had his truck bugged. When they arrived up on Portia Bench, he suggested to Hugh that they check up on Greg's crew.

Greg looked surprised to see Clint and Hugh this early in the morning. Clint complimented him on his progress and told the crew to keep up the good work; he and Hugh then began heading back to the truck. When they were out of earshot of the crew, Clint looked around to see that they were alone.

"We need another pair of eyes, or to put it another way, we need a third person," said Clint.

"I don't follow you," said Hugh.

"The Flamingo Motel is right across the road from the Fraser Canyon. We need a third person to stay in one of the rooms at the Flamingo and spy on Oscar. It must be someone from outside the organization; someone Oscar doesn't know."

"Do you have someone in mind?"

"Yes, Ted Harvey. Oscar and Kyle don't know who he is or what he looks like."

"Have you talked to him about it?"

"No, not yet. I plan to pay him a visit today. I'm heading back to the Vancouver office as soon as we get back."

Clint drove like a maniac all the way into Vancouver. All during the trip, he constantly looked out his rear-view mirror. His paranoia was really taking control. When he arrived at the Vancouver office, he called Ted into his office and explained everything. Ted found the story ludicrous, and Clint had a difficult time convincing him that everything was true.

"Come on, Ted. There's basically no other alternative. Our backs are against the wall here. Now we're facing an even bigger crisis, and the last thing we want to do is give in to an extortionist, so this is where you come in."

"What is my role in this?"

"Neither Oscar nor Kyle know who you are, so they have no idea you work for me. There is a motel located right across the road from the motel where Oscar and Kyle are staying. What I would like you to do is get a room at the motel across the road and spy on them. Our objective is to catch Oscar by himself when Kyle steps out. Then, we swoop down on him and steal the tape. Are you in?"

"That sound like an alright plan, but how long do you think it will take?"

"Hopefully not too long. We only have until next Thursday to make a decision. If we don't pay up by then, Oscar is going to the media with the tape."

"Well, that seems easy enough. I just keep an eye on their room, and wait for this Kyle guy to leave. Then I call you?"

"You got it."

The next day, Clint phoned Bill and told him the good news.

"Ted has confirmed he will help us recover the tape. Bill, when is the soonest that you can come over to the mainland?"

"I can be there on Monday morning."

"Good, meet me at my Vancouver office then," said Clint.

45

When Bill arrived at Clint's office on Monday, Clint called Ted into the office as well and outlined his battle plan. "Ted, when you check in to the Flamingo Motel, tell the desk clerk you do not want to be disturbed. Make up a story about writing a book about the Kootenay Central Railway and you want complete privacy." Clint gave Ted a pair of binoculars and a Polaroid camera. "Ted, if you ever see Kyle leaving Oscar's room, you need to call the Hope office immediately." He gave Ted the number of the motel where he and Bill were staying in case Kyle stepped out in the evening. "If either Hugh, Bill, or myself answers the phone, you will use a specific code to make it known that Kyle has stepped out. The chosen code will be, 'The blueprints are in'. Once everyone has arrived at the motel, you will come over as well. Since Oscar is not familiar with your voice, Ted, it will be you who knocks on the door of Oscar's room, and when Oscar asks, 'Who is it?' You'll say you're the maintenance man, and you're there to check the air conditioner. Once he opens the door, everyone will storm inside and grab the tape. Do you have any questions?"

"What is the Polaroid camera for?" Ted asked.

"In case another person enters or leaves Oscar's room. I am certain that he has one or more spies working for him, and I would like to find out who it is." Clint gave Ted money for the motel room, and an extra hundred dollars for groceries. "We will be travelling to Hope separately, and we're not to see each other, or even phone each other, until the takedown happens."

Clint and Bill spent most of the rest of Monday at the Hope office going over construction cost figures and estimates for the next six months. By 6:00 p.m. they decided to call it a day. There was no phone call from Ted. On Tuesday, it was the same thing, only this time, Hugh joined them. They spent all day going over cost estimates while waiting for the phone to ring. Still no phone call from Ted.

All Clint kept thinking was, *Ted must be going out of his mind by now, being cooped up in that motel room all day.*

On Wednesday at 1:15 p.m. the men got the break they had been hoping for all along. The phone rang.

"Department of Highways, good afternoon," said Clint.

"The blueprints are in," said the voice at the other end.

"Hot diggety dog! The blueprints are in," said Clint in a joyous tone.

"Holy shit—the blueprints are in," Bill said exuberantly.

It took Hugh a few seconds to clue in to what was happening, but then he said, "Right on, the blueprints are in."

"What are we waiting for? Let's go," said Clint.

The three men ran out of the building like it was on fire. Clint tore out of the parking lot with the tires squealing. As he approached the CNR crossing, the signals started flashing five seconds before, so he yelled out, "Hang on," and floored the accelerator. His car flew over the railway crossing just as the crossing arms came down.

"Whew, I betcha I'll never do that again," said Clint.

Hugh, who was sitting in the back seat, was hanging on for dear life. "Thank God for that."

When they arrived at the motel, they parked at the east end. Ted was standing in front of the building, and Clint silently motioned for him to come over to where they were standing. They tiptoed over to Oscar's room.

Ted knocked on the door, and Oscar said, "Who is it?"

"Maintenance man. I'm here to take a look at the air conditioner."

"That's good. The damn thing isn't working properly," replied Oscar.

Oscar opened the door and let Ted in. Clint was right behind him. He tackled Oscar, and once he had him on the ground, he placed him in a wrestling hold. Bill, Hugh, and Ted then proceeded to tear the room apart, looking for the tape.

"You thought you could outsmart me, hmm? Well, it didn't work. I was one step ahead of you," said Clint.

Eventually, Hugh found the tape when he was rifling through one of the drawers in the dresser in the bedroom. He yelled out, "I found it."

"Good, let's get out of here," yelled Clint.

As Hugh and Ted proceeded to leave the room, Clint noticed that Bill wasn't with them.

"Bill, where are you? What the hell are you doing?" yelled Clint.

"I'm looking for the picture," said Bill from the bedroom.

"Forget about the picture—we gotta get out of here. Kyle will be back any minute," Clint yelled back.

A few seconds later, Bill said, "I found it."

As Bill left the room, Clint released Oscar from the hold, and as he left, he said in a smug tone, "So long, Oscar, it has been a pleasure *not* doing business with you."

On their way back to the office, the men were hooting and hollering like they were teenagers.

"This calls for a celebration," said Clint. He stopped in at the liquor store and purchased a case of beer.

For the remainder of the afternoon, the men completely forgot about work. The afternoon turned into a non-stop bull session fuelled by beer.

At around 5:30 p.m. Ted said, "Clint, would it be possible for me to view the tape before you destroy it? I'd like to see what all the fuss was about. I promise I won't tell anyone."

"Come to think of it, I wouldn't mind seeing the tape, either. I wasn't there when Oscar showed it to you," said Hugh.

"There's just one problem. This tape is on VHS, and my machine at home is a Betamax. What about your machine, Hugh?" said Clint.

"No, mine is a Betamax as well," replied Hugh.

"I don't have a VCR, period," said Ted.

"I know Phil's TV and Stereo shop, which is just up the street. I hope he's still open," said Clint.

Clint phoned Phil's TV and Stereo. "Hi, Phil. I was wondering if you still had any VHS units in stock?"

"Right now, I only have one unit, and I'm using it as a demonstration model," said Phil.

"That's alright. Can I come down and take a look at it?" asked Clint.

"Sure, but I'm closing in twenty minutes."

"This won't take long. Besides, I promise to buy one."

When the men arrived at Phil's shop, Phil led the men over to where the demonstration model VCR was situated.

"This is it, gentlemen, the latest innovation in VCR technology, the Panasonic VHS. It has revolutionized picture and sound quality."

"Sounds good to me. How about a demonstration?" asked Clint.

Phil seemed to take an eternity hooking up the cables to a television set and playing with the buttons on the remote. Bill appeared to be getting quite anxious. Eventually, Phil said, "Okay, it looks like we got her going here."

Clint handed him the tape and said, "Here, use this."

Phil placed the tape into the VCR and hit the play button on the remote. A picture came onto the TV screen, but it wasn't what anyone was expecting. The scene was of someone's backyard. There were a series of tables with tablecloths and plates on them. There were balloons and streamers everywhere. There were a large number of small children milling about, and a group of them appeared to be attempting to pin the tail on the donkey.

"What did I tell you? See how crystal clear the picture quality is? And you can pick up everything they say. Is this a superior video machine or what?" said Phil.

"What the fuck is this?" Bill asked angrily.

"It looks like some child's birthday party," said Phil.

"I know it's a child's birthday party," Bill snapped back. "The point is that's not what it's supposed to be."

"Easy, Bill," said Clint. "The tape must not have been rewound to the beginning. Can you rewind it?"

Phil pressed the rewind button. When the tape was rewound to the beginning, he pressed the play button again. The scene was exactly the same; the same backyard, the same tables, and the same decorations. The scene at the beginning was of guests arriving at the party.

"Can you fast forward?" Bill asked, and Phil complied. They could see what was on the screen, but everything was in fast motion. Over the next five minutes, there was no sign of the ceremony, only the birthday party.

It was then that Clint finally came to the conclusion that this tape was nothing more than a decoy, and the real tape was moved to another location.

Just then, Bill's mobile phone rang. When he answered it, it was Premier Davenport, and he sounded hysterical.

"Bill, where the hell are you?" he said.

"I'm in Hope," said Bill.

"Are you near a TV set?"

"I should be; I'm in a television store."

"Quickly, turn on the Channel Eight News."

The men turned to look at one of the other television sets in the store that was tuned to channel eight. The anchorman was just starting to read the top story. "The News Hour has obtained proof that Premier Mike Davenport, along with Highways Minister Bill Plotnikoff, paid fifty thousand dollars of taxpayers' money to obtain the services of Edwin Baptiste, Chief of the Hope First Nations, to perform an evil spirit cleansing ritual on the Coquihalla Highway project. We have an exclusive video of this so-called ritual, which was provided to *The News Hour* from an unnamed source."

The newscast then cut to the footage of the ceremonial dance. Every word was audible, although it was censored, since it was on television. But the viewing audience could clearly hear Premier Davenport admitting that fifty thousand taxpayer dollars were spent on the ritual.

Bill was still on the phone with Premier Davenport as the news played. "Mike, I will be heading back to Victoria right away."

Right after that news feature, the anchorman went on to say, "*The News Hour* has obtained evidence to directly connect the family of Highways Minister Bill Plotnikoff to terrorist activities of the radical 'Sons of Freedom' Doukhobor sect. A never-before-seen photograph, also provided by an unnamed source, shows Plotnikoff's father, mother, and grandmother, along with eight others, staging a nude protest in front of the Nelson Courthouse," the photo was censored, "in 1957 during the trial of 'Sons of Freedom' leader Yuri Podmoroff, who was accused of bombing a Kootenay Central Railway bridge near Castlegar."

"How can it be? I have the photograph," said Bill.

"Bill, photographs can easily be reprinted. He likely had a copy made," said Clint.

"Wait until I get my hands on that Oscar bastard," said Bill.

"It's too late for that. *The News Hour* likely paid him a hefty sum for the tape and the picture, so for all we know, he could be in the Cayman Islands by now," said Clint. He couldn't help but notice the look of helplessness on Bill's face as he silently left the store.

"Thanks for all your help. I promise to buy one of those VHS units when you get a new shipment in. I guess you want to close for the night. By the way, you can keep the tape," said Clint to Paul as he and Ted left the store.

The next day, it was a raucous session in the Legislature. There were numerous calls from the Opposition for both Premier Davenport and Bill to resign. Both of them steadfastly refused, claiming that the expenditure was justified. There was even a request from an official with the Ministry of Highways office in Victoria that Clint resign as well. However, Bill spoke up on Clint's behalf, saying that Clint only went along for the ride.

46

AUGUST 1985

One week after the incriminating tape was played for all of British Columbia to see, Bill and Stan both caved in and resigned. A backbench MLA from the Peace River region was appointed interim Highways Minister. It was toward the end of July before Clint was able to make the trip to Victoria to meet with her for the first time. She promised to tour the Coquihalla Highway construction project some time in early September.

With the date for Greg's preliminary trial vast approaching, Clint realized that he completely forgot to do a follow-up with Dennis regarding his analysis into determining the exact time of Don's death. It wasn't until Margaret phoned him and reminded him about it that he remembered. However, she had saved him the trouble—she met with Dennis herself. She asked Clint to meet with her at her office to discuss the results and to give a rundown on where the Defence currently stood.

Clint met with Margaret in her office the next day. "Dennis ran a series of tests on Don's body to determine the exact time of death.

He concluded that Don finally succumbed between twelve-thirty-five and twelve-forty. Greg was last known to be with Don at twelve-ten, since Hugh said that he looked at his watch when Greg arrived, and it was twelve-fifteen. It would have taken him five minutes to walk from the jobsite to the truck."

"Alright, I guess we're in the driver's seat," said Clint.

"Yes, that will be very valuable evidence. That, along with the correlation between how the surveyor's chain was actually used in relation to where Greg's fingerprints were on it. He can determine that there was no way Greg could have used the chain to strangle Don, given where his fingerprints were found. If you ask me, we have an excellent case." Margaret's expression then abruptly changed from joy to anger, and that caught Clint totally off guard. "Alright, now I demand an explanation regarding *Willy Wonka and the Chocolate Factory*."

"What are you talking about?" asked Clint, completely dumfounded.

"Don't play dumb with me, Clint. You were asking Dennis what happens when men fuck other men up the ass, and if it could be detected. Are you bisexual or something?"

"Of course not—it had nothing to do with me."

"Why didn't you tell me that you were into men on the side? Were you and Don secretly lovers? For all I know, maybe it was you who killed him because he didn't want to give you any."

"For God's sake, no. If I *was* bisexual, Don would be the last man on earth I would ever have sex with."

"Tell me, Clint. How many men have you been with? Are you aware of the spread of the AIDS virus? If you find out that you have AIDS, then that means you have passed it on to me."

"Margaret, you're not giving me any chance to explain. If you'll just be quiet, I'll tell you why I brought up the subject with Dennis, okay? I had read about the investigation into a serious train wreck that happened in Coquihalla Pass in 1944. When the autopsies on the engineer and the brakeman were performed, the coroner discovered traces of each other's semen in their anuses. I was just curious if that was standard practice to examine every part of a deceased person's body, regardless of how obvious the cause of death was. It had absolutely nothing to do with me." Clint could tell from the look on Margaret's face that she did not believe a word he was saying.

"Clint, if I have AIDS, I swear that before I die, I will see to it that you are charged with murder," Margaret snapped back.

"For the last time, Margaret, I've never had sex with a man."

"Well, if you don't mind, I'm very busy. I have other clients to deal with."

"I didn't see anyone else in the waiting room."

"I will see you at the trial. Will you please leave?"

"Okay, but can I call you?"

"I said I'll see you at the trial—not before. Now *get out*."

On the day of the preliminary trial, the session started with both the Defence and the Prosecution presenting their opening arguments. Then it came time to cross-examine witnesses for both sides. As it turned out, the Prosecution didn't have a strong case. All of the evidence presented was purely circumstantial. The best testimony for the Defence came from Dennis. He determined that Don died at least twenty minutes after Greg was last seen with him. Hugh, Kevin, and Cody all testified that they saw Greg arrive at the truck precisely at 12:15 p.m. In addition, Dennis demonstrated how the surveyor's chain was used to strangle Don, and the manner in which it was wrapped around his neck was incompatible to where Greg's fingerprints were situated.

After all the evidence was presented, the Judge acquitted Greg. He went with the theory that someone was hiding in the bushes, waiting for everyone to leave, and then the person strangled Don, and hoped that all of the blame would be placed on Greg. The Judge would never know the real story.

After the preliminary trial concluded, Clint congratulated Greg on being acquitted, and told him his job was waiting for him. He then approached Margaret and commended her on an excellent job. Margaret was still very cold toward him.

"I will have you know, I had tests done to see if I am HIV positive, and the tests came up negative," said Margaret.

"You see? I told you. The whole thing about bringing up the subject of anal intercourse with Dennis had absolutely nothing do with me," said Clint.

"Just get the fuck away from me," Margaret snarled and stormed out of the courtroom.

Afterward, Clint approached Dennis and thanked him for his testimony.

"By the way, Margaret now thinks I'm gay, thanks to you telling her I asked you about those men who were gay lovers."

"Hey, I'm sorry she took it the way she did. I never meant for that to happen," replied Dennis.

"Don't worry about it. I could never figure her out, anyway. For someone as smart as she is, she sure is narrow-minded."

"Don't take it personally, Clint," said Dennis. "You know something, you're too smart for her. Incidentally, I decided to do some research and it turned out the City of Vancouver used to have a bylaw whereby the coroner was required to examine every square inch of a deceased person's body, regardless of the cause of death. It was claimed that the bylaw was required to tie up any loose ends. The bylaw was finally eased in the fifties. It seems kind of silly, doesn't it?"

"Well, there's never a dull moment in the field of forensic medicine," said Clint.

After the trial, Greg immediately went back to being the transit operator for the crew working up on Portia Bench. Henry's trial was due to begin in another week. Rudy was sticking by his charge of attempted murder, but Henry's lawyer, Salvatore, was working to have the charges reduced to aggravated assault.

Clint phoned Salvatore and asked if they could go over any particulars before the trial, but unlike Margaret, Salvatore was very tight-lipped about giving any details.

Unlike Greg, Henry didn't fare as well at his trial. On the positive side, he was able to beat the attempted murder charge, but in the end, he was convicted of aggravated assault. He was sentenced to one year in prison and two years probation.

When Clint finally returned to his Vancouver office after nearly a month's absence, Ted approached him right after he arrived in the morning.

"Clint, I completely forgot to return your polaroid camera when I got back here after my stay in Hope."

"Oh, right. I forgot about it, too. I don't use it very much anymore. Did you take any pictures?"

"As a matter of fact, I did. I saw some woman leaving Oscar's room in the morning one day. In fact, I have the picture right here."

Ted handed the picture to Clint. Clint gasped in horror when he realized who the woman was. It was Margaret.

"Clint, are you alright? Do you recognize her?"

Clint had to think fast. He didn't want to let on that he not only knew her, but also knew her very intimately. "She looks like someone I used to know, but when I look closer, it's not who I thought it was."

Clint took the camera and the photograph, went into his office, and closed the door. He sat in silence as he collected his thoughts. He now faced the sickening reality that he revealed all of the details of the ceremonial dance to Margaret during one of their moments of intimacy. Technically, she coaxed it out of him. He genuinely thought she loved him, but she was just using him to give Oscar the opportunity to seek vengeance on him.

Clint ripped the photograph into a hundred tiny pieces and threw them into the waste basket. He made a solemn vow never to reveal this to anybody.

47

MAY 1986

It was finally 8 May 1986, the day everyone had waited for, and the day Clint and his crew often wondered if the opening day would happen on time. With a great deal of pomp and circumstance, the official opening of the Coquihalla Highway would take place. There were many dignitaries present, including Premier Davenport, the interim Highways Minister, several Cabinet Ministers, the local MLAs, the local Members of Parliament, and the Mayors of Hope, Merritt, and Kamloops.

In the days leading up to opening day, Clint phoned Bill on two different occasions at his home in Castlegar, and tried to persuade him to attend the ceremony. Sadly, Bill refused on both of Clint's attempts. He told Clint he felt like he had let everyone in the Legislature down and he blamed himself for causing the scandal; after all, it was he who had convinced Premier Davenport to approve funding for the ceremonial dance. He said that he planned to watch the ceremony on television and that he was planning to quit politics altogether.

Clint attended the opening ceremony. After a series of lengthy speeches, Premier Davenport cut the ribbon, signifying the official opening of the Coquihalla Highway. However, throughout the morning, Clint noticed that Premier Davenport was still not speaking to him. Whenever the two of them were in close proximity to each other, Premier Davenport would brush him off and completely ignore him. After the ceremony had concluded, Clint decided to put a stop to it.

"Mr. Premier, whatever went on between Margaret and me is over now. We haven't seen each other in nearly a year, so it's not fair that you're still mad at me. I will go on the record as saying that I worked my ass off to get this highway completed on time. I worked many long hours and gave up most of my leisure time over the past three years. I believe that you should at least give me some credit for my effort."

"Need I remind you that this project has gone two hundred million dollars over budget, and I'm deep shit with the voters over the debacle with your Indian friend? But aside from that, you did a hell of a job. This is one mighty fine looking highway. Good work, Matheson," said Premier Davenport.

"Thank you, sir." They shook hands.

Later that day, Clint decided to pay a visit to Edwin at the Band office.

"Clint, what brings you here?" said Edwin.

"Chief, I want to personally thank you for taking the time to perform that ceremonial dance. I must say, it worked. There have been no signs of any spirits since, either human or animal. But I do question whether the cost was justified. I hope you guys are happy with your new ice rink."

"Oh yes, I love it. I hope our Band will turn out some future NHL legends."

"Whatever the case, I believe we've seen the last of Siaman."

"Well, that dance has been proven to be effective for many

generations, but there have been a few cases where the spirit has returned. I was reminded of this one night a few weeks ago when I had this really strange dream. I saw a young man dressed the way our people dressed three hundred years ago. He approached me, but he never said a word. He raised his arm in a manner as if he was proclaiming victory."

"That may not mean anything."

"One thing our people are notorious for is that we are not willing to accept defeat. We're a real stubborn bunch. I have also heard stories passed down from the generations that one characteristic of both Siaman and his father was that they never liked being told what to do or where to go. He would have made a great leader."

"I will admit, I was totally surprised when you included Cindy in the ceremony. I didn't think she would ever want to see me again."

"She still cares about you. She admits that she made a mistake letting Claude back into her life. Maybe you should give her another chance."

"I'll give it some thought. After all, Margaret and I split up last August."

"Yes, I heard about that."

"Jesus Christ, doesn't this community have anything better to do with their time than gossip about other people? I'm not even from here."

"Take it as a compliment. One way to look at it is that you left a lasting legacy to this town."

"Well, Chief, it has been nice talking to you. Let's keep in touch."

As Clint left the Band office, Cindy met him in the hallway.

"Hello, Clint, nice to see you."

"Nice to see you, too. By the way, I never got a chance to tell you, but you and your brothers did a fantastic job on the drums at the ceremony. Looks like it did the trick."

"Thank you. Listen, I was wondering if you would like to get together sometime?"

"I'll get back to you on that," Clint said after a brief pause.

The next day, another ceremony was held, this time at the Coquihalla Lake Rest Area. A cairn with a commemorative plaque was unveiled. Inscribed on the plaque were the names of all the people who played a key role in the construction of the Coquihalla Highway. Clint's name was featured prominently on the plaque, serving as a lasting reminder to his efforts and determination.

ABOUT THE AUTHOR

Robert Boyd hails from Fraser Valley. In his spare time, he can be found exploring the ghost towns of Western Canada and hiking the Kettle Valley Railway. He worked as a surveyor for the Alberta Department of Transportation before eventually settling near Vancouver, BC.

Portia Bench is his second published work.

ROBERT BOYD